QUEEN OF INDEPENDENCE

KAREN FRANCES

Alleisha Conway

Leah conway
xx

Karen
x xx

love
Karen Frances
x

QUEEN OF INDEPENDENCE

KAREN FRANCES
copyright reserved

Dedication

Writing this dedication is one of the hardest things I've ever had to do, even more so as you always wrote your dedications so effortlessly. So here goes...

To the one I love with all my heart, Karen. Losing you at the start of 2021 made our world collapse around us. However, you have continued to keep me going and keep me strong. The book world both in the UK and America as well as your friends within it, threw a blanket of love over our family and even although we were absolutely terrified, we all felt enormous love and support. That was all because of you! I always tried to convince you of the love and respect people had for you, but you were resistant to the truth because you only saw yourself as a wife and a mother to our five beautiful kids. Everyone else saw you as a woman that was more than that, we all recognised you as a strong, determined woman full of grace and a truly amazing wife, mother, daughter, sister and friend. Your laugh and smile lit up entire rooms, yet you didn't see the light and laughter you cast around you. You were so excited about Queen of Independence. You felt it was going to be THE ONE. The excitement around this book especially in our family motivated you endlessly, even whilst having a busy life and the daily struggles with your fibromyalgia.

Unfortunately you never got to complete Queen of Independence, your labour of love. Those who knew about your W.I.P. knew you wanted it released. With the unwavering expertise of K.L. Shandwick, ably supported by Suzie, Margaret and Pauline; your beta readers,(and many more besides), QOI is complete. I'm sure you'd be delighted with their efforts. Everyone is sure to love the story of Amelia Campbell as much as you did yourself.

All my endless love

Paul.

ACKNOWLEDGMENTS

Cover Design by
Kari March, Kari March Designs
Editing by LH Editing
Proofread by Author Bunnies Proofreading Service
Interior Design and Formatting by K.L. Shandwick

Karen's team of Suzie, Margaret, Pauline and Leah, with the support of Tracie and K.L. are all superstars. Not just for the support you gave Karen over the years, but your friendship helped her be the amazing human being she was. The support you have shown me, taking my emotional phone calls and listening to my cry at crazy times of the day and night. Thank you! It takes a whole team to launch a book and doing it fo this one was something I never thought I'd need to do. The advice from everyone has been so valuable. Kari, Krissy and Lisa, thank you for your input. Vi Keeland and Penelope Ward, thank you for all your support this year and to Kylie from Give Me Books, your knowledge and advice has been invaluable.

CHAPTER 1

*A*melia
17th July

Standing in the entrance hall of my penthouse apartment, I open the now familiar envelope with the royal coat of arms and hold the card, with its gold embossed writing, in my hands. *Not another event, surely? It doesn't seem that long since I attended the last one.* I sigh when I read the words:

Her Majesty Queen Sofia requests the company
of
Miss Amelia Campbell...

As I skim over the rest of the invitation, I realise this one is different. My heart speeds up and I take note of the date. It's sixteen days away, the 2nd of August. Two days after the Scottish referendum, *intriguing*.

"Interesting choice of date," I say aloud. The date is significant to the crown one way or another. Are they hoping to use this event as a distraction from the Scottish independence referendum? Has the date been decided in conjunction with central government in London?

It could be an interesting day, or it could be just as dull as some of the other royal events I've attended in the past. *Stuffy and boring gets my vote.*

I wonder if I can get away with not going — I just need a plausible excuse. Who am I kidding? I'll have to go. Being a close friend of Prince James, I can't get out of it.

Lottie, my best friend, stands, shifting from one foot to the other, her eyes wide with curiosity. "Well? You can't stand there reading that and not say anything. After all, I acted as messenger by bringing up your mail from downstairs." Her short, blonde, bobbed hair bouncing from side-to-side as she shuffles and waits for me to share what's on the card. She's immaculately dressed as always, in a pale blue trouser suit, and I can see the hint of white lace under her jacket. I approve, she looks completely flawless and sophisticated, yet sexy.

I glance at her. "I'm now wishing you'd left it downstairs where you found it." The fact she has a key to my mailbox is still a hazy mystery to me, but she's like a sister, which is why she also has a key card and code to enter my apartment.

"We both know you'd have avoided opening it, if I had. One of these days, you're going to miss out on some incredible news, and all because you can't be bothered to collect your own mail." She bites back a grin.

She's right, I avoid my personal mailbox, it usually contains what some would call fan mail, as well as the occasional hate mail. I have a separate box for my charity correspondence which I always pick up.

"So, come on, tell me?" Lottie urges impatiently.

"Oh, here," I say, throwing the invitation in her direction, thinking she may as well read it for herself.

Lottie loves all the attention I get, and when I happen to

receive a plus-one invite I almost always include her, because isn't that what best friends do? She's a constant support when she accompanies me through some of my more tedious days, and always lifts my spirits afterwards when we hit the town on our evenings out.

I glance at her reading the card and sigh. Stuffy parties full of pompous snobs at the palace aren't really my idea of a good time. I can think of far better ways to spend my day.

Thanks to my parents, I've been rubbing shoulders with royalty and aristocracy from the moment I was born. Back then, I was the sweet, quiet, well-mannered child that everyone gushed over.

Now, I expect I'm the one most frowned upon, especially when my weekend antics with Lottie get splashed all over the front pages of the tabloids. I curse the pictures in the press, which always display me looking bleary-eyed, and either falling into, or out of, my waiting town car, showing a lot of leg.

Not that I care what anyone thinks of me. I'm just being myself and I don't intend to change for anyone, *ever*.

"Amelia!" Lottie squeals with excitement. "It's a royal engagement party. Please say you'll take me with you?" She stops and stares at me. I can see her brain working, and I know exactly what she's thinking. Before too long she adds, "Wait, there hasn't been an official engagement announced. How come you've been invited to Prince James' party when he isn't even engaged yet?"

"Don't be naïve, Charlotte. This is how the Palace works. I imagine the announcement will be aired on the news in the coming days. You should know by now that anything arranged by the Palace is done with precision," I say, taking the rest of the mail she gave me from under my arm where I tucked it to open the invitation.

Prince James, heir to the throne, is finally tying

the knot — if they get as far as the altar. He's a bit of a rogue with the ladies. I've lost count the number of times over the years he's tried it on with me, and he doesn't take rejection well. It's only thanks to my skills in diplomacy he hasn't cut me out of his circle. I do love him, but I see him as more of a brother than anything romantic.

Lottie scowls. "Oh, is he really going to marry… what's her name again?" I can't help but laugh as she asks the question with such a straight face. "Damn, why can't I remember?"

We're both laughing in my hallway when the lift door opens and Izzy walks towards us with a bag of grocery shopping in her arms. I'm slightly confused because I thought she was upstairs in the kitchen. I could have sworn I saw her there not even thirty minutes ago.

Isabel, or Izzy, was my parents' housekeeper, and when they died, she continued to work for me. She's been in my life since I was a baby, and I hope she'll be in it for many more years. She's like family and has always had a soft spot for me, unlike my blood relatives who haven't shown much interest in my welfare since I lost my parents in a skiing accident.

"Morning Charlotte," Izzy says, heading towards the staircase.

"Good morning," Lottie replies with her usual chirpy voice. "Okay, where were we? Her name? Come on put me out of my misery."

"Effie, her name is Effie. Lady Effie Bower, remember now?"

"That's it," she replies looking relieved.

I shrug and look at the invitation again. "I didn't think their relationship was that serious. The last time I spoke to James he said she was just a bit of fun."

"She looks like an Effie," my friend says absorbing the

information. "What is he thinking, marrying her? She looks terribly plain and prim. James could have done better he's a good-looking man. I mean she'll be his future queen and there's nothing unique about her, except that name." She shakes her head. "He'll take a mistress of course, I can't imagine her getting down on her knees to give him a blow job while he sits on the royal throne."

"Ew, Lottie, that isn't an image I want in my head." I cringe, my body shuddering at the thought.

"Maybe not, but come on, she comes across as a one-way kind of girl. I'd bet money she's the type to lie on her back, taking what he gives her, and giving nothing in return. James needs someone who isn't afraid to experiment."

"And you would know *exactly* how much fun he likes to have," I say, cutting her off. Lottie knows Prince James intimately well, but I'm not sure she was thinking straight when she had a little rough and tumble with him last summer after a garden party at the palace.

We both laugh, almost hysterically, because Lottie's description of Effie is probably spot on.

I shudder again as I try to dispel the image of James and Effie in my head.

In the ten minutes she's been in my apartment Lottie's destroyed my usual quiet and is already causing havoc to my day.

My thoughts turn to today's far more pleasant engagement, and my heart leaps at how I imagine the oncology unit we're due to announce as officially open, has already begun to pay off. It's probably the biggest fundraising event I've been involved in.

I've spent time to ensure I look my best, but as the day isn't about me, I've dressed low key. I've opted for white, slim-fitting cropped trousers by Vera Wang and a black lace and silk top by Scottish fashion designer, Hayley

Scanlan. I know the look is understated and smart, but it will easily fit in with an evening out, if that's what Lottie and I decide to do afterwards. I feel it's the perfect outfit for today, it's sensible and appropriate attire for the opening of a new children's cancer wing at the hospital here in the Capital.

Although my reputation as a party girl precedes me, I take my charity work seriously. I don't think anyone would question my devotion to all the causes I've continued to support since my mother died. It's what she would have wanted; it's what I want. I miss my mum every day; she was an incredible woman, full of fire and spirit, and I know I get those same qualities from her. She gave generously with both her time and money to her charities, so for as long as using my position gains attention for one of my charities, and it helps others, I will continue to do it.

"Oh, I forgot my bag, I left it upstairs," I inform Lottie. We walk towards the stairs of my quirky penthouse apartment, which is the result of several apartments within my building being remodelled into one.

On the entrance level there are four, spacious, en-suite bedrooms. My master bedroom has panoramic views across Edinburgh's historic skyline. When I first looked at this apartment, I'd thought it was strange having the bedrooms on this floor, near the entrance. But once I had viewed the rest of it, I could see the benefit of having the bedrooms as far away from the living space and terraces as possible; parties could happen, and people could sleep without being disturbed.

The next floor is open plan, with the kitchen, dining area, and an elegant sitting room all together with floor-to-ceiling windows. The whole area from end to end is more than twenty metres long. On the same floor there is also a utility room and terrace off the kitchen for outside eating. On the third floor is my office, another sitting room, and a cloak-room, and up a final flight of stairs there's a rooftop terrace complete with luxury hot tub. The space is big enough to hold a party for fifty people comfortably. In fact, the square footage of the whole apartment is two thousand one hundred square feet.

I reached the top of the stairs and couldn't see my house-keeper, "Izzy, where did you go?"

"Here," she replies, popping up from crouching behind the kitchen counter. I smile, I'd be lost without Izzy at times. "Is this what you're looking for?" She places my large Chanel handbag up on the counter. A memory flashes of me putting it down on the floor when I went to get some orange juice out of the fridge earlier this morning.

I step towards her and kiss her on the cheek. "Yes, thank you. What would I do without you?" I say stuffing the rest of my mail into my oversized bag.

"Truthfully? The thought terrifies me," she replies, pretending to shudder through a chuckle. "Am I expecting you back for dinner or do you both have plans?" Lottie and I share a look, and Izzy just shrugs her shoulders and smirks. "Okay, I know that look, no dinner and I won't ask what those plans are either. Some things I'm better off not know-ing, although I'm sure I'll read all about it tomorrow."

"Maybe it's for the best," Lottie says softly, and consoles her by placing a hand on her forearm. "It's Friday after all."

Izzy chuckles. "Don't get arrested."

I move in and hug Izzy to reassure her. "You know, I'm a good girl. Although I think Lottie's a bad influence on me."

Lottie covers her mouth with her hand pretending to be horrified. "Me? Never." She blinks innocently and I laugh at her.

Izzy holds up her hands. "I'm not taking sides. I think you're each as bad as the other."

"Really?" I ask, amused.

"In a good way, of course, and that's why I love you both dearly," she adds quickly, and I can see she's teasing again.

"We love you too," I say planting a wet kiss on her cheek and Lottie joins in, kissing the other side.

Izzy squirms. "Don't you have someplace you need to be? Go on, get out of my kitchen. I'll leave you some snacks in the fridge, for whatever time you *eventually* come home." We leave my penthouse and ride the lift down to the underground garage.

The security in the building was also a huge factor for consideration when I was buying. I love my independence, but I like to think I'm safety aware. There are more than a few disgruntled people out there, and I tend to attract them.

The last one claimed I was his 'princess' and wanted to whisk me away to his castle in the Scottish Highlands. After I reported him for stalking me, the police told me his 'castle' was a flat in a tenement building just outside Stirling. When they searched his place, they found pictures of me he'd cut out from newspapers plastered on his living room wall. I was relieved when he was served with an order, which stops him from coming within fifty feet of me, or sending me gifts, emails or letters, because he knew my movements better than I did myself.

"So what car are we travelling in today?" Lottie asks as she stands beside my white Porsche convertible, pouting her lips and stroking the bonnet.

I shake my head, rejecting her silent hint. "Sorry no. Today we're being practical, not showing off," I say, opening the doors to the black Range Rover, with the tinted bullet-proof windows; an upgrade I was prompted to get by one of my advisors. After my stalker incident I wasn't taking any chances.

"Fine." She huffs, walking around to the passenger side. I

smile at the petulant look on her face. "What's going to happening today?" she asks as I slide into the car and she takes her seat beside me.

"Well, there will be the usual stuff — pompous men in stuffy suits, all vying for the attention of the cameras. I do have a speech to make, along with the First Minister, during the opening ceremony. I'm not sure what he'll be doing after this, but I intend to go around the new hospital wards and meet as many of the sick children and their families as I can. There's a formal luncheon to thank the donors and project management as well. You know how these things go."

"The First Minister, huh? You know he wants in your pants? He's pretty pleasing on the eye, if you like the sleazy, boring old man look that he has going on."

"Lottie," I chastise. "I'll admit he appears older in the ill-fitting suits he wears, but I'm sure some women find him attractive."

"Don't defend him. I really do get the impression he thinks he has a chance with you. I've seen the way his eyes follow you around during the events we've attended with him. That man has a thing for you. Oh, I've just had a thought." She covers her mouth with her hand and laughs.

The state she gets into laughing makes me afraid to ask. "What?"

"Our First Minister, Harold Donaldson, and the lovely Effie. Now, there's a match that would work. They'd make the perfect couple. Harry and Effie, they're each as dull as the other."

"Lottie, stop. How am I going to look at him today without thinking about those two together now?"

"But it is something to think about," she insists, laughing again.

I start the car and turn up the radio. I glance towards her, smile and shake my head when my eyes meet hers, before I drive us out of the garage. Life is never dull with Lottie, but I love that she's a part of my crazy world. Most would never believe it, but her special brand of humour keeps me sane.

Checking the time on my dashboard clock, I note we're only five minutes away from our destination. When I look up there's a black saloon car careering towards me, half on my side of the road. My heart races and I slam on my brakes, performing an emergency stop. Relief washes over me when I realise myself and the other driver have both stopped in time, before any damage is done.

Inside the other car, two guys in their late twenties, or early thirties stare back at me. Neither look shaken. *Thank goodness we're all okay.* The men are muscular types, dressed in black hoodies and they're looking directly towards me. I wonder if my initial assessment is wrong and they're in shock.

The passenger side door of the saloon opens a little, and one of the occupants takes off his seatbelt in a hurry. For a moment I think he's coming to apologise and check we're okay, when a police car comes from nowhere, blue lights flashing as if they are attending an emergency. I think they might have seen our near miss and are going to attend the scene in the centre of the road as we're blocking the traffic now. However, as the police car draws closer, the black car immediately backs up, just enough to clear the front of my SUV, and I presume it's because the driver has realised the police car needs to pass. But once the police car has over-taken, the black saloon pulls back onto the road and speeds away.

"Well damn, we were extremely lucky there. Are you okay?" Lottie asks.

I nod. "Yeah, just had a fright, that's all." By now there's a line of traffic behind me and I move the shift into drive and set off again, a little shaken, towards the hospital.

CHAPTER 2

 melia
17th July

"AH, AMELIA, LOOKING BEAUTIFUL AS EVER," Harry Donaldson says taking my hand in his, but his eyes stay firmly on my cleavage. It's no wonder he's a single man. There's nothing gentlemanly about him, *at all*. Mr Harold Donaldson is the youngest Scottish First Minister, and at only thirty-five years of age he still gives off the impression of a leering, dirty old man. Someone needs to tell him that the way he presents himself doesn't do him any favours. His dirty blond hair looks greasy and unkempt, and his pale skin looks dry. He would look more attractive with a little help from a stylist.

A loud cough from Lottie finally draws Harry's attention away from my breasts, and if looks could kill, Lottie would be falling to the floor right about now.

"Charlotte, how nice to see you again," he says addressing my friend.

"And you," she sweetly replies. *The two faces of Charlotte Gray.* I bite back a grin.

11

They're both terrible liars. Neither likes the other, which can become unbearable at times, due the icy atmosphere that exists between them.

"This is incredible. You must be so happy to see this state-of-the-art facility finally opening," Lottie says.

Harry smiles at me, a genuine smile, not the fake one I've seen him plaster on at other events we've both attended. "None of this would've been possible without Amelia's investment and enthusiastic backing for the project," he tells her.

With Lottie's words from the car journey ringing loudly in my head, I know he can pay me all the compliments he wants but he'll never be anything more than a business acquaintance.

"No, I don't suppose it would've come to fruition without her help," Lottie states firmly.

They both have a point. Initially, Harry wasn't willing to give government backing to invest in this project. However, as soon as I came on board his attitude changed, and he was falling over himself to be involved. I suspect he thinks this will help win him some votes in the upcoming independence election. Although he won't be gaining my vote; not because I disapprove of Scotland's independence, but because the man running this campaign is someone who I wouldn't let run a bath.

I glance around the room, which is filling up with dignitaries and staff, and it gives me a warm feeling to see them all gathering here. I know my parents would be proud of this achievement. My mother was always interested in children's charities especially after the death of my brother to cancer. He was only six years old when it claimed his life. Unfortunately, I was only two at the time and don't remember much about him. I was delighted when I found out this new wing was a children's oncology department, with all the latest technology and new treatments that have only been available in America up until now. My hope is that more young lives will be saved from this deadly disease that claims so many.

Harry states, "We all played our part, and it contains valuable resources for the sick, that's all that matters." His wandering eyes return to me. "Amelia, would you like to have dinner with me tonight? We have some things that I'd like to discuss before the referendum takes place."

Lottie starts coughing, and I swear I could choke her myself. I almost laugh at how perceptive she is of Harry's interest in me.

I give a small smile. "Oh, Harry, I'm afraid not. I already have dinner plans for this evening."

"Ah, okay. I'll check my diary with my secretary, and we'll make another date. It really is quite important that we speak." Someone catches his eye, and he looks excited. "Oh, there's Mr Hudson from the hospital's board of directors. I need a minute with him. If you'll both excuse me."

Harry rushes off in the direction of Mr Hudson, and even though I'm relieved he's gone, I feel a little sorry that Mr Hudson has to put up with him. Despite the doctor's appearance as a pompous old man, John Hudson is very interesting. I've found his views very refreshing, and he's been a mine of information for me whilst I've been raising awareness for this new facility.

"Thank goodness he's gone," Lottie says with a sigh.

I huff. "I know what you mean. The man's a letch. There's no way I would willingly spend any of my free time with him."

"But aren't you even just a tiny bit curious as to what he wants to talk to you about?" she asks, nudging me with her elbow.

I scowl. "No, honestly, he needs to concentrate on the things that are important to our nation. Like sorting out our health, welfare, schools, and emergency services... getting the homeless off the streets, need I go on? Do I want Scotland to be independent? I really don't know anymore. And if he does get this vote, I'm not sure he's the right person to take this country forward. His direction and focus are hit and miss at best. He's a blowhard that just wants to make a name for himself."

Lottie giggles. "Go you, Amelia. If you ever want to run for First Minister, I'll back you one hundred percent. I'm sure the nation would much rather back the fun-loving and generous Miss Campbell, ahead of that monotonous social climber, Harry Donaldson."

"I doubt it, but can you imagine some of the headlines if I did? *Drunken First Minister stumbles from town car at eight a.m. after an all-night party session.*"

"Now, that would be a headline to be proud of. It's been a while since you made the news for that reason."

I chuckle. "It has, maybe we need to rectify that tonight. Come on, it's almost time for the speeches." My best friend grins wickedly at my reply as we make our way through the crowded room to our table.

CHAPTER 3

*L*iam
17th July

MY FINGERS TRACE over the two fastened buttons on my suit jacket. I stare ahead, not quite sure what I'm looking for. There's nothing worse than babysitting politicians at a mundane opening of some building or another. My head is filled with doubts over this job, which is a different career direction for me. I've experienced some of the most dangerous missions of my life in war-torn Afghanistan; missions that were life and death. And yet here I am confused about a simple protection assignment.

My doubts about accepting the job are beginning to be confirmed. From what I can see, this gig is a case of kissing babies heads, licking the arses of VIPs, and patting the backs of all concerned with this project.

Surely, the First Minister is hardly at risk of being attacked at an event like this, not when it's for the opening of a unit aimed at saving children's lives.

Scanning the room, I can see there are already plenty of security guards around. And again, I think the risk to Donaldson's life is negligible. Why he has me here is a mystery. I'm not an ordinary security guard, I'm an intelligence led close protection officer, and he already has a bodyguard with him.

When I got the call commissioning my services for this event at seven this morning, I was surprised his department had left it so late.

For several minutes I stand watching the First Minister work the room before he comes over to speak with me.

"Thanks for coming Liam. Would you mind if we stepped out for a minute? I really need to talk." I glance towards my partner, Ross, who has come along to act as my driver for this low-key situation, and nod.

Donaldson glances around nervously, and I guess he's ensuring no one hears what he has to say. "Okay, I need to make this quick because I'll be missed," he says, all full of self-importance. "This is…" He hesitates, and I feel the weight of whatever is on his mind. His gaze grows serious. "Extremely delicate."

"Okay," I say, intrigued.

"What I'm going to tell you must not be disclosed, but I really need your help."

I narrow my eyes and observe his body language. For a man who would take on Scotland as his next project, he looks more than a little skittish.

"I'll do my best," I say.

He nods. "That's why I've chosen you. You are a man I've come to regard as above reproach."

"Thank you," I say, feeling a little weird to be praised by him. The man hardly knows me. It's my job to stay in the background and meld into the scenery.

We've hardly said two words to each other in the year I've

been part of his security team. During that time, I've ascertained Mr Donaldson is not all he appears to be. His image in the media is that of a pillar of the community, but I personally think he's a good actor. This caring version of First Minister Donaldson is what the people *want* to see, rather than who he really is. Perhaps they believe under his leadership the majority of Scottish nationalists might finally get what they want: independence from the rest of the UK.

In my eyes that doesn't make him a hero, it makes him an enabler. Real heroes are the ones who roll up their sleeves and do all the dirty, hard work, for users like him who smile widely for the cameras, shake hands, and bask in the glory of success at the appropriate time.

"You're short on time, First Minister, why don't you cut to the chase?" I say.

"Sometime during the night, I received a handwritten letter warning me that Amelia Campbell may be at risk of being kidnapped or worse."

I frown. "The party girl opening the unit today with you?"

He snaps, "Amelia isn't just a party girl, she's a society girl who moves in royal circles."

My frown deepens. "I'm sorry, I don't understand. What does she have to do with you, and why would someone contact *you* about something like this?"

Donaldson fishes a letter from his inside pocket and shows it to me. "I recognise the handwriting and I believe this is a credible threat to Miss Campbell."

The First Minister checks the time on his wristwatch as I take the paper out of the thick envelope and note the luxury, cream coloured paper, that I assume previously had a company header, but this has been cut from the top. The postmark is Lambeth, London.

"I only have five more minutes," Donaldson informs me as I scan the contents of the letter.

Amelia Campbell may be about to disappear.

Plot to remove her completely from the Scottish arena before the referendum.

I SHAKE my head and scoff. "Disappear? Why would anyone threaten her this way? What do they have to gain? She's a party girl that does a bit of charity work for Christ's sake. You're really taking this seriously?"

He glances around furtively. "Look, I don't know what they have to gain, but I do know who this is from. It's a very credible threat."

"Who are *they*? You know who sent this?"

He nods. "I do, but I can't tell you that. Will you protect her, Liam? I need someone I can trust. I need you to start immediately."

I narrow my eyes again. "What's in this for you?"

"Apart from Amelia being safe, you mean? Perhaps it's our connection and the referendum. Do I need a reason? What else do you suggest I do with this? Nothing?"

"Does she know?"

He sighs. "Of course not. Like I said, I only received it sometime during the night."

"What do you want us to do?" I ask.

"Keep her alive," he implores.

I shake my head. "You're interpreting the word *disappear* as meaning her life is at risk? If so you need to tell her about this letter."

"Not yet, and I'd rather she didn't feel threatened, if we can help it. I just need you to look out for her while I find out exactly what's going on."

I nod. "I think we're better equipped to investigate who's behind this." My business partner Ross was part of an elite intelligence force in the military, and I know his investigative skills will help us to find out who is behind the letter.

Mr Donaldson's secretary pokes her head around the door to the concourse we're standing on, which is outside the main event room. "Mr Donaldson, we're going to be starting in a few minutes," she says.

He nods at her, then turns to me again. "Will you do it?"

I rub my hand over my face. "I need more details, Mr Donaldson," I say. My tone is a warning. The more information I have the better I can assess any risks.

"You'll have them, just as soon as I can get a background file on Amelia here for you. Meanwhile, please do what I've asked. When I know exactly what I'm dealing with I'll pass it on. With the referendum only a couple of weeks away, Miss Campbell needs twenty-four-hour protection. From what we know so far, her connection to me somehow puts her at risk."

Curiosity has the better of me, I'm not a stupid man, I know he has closer men on his security team than me. The question burning within me now is, why does he think I'm the best person for this job?

His brief was simple: protect her from a distance, do not engage with her... at least until he finds out more.

It appears clear enough. Protect Miss Campbell from any flaky idiots that aren't Scottish nationalists. It feels like easy money.

* * *

IMMEDIATELY, another politician grabs his attention when he steps inside the event room.

Ross comes over and stands beside me, but he doesn't talk. He's said very little since we arrived. I whisper a brief synopsis of the conversation with Donaldson.

19

Now, we both have our eyes on the room and my focus shifts to the table at the front; the table furthest away from the exit doors at the back, and the one Miss Campbell, the woman we're here to protect, will be seated at. At least I know who I'm looking for. Everyone knows Amelia Campbell from the newspapers. She's the kind of woman that stands out in a crowd. I move around the side of the room until I'm at the wall behind the chair where her place card is.

More people enter and take their seats at their tables, and as my gaze sifts through the faces, my trained eyes dismiss everyone else until I find her. She's walking confidently through the room with her petite blonde friend by her side. She stops more than once as she makes her way to her seat, smiling and talking, taking her time with everyone who approaches her.

Mr Donaldson is standing by the table, his neck stretched, his legs straining to make him taller as he looks for her. His eyes flick briefly towards me then back on the crowd in the room. From my position I see him sigh when he finally spots her. He doesn't look like a patient man as he waits for her to reach him. I smile. I'd be impatient too, if she was mine.

I wonder what's running through his mind as he watches her coming towards us. I turn back to see her kiss an older man on the cheek before she reaches the table. She straightens her spine, her shoulders back, as she walks slowly towards Mr Donaldson.

The good friend with Miss Campbell is Charlotte Grey. She nudges her with her elbow the closer they get to the table. Miss Campbell subtly shakes her head and frowns, her eyes darting towards the First Minister. I wonder why Charlotte is distracting her, sharing a private joke perhaps? Whatever it is, according to the look on Miss Campbell's face, now isn't the time or the place.

As the ladies reach the table, Mr Donaldson reaches forward, wraps his arms around Miss Campbell, and tries to kiss her, but she turns her face to the side. When his kiss lands on her cheek she doesn't look happy with his gesture.

Ross wanders to the other side of me and leans against the wall. "Did you catch that?" I ask him.

"Yes, of course I did, he makes her uncomfortable," he replies.

My colleague's response tells me we're as in sync as always. Whatever is going on with that note, I know Ross is just the man to help me figure it out. It would appear the First Minister's protection for Miss Campbell may be in her best interests, since he's acted on the note, but with a man like him, there's always a hidden agenda. I personally would be surprised if there's any real threat to her.

It makes me wonder why Donaldson is taking this threat so seriously. Nevertheless, he does have that note and it's been enough to spook him into thinking Miss Campbell is in some kind of danger and needs my protection.

 melia
17th July

I LEAVE Lottie at the table and make my way to the stage, following behind Harry. There's a loud round of applause as the main speaker introduces the First Minister and me to the room. Silence descends as we walk towards the podium. Harry smiles warmly and I inwardly cringe at his attention towards me, not wishing for my feelings to be made public. He places his hand on my shoulder, which is thankfully brief because I'm not sure I could have hidden my reaction to him touching me a second longer.

He addresses the audience. "Ladies and gentlemen, thank you all for coming here today to celebrate the opening of our new children's wing. There has been no expense spared on this project, and I'm sure those of you who have already toured this incredible facility will agree with me when I say costs should never be cut when it comes to the health of future generations."

The attendees applaud again, and Harry takes the time to

soak up the adulation. When the clapping dies down, he continues, "Some of *the* best consultants in the world are now based here in Edinburgh. All of them prepared to put our children and their families first." More applause fills the room as he smiles proudly.

Hypocrite. If I wasn't a lady, I'd push him away from that microphone and tell everyone in this room, that Harry Donaldson wasn't prepared to put up *any* of the money for this project, even though his own MSPs were all for it. He hummed and hawed for months over this project, putting it into jeopardy, until I stepped in. Then, suddenly, he was prepared to pledge public funds and money from his own pocket. My guess is he's chasing the limelight. He should've gone into acting instead of politics if this is the case, although even his acting skills are questionable and practically laughable.

After the round of applause and cheering in response to his opening speech, my eyes scan the room. Almost everyone is sitting at their allocated table.

"Now, let me hand you over to the woman who has made all of this possible, Miss Amelia Campbell." I offer Harry a smile as further clapping ensues, while he steps aside to make room for me. I push my shoulders back, straightening my posture, and hold my head high just like my deportment teacher taught me.

I have a speech prepared, but when I look out to the crowd, I'm overwhelmed by the raw emotion flowing through my veins. I think everyone present is here for the same reason, to make a difference, or so I hope. I fold the small piece of paper in my hand that contains speech prompts, and slide it into my pocket, choosing to speak from the heart instead.

"Good afternoon everyone. I'm here to thank each and every single one of you who has helped with this project.

This is a cause that is remarkably close to my heart. As many of you know, my older brother, Finley, was claimed by cancer when I was only two years of age. Unfortunately, I don't remember the short time we had together, and that saddens me to this day. We never had the chance to experience the special bond between siblings, or the quarrels, which I'm sure, knowing me, there would've been plenty." A soft ripple of chuckles flows through the room.

I clear my throat. "But I do remember how hard my mother worked, after Finley's death, to highlight the horrific disease cancer is, and how it claims far too many of our loved ones, young and old. With this new unit, the hope is that more lives can be saved. I'm proud to have been able to play a small part in bringing the concept of this facility to fruition.

"So, we have this amazing facility, but it is the oncology experts, consultants, nursing and support staff who will help make a difference to the lives of young patients and their families. But the aim of this unit isn't only about caring for and treating the patients. It's about keeping families together, giving them vital support during difficult times until they no longer need treatment."

I pause, my eyes find Lottie in her seat at the table in front of me. Her smile is wide, and she nods her head approvingly. A warm round of applause and cheering resounds again in the room. I might make headlines as a party girl, and the press may choose to focus on that frivolous side of me, but I do have a serious side,

"I'd like to thank all of you who have donated through this joint private *and* public funded initiative. Having this facility gives the children of our nation, and their families, hope and belief that they can face this horrible disease, knowing they are receiving the best treatment possible."

I've said all I want to, there's nothing else that needs to be added. I take a step back from the podium and I'm not prepared for the sweep of emotion that runs through my body as I watch every person in the room rise to their feet and applaud.

Harry offers me his hand and I reluctantly take it as we make our way back to our table. "Brilliant," he whispers, too close to my ear, as I sit down. I wipe the memory of his imprint on my hand on a napkin I then place on my lap.

HE DOESN'T STOP THERE. "You, Amelia Campbell, are not just a pretty face." I choose to ignore his comment when all I really want to do is slap *his* smug face hard. He kisses my cheek before taking the seat beside me.

Chatter around the table is light. Harry pours me some white wine, which I accept and take a rather large gulp.

Lottie nudges me. "Miss Campbell, is there something you've omitted to tell me?" I turn to face her, she has her wine glass in her hand and is staring at me, questioning me with her raised eyebrows.

"What?" I say, probably a bit louder than I should, gathering interest from everyone at our table. "Sorry," I address the table. Harry has his eyes on me.

Lottie chuckles beside me and whispers. "You and I need to talk. He thinks he stands a chance getting into your pants," she says gesturing towards Harry.

I can't believe she's said that here and now. Outspoken should be Lottie's middle name.

I lean closer so the entire table can't hear me. "There's no chance of that ever happening. *Ever.*" I hope she hears how much I mean the words I've spoken.

"I hear you, but his number two, I wouldn't kick him out of bed. Look at him, he's gorgeous. I wonder if he looks as fine under the suit as he does with it on. What do you think? Big cock or not?"

I cover my mouth with my hand to save me from spitting out my wine as I choke on it. Without looking around at the other guests at our table, I already know they're looking at me. *One of these days I'll threaten to attend an event without Lottie.*

"Amelia, are you okay?" Harry asks, his voice laced with concern.

"Yes, sorry. Lottie just has a way with words."

He glances at Lottie and then says, "Would you care to swap seats? I'm sure Doctor Wilson would much rather be sitting next to you."

I look over past Harry at Doctor Wilson, who looks like a lovely man and I smile. The distinguished tall man in his sixties meets my eyes and smiles back. The smile reaches his dark brown eyes, and they soften. He's good-looking with flecks of grey in his dark brown hair. "I'm fine where I am, and anyway, I'll have plenty of time to talk to Doctor Wilson after lunch."

"You will?" The pitch of Harry's voice suddenly rises.

"Yes, I'm taking a tour of the facility."

He frowns and says, "But you've already been escorted around it."

"Yes, but I want to meet some of the children."

His face lights up. "This could be a great PR opportunity," he says, and I can already envisage the conversation he'll have with one of his many advisors. Harry Donaldson is an opportunist who is always looking to spin any situation to make himself look good.

I scowl. "I don't think so, Harry. This isn't up for debate and it would be crude to use sick children for your political posturing. Think of the privacy of the young patients and their families. I won't allow you to use me, or them, to gain momentum for yourself before the referendum." My protest is louder than I expect, but what he wants to do is wrong Exploiting these children would be morally abhorrent.

He smiles at the people across from us and then, without moving his lips, whispers to me, "Keep your voice down."

"No, Harry, I won't. I think Doctor Wilson will agree with me on this one," I say, drawing the eminent oncologist into the conversation.

He nods his head. "I do, Miss Campbell. The children's privacy has to be respected at all times," he says, bluntly. Harry doesn't look so smug now. His self-importance is an ugly trait. First Minister or not, if he needs to be brought down a peg or two, I have no problem in being the one to do it. Surely, he knows that.

Turning my attention to Lottie, I can see she's almost giddy from my interference in Harry's plan, but doesn't laugh. She knows how much she can get away with. I'm looking forward to our night out and I'm sure we'll revisit the topic of Harry Donaldson at some point during the evening. I already know she agrees with me, Harry gives us both the creeps.

The food is lovely, as one would expect, and the company has been exceptionally good as well, considering Harry has kept his beady eyes on me the whole time. I've tried to ignore him, but damn, it's been hard. He's a trying man and I'm not a patient woman.

"Miss Campbell." I turn my attention to Doctor Wilson's voice. "Shall we?" He stands and walks the short distance to me, and offers me his hands, which I accept gracefully with a smile.

"I'd love to come along," Harry states pushing his chair back.

I stand at the side of Doctor Wilson as he tells Harry, "I'm sorry Mr Donaldson, I don't think that's wise, all things considered. A few of the children know that Miss Campbell is coming to meet them, along with her friend, and they are excited about seeing her." Lottie stands and I'm scared to look at her because if there's even the slightest hint of smug satisfaction on her face, I may not be able to control my laughter. Harry sits back down in his chair, frowning and mumbling under his breath.

"Ladies, come with me."

"Doctor Wilson, I know the facility is new—"

"Please, Derek is fine," he corrects. "I hate all these formalities," he says putting me at ease. I relax with his request that puts us all on a first name basis.

"May I say, Derek, we are so thankful you took a position here. When I saw you were joining the team, I read about the incredible work you've been doing. The stem cell trial you ran was groundbreaking."

"Indeed, but there is much more to learn," he replies playing down the herculean effort he's put into his cancer trials. He looks awkward with my praise, so I change tack when I sense his embarrassment.

"Okay, Derek, I was going to ask how many patients are currently in the unit? "

"We have three full-time patients. Two girls, both aged nine, and one boy who is six."

I stop and glance between Derek and Lottie. The sadness on my friend's face tells me she knows what I'm thinking.

Derek continues, "Amelia, I'm sorry I didn't know about your brother until your speech," he says as if reading our minds. "If this is too distressing, you don't have to meet the patients." His eyes meet mine and I can see the sincerity there.

"No, honestly I'll be fine." I straighten my shoulders and carry on walking.

He holds out a hand in the direction of some fire doors. "There will also be a few patients in our day care ward. I should mention that we have a baby in the facility. I'm hoping she'll be well enough to go home in the next few days."

"A baby!" It's Lottie's faint voice beside me. I take her hand. There's an ashen look on her face and I know there won't be a dry eye between us soon. *How does a new life end up with this awful disease?*

"Yes, she's only seven months old, but she's responded well to our new treatment. Her parents are a lovely young couple who are coping well under the circumstances." I hear his words but wonder how any new parent deals with the fact that their baby has cancer. I can't imagine what they are going through. My heart is already breaking for them and I haven't met them yet.

We enter the hospital wing and Derek introduces us to a few members of the nursing team that are here to greet us. The conversation is light, and we are told we are meeting the three patients and their families who are currently being treated in the unit. I try to control my breathing, but it's so damn hard because it's coming in quick gasps.

Slow and steady. Slow and steady, I repeat over and over, hoping it helps.

We are led to a day room and Derek speaks to me the whole way, telling me everything he hopes to get out of this new facility. I could listen to him talk all day long; he's so enthusiastic and his passion for his work shines through when he speaks.

When the room door is opened, I'm not prepared for the gasp from Lottie. I take her hand and squeeze it in the hope it gives her a little reassurance. She smiles and gives me a nod of her head.

"Are you both okay?" Derek asks.

"Of course," I reply, trying to convince all of us.

"If at any point this gets too much, please just say."

I offer him a smile, but if these patients and their families can face the ordeal of their child being gravely ill, then Lottie and I will stay strong to show our support as well.

Derek leads the way, and the two girls are sitting happily watching TV, their parents are at a table drinking tea or coffee and chatting.

"Grace, Emily, we have visitors," Derek says approaching them. Two beautiful little girls turn around, smiles cover their perfect little faces and... *good grief*, my heart breaks in two for what they are both going through. Both girls have lost their hair.

I crouch before them. "Hi girls, what are you watching?" I ask, careful not to block their view of the TV screen.

"It's a musical. We both love it. You're very pretty," Emily says.

"So are you," I reply, trying to sound cheerful.

"I'm not pretty without my hair," she says, and Grace nudges her, frowning.

"Well, I happen to think you are extremely beautiful. You both are. Your smiles could light up a room. and I'm sure your parents agree."

"Girls, do you remember what I told you?" Derek asks.

"Yes, that if it wasn't for Miss Campbell, we wouldn't have this new centre," Grace says looking at him. She turns to me. "Thank you, we're glad Doctor Wilson is helping us."

These kids have had to grow up too quickly, and that is so sad. I hear Lottie swallow roughly behind me, and I dare not turn around to look at her because I know I'll cry if I do.

"So, you are both aiming for going home soon?" I ask with a smile.

They both nod and tell me what they are looking forward to, and Derek encourages both sets of parents to talk with us. I'm truly overwhelmed by the positive attitude of both children and their families. I hear how tough it's been on them, but how much the new facility has helped keep their family units together. From listening to their shared stories, it's clear that strong friendships have been formed between not just the girls but their parents too.

I could spend all day with them, but Derek encourages me to move to the day unit. I ask if it's okay if I can be updated with both girls' progress and also ask if they wouldn't mind me coming back to visit. Both families agree and I leave the girls, happy to have met them.

We enter the day unit and it's me that has to mentally talk myself out of crying as I see the parents standing over a cot. *Oh no this is heart-breaking.*

"Amelia, Lottie, this is Luke and Katherine and this precious little one is Angel," Derek says by way of introduction.

Luke stands and offers us his hand. I'm trying to not to show my emotions and Lottie, well, she's so quiet I know wants to cry.

Derek asks, "Lottie, do you need a minute?"

She looks embarrassed and shakes her head. "No, sorry, I'll be ok. I just feel helpless."

Luke gestures to where he was sitting. "Here, please take my seat." He smiles kindly. "Don't feel sorry for us, please." He turns to face me. "We know our baby girl is getting the best chance at life, and that's thanks to you."

I feel so humbled being here with you, it's such a privilege to have been involved with this project. When I see what you're going through, it doesn't feel like I've done nearly enough," I say.

He shakes his head. "No, you have. I've followed this story from the start and if it wasn't for you this centre might never have been given the go ahead. You've campaigned tirelessly and put up most of the funds."

I smile warmly. "If being involved saves lives, I'll do it every single day."

Luke's wife, Katherine, studies me for a moment. "I think the media and the public has you wrong," she says softly.

I grin, a little embarrassed that she sees me for who I am. "Shh, it's my biggest secret. I'm human and I've made more mistakes than I care to mention but when I believe in something, I'll do whatever I can do to help, or make something happen."

Derek smiles and the young couple do the same.

Katherine asks me, "Would you like to hold Angel?"

I'm surprised by the question. "I won't hurt her, will I?"

"No," Derek says with a broad smile.

"Okay," I say nervously. Katherine stands, giving me her seat, and lifts her gorgeous daughter out of the crib before handing her to me. Gosh I'm nervous. "She's beautiful," I say looking at the tiny girl in my arms, and tears fill my eyes. She's peaceful despite all she's going through.

I look at Luke and Katherine and can't imagine the strain they are under. "How are you coping?"

Katherine's tired eyes meet mine and she smiles. "We don't have a choice but to make things work. We've only been married for two years and barely had time to let that sink in before we found out we were expecting Angel and now this…" her voice trails off and she casts a worried look towards her baby again.

Luke sighs and takes her hand. "It's been hard. I gave up my job recently because I wanted to be here to support Katherine."

"What did you do?"

"I was a bricklayer, but I juggled my job with visits here to the unit when I could. Working filled me with guilt for leaving the burden of Angel's illness on my wife's shoulders."

"That must be a financial strain," I say.

"Money is tight, but we wouldn't have it any other way, especially now that Angel is getting better."

Derek then cuts in and explains Angel's cancer diagnosis and the tailored treatment plan the oncology experts have devised for her, which she has responded exceptionally well to. Katherine asks if they can have a picture with me and who am I to deny them? She hands her phone over and Lottie takes a few photographs.

It strikes me, this little girl in my arms has a fighting chance. One that, without this facility, may not have been possible. My tears fall as thoughts of this new young family fill my head. Life can be so cruel, but they are showing the strength of determination that some can only dream of. But most importantly, all I see before me is their deep love and commitment to each other and their daughter.

After spending more time with the family than I imagined, we reluctantly leave. Derek is talking to us, but I don't hear a word he says; my head is still in the room we just left.

He opens another door, and we enter living accommodation. A home away from home. And sitting on a sofa is a gorgeous boy, and my heart sinks, because not only is he the same age as my brother Finley was, but the boy's bald appearance looks similar to some of the photographs I have of my brother.

"My mummy reads stories about beautiful princesses, but I didn't know they were real. Are you a real princess?" he asks with his eyes on me.

I close the distance between us. A nurse is tending to him and his mother is sitting holding his hand, a sad smile on her face.

I tell the boy, "I'm not a princess but I am real. And real princesses do exist. Keep listening to those stories, promise?"

He nods. "Yes, I promise."

I spend time with Callum and his mum, and I'm so taken

aback by the positivity they have. That's the one thing I didn't expect, but I think staying positive in such a situation gives everyone strength to keep going.

When our time comes to leave the unit, I'm so emotional, which of course I expected, but I want to do more than I already have done. If there's a small way I can help any of these families, then I want to do it. They are all so special. My thoughts are with Luke and Katherine and how tough their situation must be for such a young couple at the beginning of married life.

Life can be so cruel, and yet they don't look like a couple who is suffering.

My mother always said a baby was a gift from God, and today I think I've finally realised she was right. Angel is the perfect name for their baby girl.

CHAPTER 5

$\mathcal{L}$iam
17th July

THIS IS RIDICULOUS. Our principle — the woman First Minister Harry Donaldson's hired me to protect — left the room ages ago with her friend and a doctor. I had been about to follow when Donaldson grabbed my arm and told me to leave her with them after telling me the site is secure. *If it's so secure what are we doing here?*

The minute she leaves this site, we are to take over. I'm getting restless with every minute that ticks by that she's gone, because we're either doing this half-arsed job, or we're not.

"You're antsy," Ross says.

"I am," I say turning my head to face him, and I see he's smirking.

"What has you this wound up?" he asks.

I frown and shake my head. "Truthfully, I'm not sure. I

suppose it's instinct. Do you think he's perhaps infatuated with her?

Ross scoffs. "Can you see the First Minister and that gorgeous woman as a couple?"

"We're not paid to match make," I remind Ross.

He shrugs. "Well for what it's worth, I don't think this job is going to be all that bad. Amelia Campbell is a serious piece of eye candy."

I shake my head from side-to-side at my friend's lack of professionalism. Ross is ever the player, trust him to focus on her looks. Not that he's wrong in thinking how stunning she is, I just wouldn't voice it like him. However, I can't hide my smile, and the icy atmosphere that was there only moments ago is now gone. Buried again for the time being.

"We'll need to go and speak to Donaldson again," I say.

"Yes, we will. But looking at the flurry of non-stop visitors to his table, you might not get a chance before the principle comes back."

Ross isn't wrong, there is always someone stopping by to have a word in the First Minister's ear.

"What do you think of him?" I ask.

"Who, Mr Donaldson?" I nod and he scrunches his brow for a moment. "Personally, I've yet to meet a politician I like, and from my limited knowledge of him, I'm not expecting my opinion of them to change. He seems to enjoy the lime-light, but when it comes to his policies they're pretty vague or full of holes, and that won't get him the votes he needs for independence."

And that's where I'm also at with the First Minister.

"Come on," I say, straightening my shoulders. We walk around the outside of the room, saying hello to a few members of Donaldson's own security team. No one asks why we're here, so I presume they've had a briefing of some kind or another, but not on the real reason we're present.

We stop at the side of his table. At the same time a woman pulls out the chair beside him and sits down extremely close to him. I recognise her as the MSP Education Secretary, Miss Beverley Harper. Donaldson hasn't spotted us as he leans toward her and whispers in her ear. She wraps her arm over the back of his chair, but her fingers trail up and down his back. He doesn't appear upset with the attention she's giving him.

Are they a couple? If so, why is Miss Campbell at risk and not Miss Harper?

"Is it just me…" I begin.

"No. I see it," Ross says quickly with his voice lowered so our conversation isn't heard. "I personally don't see the attraction."

I smirk. "Well, unless you're keeping something from me and you want to choose now to come out the closet, then I wouldn't expect you or I to see the attraction of him."

"Arsehole," he replies. "Now, if he's after Amelia, why would he be allowing Harper to paw him like that?"

"No idea, but I think now is the perfect time to interrupt our Mr Donaldson."

Ross agrees and we both approach the table. "Excuse me, First Minister," I say clearing my throat. Poor Beverley Harper almost jumps out her skin and there's a small, tiny part of me that feels sorry for her, but that thought quickly diminishes.

"Ah, Mr McKenna," he says rising to his feet. "And this must be Mr Phillips, good to meet you." Donaldson holds out his hand to Ross, but his attention is pinned towards the door. We were talking less than an hour ago and he's pretending we didn't. I try to hide my smug grin when I see Donaldson flinch as Ross shakes his hand with a firm grip the First Minister isn't used to. Ross has a bone crushing handshake.

Donaldson steps away from the table, obviously not wanting anyone else to hear our conversation.

"Miss Campbell will be back any second. Remember you are shadows; she doesn't need people to be aware she has security with her."

I don't allow my focus to waver, it stays firmly on Donaldson, who is sounding disjointed and nervous as his gaze travels everywhere but at me. One of his security guards moves towards us, I put my hand up shaking my head. The First Minister also shakes his head, halting the guard in his tracks.

"Can you be any clearer on what I'm keeping her safe from?" I ask, irritated that I'm still trying to get answers from him.

"You saw the letter. With the impending referendum I can't take the chance with her safety. You're to trace Miss Campbell when she's out and about until she's home safely."

"Of course, Sir," I say quickly, thinking I don't care much for our First Minister. Right now, he's coming across as a bit of a paranoid prat. "We'll start as soon as she moves."

"Thank you, I hope you can understand I won't risk anything happening to her." His statement is one I could understand coming from a man who cares, but from what I've seen, I don't think Donaldson is capable of caring for anyone but himself. He seems driven by the referendum, and the possibility of Scotland gaining independence.

Amelia Campbell re-enters the room and makes her presence felt as she moves through the donors, and I note Ross isn't wrong; she's breathtaking. Donaldson continues to talk but I'm no longer listening, as the beautiful woman I'm here to protect is walking directly towards us.

 melia
17th July

I stop as we near the table we were sitting at earlier for lunch. Harry has his back to me and is talking to the two men that I had noticed standing behind me when I got up to make my speech.

Lottie nudges my arm. "What in the devil's name have we stopped for?" She grumbles then follows my gaze and notices who I'm looking at.

She tilts her head. "I noticed those two earlier, who do you think they are?"

I shrug. "I've no idea."

I dismiss them as two of the venue's hired hands and wonder what excuse I'm going to tell Harry Donaldson for leaving earlier than he probably expects me to.

Harry steps away from the men and throws an arm around my shoulder. "Amelia, darling there you are." I'm shocked at his use of the word 'darling' as he leads me away in the direction of the door. I'm glad because my exit from the event will be all the smoother for it. Lottie follows us, a few steps behind. As soon as we're out of earshot I shrug out of his hold and cross my arms over my chest. The man makes my skin crawl. He ignores my manoeuvre and asks, "How did the tour go?"

I sigh, trying to rein in my emotions. "It was harrowing seeing those poor children, but I'm glad I revisited the unit. I can see how much it's already achieving."

Laughter in the room distracts us, and I turn away in the direction of it. I feel Harry reach out and take my hand. With a shake of my head, I pull my hand from his and refocus my attention. "Harry, I'm sorry but we're leaving," I say.

He pouts. "So soon? I was hoping we could at least find a few minutes to talk since you can't do dinner today. Who knows when we can get together, because it's so close to the referendum, and my diary is filling fast."

I hold back an eyeroll. "Harry, I don't have anything to do with your referendum, and now that the unit is up and running, most of my work here is done. My only obligation is to support the charity arm of the unit in helping them raise funds for the continuation of the families' hospitality." As sweetly as I can, I add, "Please accept my apologies for not being able to stay for the remainder of the day."

I turn on my heel ready to walk away, because if I stand any longer I'm going to say something that I might regret, with regards to him trying to use me to gain votes.

"Nice meeting you again, Harry," Lottie says flippantly over her shoulder, as I begin to walk away, and she quickly joins me.

"What the hell just happened? That man has been all over me since the moment I arrived," I say as we walk toward the exit.

Lottie giggles. "I told you, he wants to get you into bed. He sees you as the woman who'll be by his side as he leads our country to a great victory. I mean you're beautiful, and he needs all the help he can get. I wouldn't put it past him to think you'd make a power couple... Like Posh and Becks."

I snort and freeze on the spot when she says this. I glare at her. "Over my dead body."

She raises her eyebrows. "Oh, no, he wants you very much alive. As limp of a dick as he is, I don't think he's into necrophilia. Just think, Amelia, you could be Scotland's answer to Jackie Onassis or Michelle Obama. If you marry him and he wins you'd be the first lady. Think about it. You're a catch. Hell, if you'd given into Prince James' advances, you could have been our next queen." She nudges me and chuckles. "There's still time, they've not announced anything about Effie."

As we start walking again, I shudder at the mere thought. "I have absolutely *no* desire to be queen *or* first lady. I could never imagine being married to James." I cringe. "Can you imagine how miserable I'd be? Do you honestly see me playing the dutiful wife? I'm too free thinking and opinionated to fawn around behind a man's coattails. I'm not saying I don't want to get married. When I do, it will be for love, not to support someone to do their duty, or to make a man look more powerful."

Lottie laughs, knowing that I mean what I say. I glance over my shoulder when I reach the end of the corridor and Harry is still standing where I left him. He's watching me, and I find his attention unsettling. I'm slightly mindful of him though, because he does wield some power. I honestly don't know what to do about him, but I'm sure I'll think of something.

My friend links her arm with mine as we exit the building. "Are we going to that new celebrity wine bar that's just opened on the mile?"

I nod and I tell the member of staff at the door not to get my car, and that I'll have it collected tomorrow.

* * *

"WHERE DID THEY COME FROM?" I ask, noticing the two men I saw at the event a couple of hours ago."

Lottie glances in the direction of my gaze. "Who, those two? The ones from the event? It's odd but we're not far from the unit, so it's probably coincidental they're here. Maybe Harry left not long after us," she suggests. "If he and his cronies have gone there'd be no need for a lot of security."

"Funny you should say that, because I thought they were security guards as well. Must be the suits," I say.

I look over my shoulder and both men are sitting in seats facing one another with glasses of water before them. Neither of them is talking, and they occasionally glance in our direction.

Whoever they are, I think they're interested in us.

"You're probably right, it's a coincidence," I say turning back away from their watchful gaze to pour us both another glass of champagne.

"You do know this is fucked up, right?" Lottie says. I frown in confusion and take a sip of my bubbly while she continues, "They're two hot-looking guys... we could have a lot of fun with them."

"If they were interested, they'd come over. Perhaps they're waiting for someone?"

"Yeah, maybe they are. It's the only reason I can think of that would make them pass up the opportunity to get to know us," Lottie says, sounding big-headed and sighs wistfully. "Pity, that one in the navy suit looks like he knows how to party." She raises her glass to mine with a smile before taking it to her lips. Instead of an elegant sip, her mouth opens wide, and she almost finishes the contents in one.

I glance over my shoulder and it's clear that the taller of the two men appears to be studying me intently. My body, for some strange, unknown reason, seems attuned to his. I sense chemistry between us, which is absurd since I've never seen him before today, and I don't know him.

Let him look.

With a smile on my lips, I turn my attention back to Lottie and finish my drink.

My thoughts turn to Harry, and I hope that whatever grand ideas he imagines about us becoming a great Scottish romance story will fade very quickly.

"Ladies!" We both lift our heads to see two very well-presented men, standing beside our table with a bottle of my favourite champagne. "May we join you?"

Lottie and I exchange glances, and she nods. "Of course," she says, making room for the men to pull up two chairs.

Looking over my shoulder, I can see the two suited men from earlier talking, but it's the taller one that has my attention again. His seated pose is stiff, leaning slightly forward, his huge hands on his knees as he scrutinises our company. His suspicious gaze makes me smile. He's so attractive, I'm struggling to take my eyes off him.

Maybe I'm imagining it, but I feel there's a strong possibility the grim look on his face has nothing to do with his job. My imagination is playing tricks on me, I think. My judgement is impaired because I've already had a few drinks, but it warms me to think he's a tiny bit miffed by the men's intrusion. Was his intention to make a move spoiled by our new friends' arrival? If so, I love a jealous man.

On impulse I decide I don't care. He should have come over if he wanted to talk to us. Laughter rings loudly at our table and I turn my attention away from him. I remind myself I agreed we should make headlines and choose to focus on that.

Since we're at this new celebrity haunt in the city I know I'm guaranteed there will be someone outside ready to take our picture when we eventually decide leave. Hopefully, it will make me appear scandalous enough to scare off the advances of a man with designs on using me to his advantage to gain an edge in his pursuit of an independent Scotland.

CHAPTER 7

$\mathcal{L}$iam
17th July

BEING SLOWLY TORTURED in a basement somewhere would be preferable to my Friday night as it now stands. I should be at home with a glass of whisky in my hand after exerting myself in bed with a nameless woman; someone that would've helped clear my mind of some of the sights I've seen in the past that haunt me in the dark.

Instead, Ross and I are sitting here in an upmarket wine bar, each with a glass of flat lemonade in front of us. We're doing our job, such as it is, of keeping a watchful eye on our principle, the beautiful, rich socialite who's downing Dom Pérignon like it's a fiver a bottle.

"How long are we going to sit here?" Ross grumbles, because he's not as patient as me in the field. His expertise is usually as a cyber intelligence operative, tracing people online, not physically following them. He only agreed to drive me today because he was at a loose end.

I shrug without looking at him. "I'll be here until she's ready to go home. You can leave whenever you want, this stupid detail doesn't take both of us."

"I'm not leaving you all alone. What kind of friend would I be? You'd look a real sad sack sitting here on your own. But I am going to pop outside to make a call." He stands and shakes his trousers out before he straightens up.

"Okay, go and apologise to whomever you were meant to be shagging tonight," I say with a smirk as he leaves the table and doesn't look back. Knowing Ross, I would guess his date was hot. But I'd bet my right testicle she isn't as hot as Amelia Campbell. I feel pissed I'm so attracted to her.

Fuck.

As if she knows what I'm thinking, she raises her gaze and looks over at me. She's laughing and talking to the slick city boy who is sitting beside her, his arm slung casually over her shoulder. He looks smug, and right now I'd happily punch the fucker in the face. Not the most professional of thoughts from me tonight, but there's no need for him to get handsy with her. I tell myself this is my protective instinct towards my client, which I know deep down is bull shite, but the guy chatting her up reminds me of the turd who hired me – Harry Donaldson – they're both sleazeballs. I grin.

Amelia smiles at me raising her champagne glass to her lips, and I lift my soft drink. She thought I was smiling at her. "Cheers, yourself," I say before taking a drink as I try to look as if this is a chance encounter, and I haven't followed her here.

Ross sits back down beside me. "Fuck, are things that bad, that you're talking to yourself now?"

"I'm beginning to wonder what I've let myself in for taking this job on," I mutter.

Ross takes a sip of his drink. "Well, you're here now. I'm only here to do your donkey work."

Ross is modest, if my work with Miss Campbell continues, he'll be doing a lot more than that. If I find out the threat towards Amelia Campbell has substance, I'm hoping he'll be able to use his intelligence skills to find out who or what the danger is. Donaldson was surprised when I said I needed a driver to take me to the event today, and as far as he's concerned that's what Ross is, just a driver. Looks can be deceiving because there's a whole lot more to my business partner than a driving licence.

Ross has done everything from disrupting kidnappers to organising covert rescue missions for the military. Skills he rarely gets to use these days due to our new venture since we've been on civvy street.

I shake my head and narrow my eyes. "If this job stretches out, I'll need you to do some digging."

"Do you think we'll actually find something?"

I scoff. "Don't you, after meeting him earlier? For a guy who wants to run the country, he looked like he had more chance of running a raffle. You never know, he may actually have something he's not telling us. Even if it's only that someone might try to kill her to save her from a fate worse than death by letting Donaldson screw her."

"Yeah." Ross chuckles.

We continue talking and watching, and my frustration grows by the second with the woman seated across the bar. She should be heading home. Various people wandering past their table stop and make small talk with Amelia and her friend, which I'd expect since she's instantly recognisable. It's mainly men who show interest, but the two letches hanging around their necks have chased every other guy away.

Even the patience I pride myself as having is wearing thin, and my arse is sore from sitting on this uncomfortable, thin padded seat; it's been a long and tedious day.

"Get your…" I'm already out of my chair the second I

hear Amelia's clipped tone, and in six strides I'm dragging city boy's body from his seat and pushing myself between him and Amelia with ease.

"Oh!" she manages before hiccupping.

Great she's drunk.

The inebriated city boy snarls. "Who the hell do you think you are?" He grabs my arm and takes a weak swing at me with a tightly clenched fist.

I stop him swinging and crush his fist in my palm. "You really don't want to do that," I warn through gritted teeth.

"Fuck you," he slurs, but I see the anger dim in his eyes and it's replaced by pain when he feels the strength in my grip. He knows instantly he's defeated.

"Come on, Tristan," his posh skinny friend says, as he attempts to pull him back.

Ross is standing with folded arms, assessing the situation and looking amused. He'll only interrupt if he thinks I can't keep things under control, which I can, of course. I see a member of staff speak to my partner, and I'm sure Ross is telling them I've intervened to help the two women, I don't want any trouble, I'm preventing it.

"Get off me, I'm not interested in this stuck-up bitch." *Says the man who had no chance.* He had no idea Amelia, and her friend, were merely amusing themselves with him and his friend.

"I think you want to go that way," I warn, nodding away from the table. He pulls out of my hold and stumbles backwards, his eyes darting between where Amelia is still sitting, and me.

"Gentlemen, it's time you left," the bar's bouncer suggests.

Tristan's friend pulls him away from the table remarkably easily after this. Ross steps forward blocking city boy, Tristan from me, and ensures both men leave.

"Are you okay?" I ask Amelia.

She narrows her eyes at me. "Yes. You should know, I can handle gropers like him by myself."

"If you say so."

She takes another sip of champagne and Lottie giggles. "I do say so…" Miss Campbell chirps like a petulant child, puts her glass down and folds her arms across her chest in a huff. My eyes fall to her cleavage and she quickly swivels the top half of her body away.

She caught me looking.

"Don't you think it's time you both went home?" I ask them as Ross re-joins us, standing next to Lottie.

She reaches down and squeezes his arse. "I'll happily go if I can take this one with me." She giggles, gazing up at him. "Amelia, you can have Mr Broody and Moody."

Ross comes closer to me. "There are some reporters and photographers outside."

"And why is that a problem?" I ask quietly.

"You know what I mean," he says nodding at both women. "They're three sheets to the wind."

My gaze is on Amelia and Lottie, and he's right. I imagine their drunken state is what gets them the reputations they have. "Can you get a taxi for me and drop her friend home in the car ?"

"Of course. Do you want me to take Lottie outside first?"

"No, we'll leave together. Let's not give the reporters anything else to speculate on." I sigh heavily, thinking about how the four of us leaving at the same time will look to the waiting paparazzi.

"Miss Campbell, is it?" I ask like I'm unsure. "I'm going to see you get home safely," I say and gesture towards the cloakroom.

She snarls. "You think so? I don't even know who you are.

49

For all I know you could be worse than the guys you saw off. How do I know you're not going to take me down some dark alley and slit my throat?"

Her words tell of the very thing that I'm trying to prevent, but I don't say this. "Look, I saw you today, nice speech by the way... very moving. I'm a friend of Mr Donaldson's, you can trust me to see you home safe."

She laughs. "You're a friend of Harry's, and I'm supposed to feel safe with you?" Her friend joins in her laughter.

I begin to see why Donaldson doesn't want her to know what he's learned. It feels as if she doesn't trust him in the first place. Frankly, I feel her judgement isn't all that impaired, despite the drink, because I don't think I trust Harry Donaldson either.

I try again. "Please listen, I promise I don't want to hurt you. That drunk guy was angry and may be hanging around outside. I'd hate to think he started something with you again, since I interjected already."

She blinks a few times, then stares intently at me and I wonder if she's considering whether she really is safe with me. Eventually, she nods, and I'm relieved she's letting me do this without a fight.

Lottie giggles. "Oh, Amelia, he's taking you home and I bet he's—"

"Stop it, Lottie," Amelia snaps, holding her finger up to prevent her friend from finishing her sentence, and I immediately wonder what she'd been about to say.

"Fine." Lottie huffs, handing over a raffle ticket to the cloakroom attendant. She collects her suit jacket and grabs her bag. "We're leaving."

Amelia reluctantly pulls on her coat and I stay with the ladies whilst Ross goes outside to bring my car around to the front of the building. I wait longer knowing he also needs to hail a taxi for us. He knows I want to speak to Miss Campbell alone to see if I can glean anything worthwhile from her that will make Donaldson's demand to watch her feel valid.

It's easy to see how they've both been caught on camera in the past when leaving establishments like this. Neither of them is remotely sober.

A few minutes later my phone beeps and I check the message from Ross, he's waiting out the front. "Ladies, my colleague Ross is outside," I say.

"Time to run the media gauntlet," Lottie tells me as she hooks her arm in mine, and Miss Campbell raises her eyebrows at her friend. I'm not sure I'm ready for this but she apparently is. She calmly smooths down the front of her coat, steps in front of me and, after taking a breath, she begins staggering casually with confidence towards the exit. She's one step away from being a fall down drunk and I hurry beside her, slip my hand around her waist, and use my hip pinned to hers to guide her. My intervention makes her look more dignified than she would otherwise.

When the door opens, a flurry of camera bulbs flash repeatedly. It feels like strobe lighting from a 70's discotheque, and the light blinds me for a second or two. Simultaneously a barrage of pressing questions is hurled towards Miss Campbell. She's smart and ignores them otherwise they'd hear her voice slur.

There's a taxi waiting, the engine idling, with Ross nearby and our car is parked in front of it. I glance back and see the bar's doormen are keeping most of the waiting vultures at bay.

Ross quickly arrives beside me and takes Lottie's arm from mine. Someone steps towards Miss Campbell, his arm outstretched, and makes a grab for her. I intervene and put my body between her and the unwelcome attentions of the man in his fifties. "Move back, please. Give Miss Campbell some space," I say in an aggressive tone that makes the man stop in his tracks.

Pushing him out of the way, I pull Miss Campbell closer to my body, shielding her with it, and I make a sweeping motion with my free hand, steering her clear of him.

Questions are now aimed at me, but with my professional head on, I don't answer. I expect I've already given them something to report by leaving with her and squaring up to the man who tried to accost her.

I steer her towards the waiting taxi and gently guide her inside before hopping in myself and immediately closing the door behind me. Another flurry of flashing bulbs blinds me when I look over my shoulder through the taxi's back window. When Ross sees we're free and clear he gets into my car with Lottie.

I growl, "Have these people got nothing better to do on a Friday night, than hang about in the dark, waiting for an image that might make the papers?"

"Fools!" Miss Campbell's outburst draws my attention. I glance at her as she mumbles, and fumbles through her bag. She looks up at me. "Who the hell are you?"

"Liam McKenna. You looked like you could do with a friend. I'm just making sure you're okay," I say, because she's drunk and I don't want to scare her by mentioning what Harry Donaldson told me.

"I'm perfectly fine," she slurs.

"Glad to hear it," I say, stretching over her and pulling her seatbelt. My face is close to hers and for a long moment our gazes meet. She has amazing eyes; hazel coloured with little flecks that look darker. My body is half over hers as I untangle the belt, when I see her attention drop to my lips, then she swallows. Her gaze drifts back to mine and she licks her lips as she stares at me shaking her head. She blinks once, long and slow, and it tells me she's not thinking straight; after all she's allowed me to bundle her into the back of a car and she doesn't know me from Adam. Maybe Donaldson has a point after all, and she really is at risk. I tug on the seatbelt and buckle her in.

She rummages through her bag and pulls out her mobile phone. She takes a snap of me and starts texting with one eye open to focus better.

"What are you doing?" I ask.

"Sending a photograph of you to my housekeeper. If you rape me, or kidnap me, everyone will know who you are," she says, brazenly. "I can't believe I got into a taxi with a stranger. Izzy will kill me when I tell her." She scrunches her brow for a moment. "Oh no, I think I'm going to be dead either way," she says and blinks again.

I glance towards the taxi driver who is taking rather too much interest in our conversation.

I straighten in my seat. "I told you, I'm not going to hurt you. Look at you, you've left yourself so vulnerable tonight. You should learn when to stop."

"And who are you? My dad? No wait he's dead… my …" She shakes her head, trying to make sense of things.

"I told you who I am, and it won't be long until you're back home safely."

To my surprise she pulls a 500ml bottle of water from her bag and drinks all of it. "I'm fine I sober up quickly," she informs me.

Something in me doubts this, but I could be wrong, stranger things have happened.

At least I know I've done what I was asked to do. She's safe. In ten minutes, we'll be at her building according to the address she gave the driver. I steal a quick glance and wonder again why anyone would threaten her. She looks harmless sitting beside me staring out of the window into the moonless night sky. Despite being drunk she looks thoughtful, and I wonder what's going through her mind.

melia
17th July

"Do you always allow yourself to get into this state?" I wake to a pair of strong hands gripping my upper arms as he pulls me out of the back seat of a taxi. I begin to protest and struggle, close one eye for better vision, and remember the man from the club. I think how handsome he is, which is a weird thought to have, since he looks pretty annoyed; his plump lips pressed into a line. There's a strong fresh wind blowing in my face and it's sobering.

I must have dozed off, and whoever this man is, he's right; I did drink far too much. He told me his name, but I can't remember. I'm not half as drunk as I was when he helped me into the taxi. The scene outside the wine bar floats through my mind. I remember drinking my water in the car, and the nap must have helped me sober up a little. *I can't believe I fell asleep beside a stranger in a cab. I'm never drinking to that extent again.*

I check my phone that's still clutched in my hand and see

I actually sent a text Izzy, and that at least *that* part of my actions wasn't a dream. She had replied wanting the taxi cab's license number.

The handsome man leans me against the front wing of the taxi, by the passenger door's open window. He holds me in place by leaning his body over mine until he finishes paying the driver, then closes the rear cab door. As the taxi rocks a little with the impact, he pulls me off the metal and close to his side. The wind whips my hair and I dip my head and inhale his cologne.

"You smell as good as you look."

I think he must've heard me because his head has reeled back and he's staring into my eyes. My hot, dark haired, saviour is scowling, his brows knitted, as he continues to think I need steadying before he walks me inside. I close my eyes for a second to prevent myself from fixating on his face. It doesn't work because behind my eyelids I can picture it from memory. Something in his piercing blue gaze tells me this man holds many secrets from his life. I have a strong urge to stroke his square jaw. It was clean shaven the first time I saw him, but now it's dusky with a sexy five o'clock shadow. An unexpected sigh falls from my lips, when I realise how attractive I find him.

I'm not so sure it's a good idea that he's leading me into my building because of the insane chemistry I feel, if my judgement wasn't so impaired, I'd swear he felt it as well. This wired buzz hums through me as his strong hand grips me around my middle.

"Lottie?" I ask. *Where did she go? Our golden rule has always been to stick together when we've been drinking, unless we know other people, we're with.*

"She's fine. Ross, my colleague, is driving her home because I wanted to talk to you. I'm having second thoughts about doing this tonight now I've seen the shape you are in."

"Doing what?" I ask then remember I asked about Lottie. "Poor Ross," I mumble, sarcastically, even though I don't know the man. "He won't know what's hit him when Lottie gets him in her bed." I know she'll sleep with him. The girl can't help herself. "Who is Ross anyway?" I realise what he said. "Wait, you wanted to talk to me? What do you want to talk about?"

He keeps a stern expression on his face. "It'll keep until tomorrow, but I'd like to come back and see you when you're… ready. And I wouldn't worry about Ross, I'm certain he can handle himself," he says flatly as I stumble again. He reaches out, preventing me from falling. "I've got you." And with those words he has my full attention. His searching eyes hold me captive in his gaze while his lips are only a breath away from mine. I can feel him exhale against my skin, smell peppermint on his breath from the gum he was chewing earlier. He's an extremely handsome man and I'm not at my best. He handles me with confidence, and I'm surprised when he doesn't immediately step back.

If I wanted a one-night stand he'd be exactly who I'd pick, but something tells me he won't take advantage, even if I sense he'd like to.

We enter the building and there are two men in the lobby that I've never seen before. They're sitting at the guest reception area. "What time is it?" I ask, eyeing the men in dark suits who are obviously not waiting there for fun.

"Eleven forty-five," the man, with his arm wrapped around me, says.

"What did you say your name was again?"

"Liam McKenna. Do you know those men?" he asks, and I shake my head.

"Do you think they don't belong here either?" I ask and see Liam's eyes narrow as he studies the men further.

"Evening Miss Campbell," the doorman, dressed in a navy-blue uniform, says.

"Hi, Ronnie," I say, lifting my bag and fishing out a credit card holder. I take a blank card from it and gesture towards the last lift in a row of three.

"You have visitors upstairs," Ronnie tells me.

"Visitors?" I ask, confused. His eyes dart to the two men, and I see Liam's stance physically grow. "What visitors?"

Ronnie leans closer. "A *royal* visitor."

Liam says, "Since I brought you home would you mind letting me use your bathroom before I head off?"

He distracts me from assimilating the doorman's answer, and my mind focuses on re-evaluating Liam's intention, and whether he thinks this will be a hook-up. *Usually, when I choose to be intimate with a man, we use a hotel.* I glance at the serious look in Liam's eyes and think he could never be a one-night stand. In any case, I'd likely go insane if I had a real taste of this chemistry that's buzzing between us like an electrical current, and then had to walk away afterwards.

"Sure," I reply, knowing Izzy's upstairs, and after my text to her there's no way she'll go to bed until I'm safely inside the apartment. Liam eyes the men again, slips my key card out of my hand and presses it to a panel beside the lift door. It opens and Liam ushers me inside. I rub my temple; my alcohol level is dropping, and the effects have begun to wear off. A headache is brewing, and I can already tell I'm going to have the mother of all hangovers in the morning.

"Royal visitor?" Liam asks. "Did you know those men in the foyer?" He frowns down at me.

"I think I've seen one of them before somewhere, but I can't place him. What royal visitor?" I ask this time, when I hear him remind me what the door security man said.

The lift comes to a soft halt and the door swishes open into my apartment hallway. Izzy comes running down the stairs into the spacious, light hallway with its marble flooring. She comes to a halt by the small crucifix hanging on the wall.

"Amelia, thank goodness you're okay," Izzy says with wide eyes.

I smile sheepishly, aware that I've scared her. "Sorry, he really was just seeing me home," I mumble, gesturing with my thumb towards Liam.

"You have a *special visitor*," she says, and her eyes flick upstairs like she's trying to tell me something. I glance at Liam and look back at her. "It's okay, he didn't mug me and I'm in one piece so who is it?"

She gives a small cough like she doesn't want to say.

I shake my head. "Jesus, Izzy, just spit it out. It's almost midnight, so my guess is it's a man."

"You have royal bootie calls to your apartment?" Liam says in disbelief.

I gasp. "No, I do not. Come on Izzy who is it?"

Izzy sighs. "Very well, Amelia it's His Royal Highness, Prince James."

I scowl. "James? Here, in my apartment? He's never been here before. What does he want?" I glance from Izzy to Liam and see a deep frown line in his brow. "He's a friend," I say with a sigh, although I have no idea why I'm explaining this to a man I still don't really know.

"Bathroom's through there," I say, pointing to a guest bedroom when I remember why Liam came up to my apartment. He looks as if he's debating something in his head but eventually steps past me. He doesn't look fazed at all that my visitor is the UK's heir apparent.

"Shall we go upstairs?" Izzy asks. "His Royal Highness shouldn't be kept waiting."

I don't move, my eyes are fixed on the door Liam has just walked through.

What is he doing here? Why isn't he in London with his fiancée?

My heart pounds in shock that a very senior member of the royal household feels such an urgent need to visit me in the dead of night. *Something must be terribly wrong.*

An array of emotions flood through me. Fear and anger bubble to the surface because I know whatever he wants will entail a serious discussion. I'm not at my best right now, and although we are friends, I've never received him into my home before.

I feel I must be in some sort of parallel universe. First, a stranger feels the urgent need to see me home, and now Prince James in my apartment. When the day started out at the hospital, I could never have imagined any of this. The shock of his visit has sobered me up a lot, but I'm not quite my usual self yet.

I stop when I see the prince standing with his hands against the windows, looking out across the city skyline.

I clear my throat. "James? What are you doing here? Is everything alright?"

He spins around quickly, and his eyes meet mine. My initial assessment — his smile — means there's nothing wrong.

"Good evening Amelia." His eyes shift past me to Liam when Frazier Beattie, the prince's close protection officer, steps in front of Liam obstructing him from advancing into the kitchen at the top of the stairs. "Who is this?" James barks, obviously taken aback that someone is with me.

"James, this is *my* home," I plead, when I really want to ask who gave him the right to challenge a guest in my own apartment.

His eyes narrow on Liam. "Excuse me, but we need to speak alone." Liam is respectful but has stepped to the side of Frazier and moved further into my living area, their gazes linger on one another for a moment. "Who is this?" the prince demands, addressing Frazier rather than me, and I sense some agitation in his voice.

"Her personal protection," Liam responds, clearly irritated that James dismissed me so easily in my own home.

"What?" I ask, spinning to look at Liam, but the look on his face tells me he's serious. I almost applaud Liam on his quick thinking as to excuse why he's in my apartment with me.

"Does anyone need anything?" Izzy asks, knowing full well she's breaking protocol of only speaking when spoken to, in the presence of the prince. Her question disrupts the sudden tense atmosphere in the room, but it's a gentle reminder to everyone they are all in *my* home.

"You need to leave," Frazier urges Liam, and my breath hitches at the audacity of James' man, dismissing Liam with authority.

I shake my head. "No, he's staying," I say out of pure fury that these two men are in my home late into the night and have gained entry when I wasn't even here. The men downstairs now make sense; they're also with James.

"Izzy would you please show Liam and Frazier to the lounge upstairs?" I ask with a smile.

"Of course," she says softly, her gaze narrowing on me. Izzy's a good ally but I wish Lottie had come home with me; she would certainly know what to do about Prince James' sudden visit.

At first, Liam appears reluctant to leave me, but I signal for him to go with the others and slump into the only chair, ensuring that James will have to sit on the sofa and not beside me. Eventually, Izzy ushers Frazier and Liam upstairs.

"So, we're alone; why are you here, Your Highness? What's with the late-night visit?" I ask. I know by following protocol and addressing him as 'Your Highness' I have irritated him. But he was the one trying to pull rank in *my* house, and this is my way of putting him back in his place.

He sighs and shakes his head as he tugs at the knees of his expertly pressed trousers and takes a seat on the sofa. "Stop this nonsense, Amelia. It's me, James, you know me better than that. Forgive me for the late-night intrusion, but being who I am, it's not easy to be discreet. As you may have guessed by my house call, the matter at hand is a most delicate and urgent one. There is something I need to discuss before the referendum and the announcement of any royal engagement."

I shake my head incredulously. "And you needed to discuss it tonight? Right now? Couldn't you have called? What is it about this damned referendum that has all you men acting crazy? I'm not interested in it, not in the slightest."

He shifts off the sofa and comes over to kneel before me. I instantly feel perturbed. It's not something I expect the future king to do. A weak smile plays on his lips but the worry lines prominent around his normally flawless eyes tell me something major is on his mind. James isn't a soft man, and his actions make me unusually suspicious of him.

"Amelia, the referendum is extremely important, who else has been talking about this?" he pleads with me, taking my hands in his. I stare down at them and note how smooth and soft his skin is. They're not working men's hands.

"Harry."

"Harry? As in, the First Minister, Harold Donaldson?" I nod my head to confirm this, and he clenches his jaw. "Good God. Has he said anything to you?"

Again, I shake my head but this time in confusion. "What's going on? I have no idea what you're talking about, James." I sigh. "Look, I'm exhausted, so whatever it is that has brought you all the way up here to Edinburgh, can you please just explain it to me?"

He fixes me with a stern gaze. "Harry intends to make dramatic changes as soon as Scotland has independence."

"Obviously. Scotland will be a country outside the United Kingdom. But, then again, he might not get the vote," I remind him. "Is there anything in particular you're worried about?" I ask nervously.

"But of course," he replies quickly. "In simple terms, he plans to dredge up the settlement act from 1701. If Scotland breaks away from the United Kingdom, he wants to challenge the monarchy's right to the Scottish throne.

I laugh. "He wants to use your family history to challenge Queen Sofia's position as Queen of Scotland?" The thought is absurd, but I remember my family's secret, and Harry's intention –if this is really what he is focused on doing – has *some* validity. Not in terms of me being Queen of Scotland, this could never happen in retrospect, but drawing attention to my lineage could present enough interest for a discussion as to whether the monarchy, in its current form, should continue to rule Scotland in the future.

James glares at me. "Personally, I see nothing humorous about this dire situation. Can you imagine the issues for those hell bent on focusing on breaking up the monarchy? It could even drag up old feuds between our two countries. If Harry Donaldson fans the flames of this issue with his plan, this could have a devastating effect to the stability of Scotland itself, and for the rest of the union."

I frown, stunned at the thought. "This is utter nonsense. Your mother is the Queen of the United Kingdom, of Great Britain, and Northern Ireland…" I say, but I know the issue he's talking about runs far deeper than this.

"Not if the First Minister gets his way, that's why I'm here. Rumour has it he has discussed using your family's connection through James Francis Edward to Mary Stuart and the throne. Our intelligence tells us he intends to use it to try to disrupt the Royal position here."

I sit back in my chair, staring numbly at him. *I'm definitely sober now. This has got to be someone's idea of a joke.* I can see the gravity of the situation clearly in James' eyes. I know he speaks the truth. Secrets and lies always have ways of surfacing. I'm surprised my deep family connection to the Stuarts has remained dormant for all the centuries it has.

"This explains why Harry's so desperate to meet with me," I finally say, understanding the enormity of the situation I find myself in.

"Do you know something of this?" James asks.

"Why would I?"

He narrows his eyes. "Why do you need close protection?" he asks in return.

My thoughts turn to Liam. Is that what he was doing at the venue? And at the wine bar? Is the real reason he's brought me home, because someone has asked him to?

If so, who? Harry? Does Harry Donaldson feel I need protection from the Palace?

"Who escorts me around isn't your business, James. Or do you think I feel a need to protect myself from the Palace after what you've just told me?" I ask.

I suddenly feel like a vulnerable pawn in the whole situation when I realise that I sit at the centre of something constitutional. My brain won't allow me to fully understand the far-reaching implications of my family's lineage being thrust upon the Scottish public.

He scoffs. "The Palace is naturally concerned, Amelia. You must know how this could play out."

"And Charlotte thought Harry had a romantic interest in me," I muse. "How wrong she was."

"He's not the only one," the prince says in a moment of

humour, before his face turns serious again. "But in Harry Donaldson's case, his advances have a far more sinister motive than mine."

"That brings me to *your* motive for being here. What is it that you expect from me?" I probe, feeling brave for the small amount of alcohol that's left fuelling my boldness.

His deep blue eyes study mine for a few seconds before he speaks. "You know I've always been attracted to you, Amelia."

I chuckle and pull my hands away, initially shocked by his diversion, and stifle a groan that threatens to escape from my throat. "You're the future king, James. Nothing can ever happen between us," I say playfully, trying to lighten the serious situation. I know he's asked me out many times in the past, but I've always let him down gently. "You know I'm not one to be tamed," I say and smile, praying he gets the message. "But we digress, what do you need me to do?" I ask, knowing there's more.

"Harry Donaldson must be stopped. We can't risk him carrying out his plan."

"Then the powers that be are who you should be talking to, not me... unless you want me to assassinate him?" I say, when my absurd black sense of humour bursts through the significance of circumstance I've found myself in.

"No." He chuckles. "There's a much easier way to resolve this," he says. "You could marry me."

I burst out laughing, but when I realise he's not laughing with me my heart falters. The future king almost falls on his backside as I jump out of my seat and storm past him. I pace my room and turn to face him again. *This is ludicrous.* The shock of his request renders me completely sober. What he's asking doesn't make sense. *Me... and him? All this over a rumour?*

I stand there pulling on the ends of my hair, not knowing what to think, until I settle upon the thought that politics makes people insane. "James, are you telling me that this far-fetched fairy-tale is honestly what's brought you up here to Scotland?" I ask, walking back towards him and looking him straight in the eye. As he rises to his feet, his frustrated expression tells me he's serious, but I continue, "If by some twist of fate, Harry succeeds in gaining the vote, I will simply refuse to go along with this idiotic plot," I say, decisively.

He shakes his head. "If only it were that simple," he says, his tone much harsher. "Can you imagine the uproar if you did that? Do you think you could live your life normally if you were seen to be turning your back on your country?"

"Turning my back? That's absurd. Surely no one would believe anything should be done. No one would expect anything of me." When James' stare pierces my gaze I shrug, helpless. "Tell me, what else could I do?" I ask, reluctantly.

"The best way to stop rot in its tracks is for you to marry me. If you do this, he will have nothing to say because you'll already be married to the future monarch."

I laugh again, but this time it's partly hysteria and I almost choke when I see his frustrated expression.

Desperation rolls off him as he steps closer, too close for comfort. "Stop laughing, Amelia, this isn't in the least bit funny." The move is not only an invasion of my personal space, but from a female perspective it feels almost threatening. "Amelia, please do this," he says with a tug on my top. I grab his wrist with my hand to keep his arm still, but I know better than to struggle. "We need to do what's right for our great nation. Think of the religious discord it could cause, not only to Scotland, but to all four nations of the United Kingdom." *He's right. If Harry got his way, it could destabilise the tenuous religious harmony that exists between the four nations.* "Together, you and I would protect the realm for generations to come."

I stare at him for a lot longer than I should, wondering how on earth to respond. *How do you turn down a prince?*

"Say yes," he begs.

I always imagined when someone asked me to marry them it would feel magical, and it would come from someone I loved. I want the romance I deserve, not a simple business transaction for the greater good of a country, no matter how noble the request may be.

"This is all... sudden," I whisper. "I need time to... James?" I say, my tone pleads with him, and he lets go of my top and steps back. I can see in his eyes he thinks he's won.

"Think about it, Amelia, you and I..." I suppress a shudder and move away from him. Wrapping my arms around my body I hug myself.

"There must be another way," I shout louder than I had intended and push past him again, shaking my head at his preposterous proposition.

He growls, "Amelia, it's the *only* way."

"Not if Scotland doesn't get independence. If Scotland doesn't win, this problem goes away. If Harry dies, this problem goes away. Look, I've heard what you came here to say. I need time to think. What about Effie, the great love of your life, the woman you're due to marry?" I realise my voice sounds loud and high pitched, as I struggle for reasons why he needs to look for the answer to this problem in another direction.

Footsteps come thundering down the stairs.

I tell James, "Your position is safe as long as Harry doesn't win. I don't think Harry Donaldson, as First Minister, is confident he's done enough to make it happen."

Liam comes into view. I doubt he's heard most of what we've spoken about. "Everything all right here?" Liam's voice booms through my apartment. Frazier is right behind him, his hand on Liam's shoulder. *This isn't good.* Liam puts his body between mine and James', and I can see Frazier going for the gun I know he carries. All royal protection officers wear them.

"Don't even think about it," Liam warns, his voice menacingly low.

"You need to leave," Frazier tells him.

"I was invited here…" Liam begins.

"He's staying," I announce. Based on the fact he brought me home safely when he could have kidnapped me, or worse, my gut tells me this man won't harm me. The others I know well, but I'm not as confident about their intentions right now, if I don't say what James wants to hear. "I need to think James."

"I demand your answer. Remember, I wouldn't ask if the situation wasn't perilous for the country."

I blurt out, "No. My answer is no." He has pushed me too far. "And I think you should go back to whomever sent you here on this mission. I presume its someone of high political rank who has prompted this visit. Please tell them they need to find another answer to this problem."

James clenches his jaw and speaks through gritted teeth. "I'm going to give you forty-eight hours to think it over. I'm staying in Edinburgh. Please meet me when you've had time to think and don't discuss this on the phone."

"I'll see you both out," Liam says, his booming voice full of authority. James pauses before he begins to leave with Frazier in tow.

"Are you sure you want him to stay?" Frazier asks, gesturing towards Liam before he makes for the stairs.

I fold my arms across my chest, defensively. "He's the only person who hasn't asked anything of me, so I trust him the most, right now," I reply.

Prince James has already made his way down most of the stairs to the elevator and Frazier continues to walk away.

When I hear the buzz that tells me the lift to my penthouse is closed, I flop onto the sofa.

"I don't know what to make of his visit," Izzy says hanging over the banister halfway down the stairs.

"You heard?"

"Not what he came for, just your raised voice near the end. What does he want?"

"I can't discuss it at the moment," I say, my eyes flicking towards Liam, because I still don't know who he is. "I could really use some strong coffee, Izzy," I say. She looks from me to Liam, nods and walks away.

I feel too nervous to stay here alone after what I've learned. My stomach tightens, but I know I need to trust someone. I don't know why, but Liam McKenna makes me feel safe.

"Did we really just meet or...?" I don't even know what I'm asking, but after the prince's visit I don't know what to think.

He fixes me with a serious gaze. "Harry Donaldson hired me to look out for you."

I frown. "He did? Do you know why?" My heart is beating out of my chest with the panic I feel at knowing someone else knows my family history.

Liam sits down beside me. "When he called me suddenly to come to the event, I wasn't sure what was so urgent." He pauses for a moment as if he's unsure if he should share something with me. Seeing Prince James here just now is giving me food for thought. What I'm going to tell you isn't to frighten you, but what Donaldson showed me was enough to keep me with you all night and see you safely home. To be honest, I thought it was BS until I saw Prince James here. Now, I'm inclined to believe something may be going on that is indeed putting you at risk." Liam eyes my open handbag down at my feet and his eyes grow dark. "Can you open that?" he asks. "Did Harry speak to you?"

"What?" I ask, confused, and look at the unopened envelope he's pointing towards. "Sorry, I have no idea what you're talking about."

"That letter."

I look at it and all that's there is my name, Amelia Campbell, it has no address and I realise it was among my mail that Lottie brought up to me with the invitation from the Palace.

"Can you open it for me please?"

When I open it, the first thing I notice is the header has been cut off. I frown and unfold it. It's handwritten just like the envelope.

Miss Campbell, there are some who would use who you are to question and perhaps destabilise the crown. If you know your family history, you understand what could be at stake.

Tears prick my eyes as emotions sweep from deep within me and clog my throat. Fear streaks through me. I had known Prince James' visit was serious, but seeing the threat written down and delivered anonymously, makes it all real.

"Oh my God," I say, covering my face with my hands. I feel lost which isn't like me at all. I've received threats in the past, but never anything as serious as this. And I don't need anyone to tell me, this time, the threat is far from an empty one.

I can't be alone.

"If I ask you to stay, you would be working for me not Harry Donaldson."

Liam gives me a small smile. "I stopped working for him the moment I saw Prince James here."

Relief washes through me. "Would you mind staying the night? I don't want to be alone. I'm not sure I can trust anyone else."

"It would be my pleasure, Miss Campbell. But before I do,

I'll need to understand if this is a general request for protection or if there is a more specific reason for the threat you know about? I can't work blind. If I'm to keep you safe there can't be any secrets between us."

"My head is pounding," I plead. "I'm safe here. And please call me Amelia, Miss Campbell makes me sound like an old Scottish schoolteacher," I tell him. "Can we talk, and figure all of this out in the morning?" I ask, trying to buy myself time to consider what's happened, and then work out how to digest it.

How ridiculous is this situation? For centuries my family lineage hasn't been mentioned, and now it's in danger of being disclosed publicly.

CHAPTER 9

$\mathcal{L}$iam
        18ᵗʰ July

I CAN TELL Amelia's avoiding the conversation we need to have. She's not drunk anymore and the fact she's asked me to stay the night tells me she doesn't feel safe. Seeing her letter which is in the same hand as the one Donaldson showed me, and hearing the alarm in her tone when Prince James was here, I tend to agree.

"We need to talk right now. If you really are at risk I don't want to wait until morning. To be frank, I don't know how to handle this until I have more information. Is there some connection you're not telling me about that would mean all of this makes sense? I knew you moved in the same circles as Prince James, but I had no idea you were personal friends."

She smiles briefly. "I know how absurd this must all look to you. I mean who else finds a prince in their apartment when they come home from a night out?" There isn't a shred of humour in her tone.

I try again. "If you really want me to protect you, I'm going to need honesty and *all* relevant information you have, for me to do my job properly. You can trust me, Amelia, I've kept state secrets in my past. Yours would be regarded with as much privacy as those. Perhaps you should tell me why Prince James was here? I heard very little of your conversation but am I right in thinking that his visit has something to do with Harry Donaldson?"

She nods. "It did, but the purpose of the visit felt ridiculous. However, the First Minister hiring you makes perfect sense if what Prince James says is true."

"What did he say? What did he do that made you raise your voice? If you don't mind me saying, since the prince's visit you've looked uneasy. If there's some kind of credible threat to you, like that letter suggests, I need to know what that is."

She fidgets nervously, and this show of nerves is out of keeping with the public image I've seen so far. The air of confidence she had was sexy until she stepped foot inside her apartment tonight.

She huffs and blows out a breath. "The future king has just proposed marriage to me." She giggles nervously and I can see how absurd this appears to her.

My jaw drops in shock, but I quickly recover and wait to hear more. When she calms down, she stares at me, all traces of humour gone again. "The soundproofing in this apartment must be better than I thought, seeing as I couldn't control my temper. What exactly did Harry say to you when he hired you to protect me?"

"Do you mind if I sit down?" I ask, because me standing could make her feel on edge and I can see she feels uneasy after her royal visitor, despite her brave appearance.

"Of course not, please." She gestures to the sofa and I take a seat on the edge, holding clasped hands between my open knees.

Izzy chooses now to return to the room with two steaming cups of coffee. She hands one to Amelia and the other to me, I smile in thanks. "I'm going to take mine to bed unless you need me for anything?" Izzy says softly.

"No, thank you Izzy and feel free to sleep in." Izzy pats Amelia's shoulder before leaving the two of us alone.

I'm not sure us being alone is such a good idea after our brief encounter downstairs, when her lips were just there for the taking. I shake the thought away because circumstances have changed, but she makes my thinking cloudy.

I urge again, "I think you need to explain exactly what you know, don't you?"

At first, she looks hesitant and even though her life has been threatened she's cagey about what she knows. This tells me whatever information she does have, is a big deal.

"I do," she says eventually, having stared me down for a good minute. "But I need you to be open with me, first."

I hold out my empty hand in a gesture that I hope is reassuring. "What do you want to know?"

She lets out a tired sigh. "I want to know exactly what Harry Donaldson has said to you, and what your instructions were."

I take the hot mug in both hands again and relax back in the chair. "Mr Donaldson called me this morning and hired me as your personal protector. He insisted that where you go, I go, unless you are here at home in your apartment. He showed me a letter that said you were at risk. He appeared genuinely worried about something happening to you."

"He said nothing to me. I had no idea until this letter," she says picking it up from her lap. "If he thought I was in danger, why didn't he tell me?"

I shrug. "He didn't want to scare you until he knew more."

She throws her head back and laughs almost hysterically. "I'm more afraid that no one warned me before Prince James showed up here."

"Well, in all honesty, he made it all sound urgent, and told me he'd share more information as he got it, but until then he didn't want to take risks with your safety."

She takes a sip from her coffee and stares ahead, as though carefully choosing her words, and her eyes narrow on me, like she's assessing whether to trust me. "The writing? You say it's the same person who wrote Harry's letter?"

I nod. "It is, I recognised the cursive swirl immediately. In my line of work attention to detail is all important. So, what do you know that can help me do my job?"

"I don't have all the pieces of the puzzle yet," she says, tapping her lips with her fingers.

I'm not sure I believe her and think she does know some of it. "Tell me the parts you do have," I insist.

There's a long pause until she puts her cup down and begins wringing her hands. "This… has to do with my family history," she says, the words rushing out. "There's something there that could cause… issues for the monarchy if Scotland wins independence."

I shake my head and frown. "What family history?"

She cringes. "As history would dictate in my lineage, some would say I had a claim to the Scottish Throne."

I widen my eyes. "Are you fucking kidding me?" I shriek, before I pull myself together and apologise. "Sorry, but that sounds incredulous."

She sighs, a look of despondency appears in her eyes. "It does, but it's true. But I don't, it's a long story and I won't go into the boring history of it right now, but Prince James says that Harry wants to use *me* to bring up the question of the monarchy in Scotland if the referendum result is a yes."

She goes on to tell me that's what brought Prince James to her home to visit.

The news that she's a direct descendant of Mary Queen of Scots and could potentially be a talking point for the nationalists is the last thing I'd expected to learn. It changes my view on her safety dramatically. Harry Donaldson has every reason to make sure she lives. However, with Harry's intentions, not only is Amelia at risk from royalists, but her Catholic religion makes her a target from Protestant nationalists alike; since it was the anti-Catholic riots that made King James VII – the king in question – flee from his throne in the first place.

With Ross's help, we'll get to the bottom of this, whatever *this* is.

After a moment to take it all in I say, "So, Prince James' plan is to marry you?"

"He… *they* think it would make the problem go away. I'd already be married to the future king and Harry's challenge wouldn't have nearly the same merit."

"Who are '*they*'?"

She shrugs. "The establishment… senior politicians, the Crown, the Palace… I don't know."

"Right," I say, realising the gravity of her plight. "Okay, we'll figure out what needs to be done and do it. Amelia, you can count on Ross and me to do everything necessary to keep you safe."

"I'm trusting you with my life, Liam. You can't tell Harry about the prince or anything else I share," she says turning and looking anywhere but at me.

I don't point out the fact I'm never usually hired unless there's a potential risk to life. Which had confused me when Harry called me in the first place, but with the crazy story she just told me, and with knowledge of her birth right out there, and the Scottish referendum pending, there's an outside chance she may fall into this category. I know this will have to be discussed with her at some point soon, but this isn't the moment for that.

Right now, she looks lost. Nothing like the confident drunken woman I held in my arms in the taxi who was silently begging me to kiss her. For a nanosecond I almost gave into temptation. *Fuck!*

I've never been attracted to a principle before, and I seriously can't afford this now. Her life could depend on me staying focused on the job of keeping her alive.

Distraction leads to mistakes.

With my eyes on her, I continue drinking my coffee and my mind drifts back to the taxi again. What would've happened if we'd shared that kiss? I'm glad we didn't, because I would've had to walk away, and now more than ever, Amelia Campbell needs someone she can place her absolute trust in.

I stifle a sigh because no matter what, I need to keep my mind on my job and remind myself I'm here to protect her.

* * *

I TOLD Amelia to get some sleep and she showed me to a bedroom that was right next door to hers. On the other side of my room was the lift. She told me Izzy always sets the security alarm for the main door and the terraces before she goes to bed each night. I asked her to check this had been done. When she retired, I opened the lift door and jammed it to ensure no one could reach the apartment by this method.

I took a shower and laid my suit on a chair. Pulling out my phone I saw the background file for Amelia had been sent to my email. The contents inside were sparse. Mr Donaldson was mentioned, along with our principle's name and personal contact information, as well as brief details of the person we're commissioned to protect: Miss Amelia Campbell.

Curiosity had got the better of me when I met with Harry yesterday and it turned out that he had a personal investment in keeping Amelia safe. I'm not a stupid man, I know he has his own security team, but the real reason he called upon me was because he couldn't risk anyone in his team finding out his plan to use her.

While Amelia sleeps, I decide to carry out my own due diligence. I open my phone's internet browser and enter Amelia Campbell's name into the search bar. Picture after picture of the stunning brunette, with a sexy as sin pout, have me enthralled. She has the kind of smile that draws men in and renders them weak.

Studying her face, I click through the pictures on the screen avoiding the headlines that accompany them, because I've seen most of these stories before. I've never taken an interest in the life of Amelia Campbell, but I do know who she is. She's a rich socialite, and now I know she's also connected to the royal family. With each picture I see I can't quite believe this party girl is truly who she is. She's no airhead, given she has a law degree and holds patronages from some serious fundraising charities.

Unfortunately, most of the articles read much the same and there isn't a lot of useable information I can glean from the internet.

Miss Amelia Campbell, daughter of the late Rt Honourable Colin and Celia Campbell. She lives in Edinburgh. Parties hard. Works harder for charitable causes. Studied law at university and earned herself a degree. No steady boyfriend if the press is to be believed, although Mr Donaldson has intimated, they're romantically connected. No real scandals except the stuff that is in the media. They seem to focus on the party girl side of Miss Camp-

bell. Has been linked to various men but nothing serious to write home about.

Since leaving the military I'd been used to protecting high risk foreign dignitaries during their visits to the UK. This is what I'm trained to do. Something about this job tells me I will never again have a job where the stakes are higher.

melia
18th July

LYING IN BED, my head is a toxic cocktail of the threat towards me, the ludicrous proposal from James whom I've never even dated, and the attraction to the man who's now charged with keeping me safe.

It has been a long day but for whatever reason I didn't want to drag myself away from Liam and retire to bed. My eyes are bleary, but I feel safer in his company. I keep telling myself I'm only scared because I'm tired and I drank too much, and that come daylight when I wake up, I'll be ready to take on the world. I'm not sure I believe it. My mind retraces the previous ten minutes before I got into bed.

"You should probably get some sleep," he'd said softly. His tone gentler than I'd heard it before, and his eyes filled with concern for me. I'd stared at him for a long moment and, he'd returned my gaze.

Sleep.

It's weird. I should be wary of Liam McKenna. Afterall, he looks dark and dangerous, but I'm not wary at all.

I tell myself he's now protecting me for the right reason, and what is helping me trust him is that he wasn't aware of the full picture when he was hired by Harry Donaldson.

What is the full picture?

"I'm past being tired," I'd lied when he'd suggested I get some sleep.

He'd smiled, his eyes brightening despite his own tiredness and he looked unconvinced. "Miss Campbell has no one ever told you it's not good to tell lies?" The corners of his mouth had tugged into a wider smile as he'd tried, but failed, to hide his amusement.

"Perhaps, but I'm sure you've read stories about me, I rarely listen to anyone. I'm known as a rule breaker, not one for compliance."

He'd stared at me intently and a small thrill had run down my spine at the way he'd studied me. It wasn't as if I hadn't stared back, because his gorgeous, even features looked striking. It confirmed what I'd suspected, we do have a mutual attraction. I've known him for less than a day, yet he feels familiar and safe.

"You like to make things hard for everyone," he'd said.

I had tilted my head and raised an eyebrow. There was a flirty side to him that strained to break free, but I'd felt he was being too professional to let his guard down.

"Hard, that's a good word. Am I making it hard for you?" I'd asked, dropping a double entendre into the conversation. "Besides rules are there to be broken," I'd finished before there was a shift in atmosphere between us.

"I think after the day you've had you should get some sleep. I imagine you'll need your wits for the day ahead. I think you've had too much to drink, and your emotions have been rattled."

His response had felt like a rejection of sorts and I'd moved quickly towards the stairs with frustration flowing through me.

We're attracted to one another and we have chemistry, it's making me act irrationally. I want him and I know he wants me. I saw it in his eyes in the taxi earlier, and I saw how he looked at me while we sat on my sofa.

"Amelia…," he'd said as if he knew I was feeling let down. I had turned and looked up at him from the bottom of the steps, and watched as he came down next to me. "I need you to check the apartment alarm," he'd said. I'd felt the pull between us like he had wanted to say something else, but he didn't. *He doesn't like that he's turned me down.*

Now alone with my thoughts again, I slip back out of bed and wander across the room to stand in front of the windows. I look out across the city where the night sky is slowly changing with hints of lilac and copper, and I'm certain it won't be long until dawn breaks.

Sunrise will bring a new day and I'm not sure what lies ahead. Maybe I am; problems and challenges that are all connected to a member of the opposite sex. Harry, Prince James and now Liam. *Although the last one doesn't need to be a problem.*

I get back into my bed alone, frustrated that the man I want lies next door. But he's only here because I'm paying him to protect me.

Why am I focusing on him? I'm becoming infatuated and I don't need the distraction. He should be the least of my worries. I should be concentrating on the situation Prince James warned me about involving Harry Donaldson.

I stretch and yawn, toss and turn in my attempt to get some sleep.

* * *

AFTER A RESTLESS NIGHT where a million thoughts have run through my head, I don't look as exhausted as I feel. Lottie has tried to call twice already, and I've only just stepped out of the shower. I ignore the voice messages and get dressed as my mind runs over everything that happened before I went to bed. To save face I know I must carry myself with my usual confidence and pass off my clumsy flirtation towards Liam as me being emotional and having had too much to drink.

How can I expect him to fall for that when I don't even believe it myself?

Regardless of my instant attraction towards Liam, I need his expert skills and assistance, but first I need some assurance he's working for me and no one else.

With a deep breath I take one last look in the mirror. Despite my overindulgence with champagne last night, I'm satisfied that I look presentable. I leave the comfort of my bedroom wearing tight blue jeans and a black vest top. I've piled my hair into a bun, that's taken far too much time to do, and my make-up is light. I appear casual and relaxed; a carefree look that hides the turmoil I feel inside after learning about Harry Donaldson's plan for me.

As I reach the top of the stairs, I can hear Izzy talking to Liam. My confidence isn't as high as I'd like but I'll smile and hope it's good enough to hide my inner anguish.

"Good afternoon," I say, entering the kitchen. Liam is sitting at the table and I try to avoid looking at him, whilst Izzy is cooking food on the stove.

"There you are," Izzy says looking up as she stirs something in a pot. "What time do you call this, child?"

"I'm far from a child," I scoff. "I must have needed to sleep."

She narrows her eyes. "It doesn't look as though you've slept much to me."

I shake my head in disbelief. If I didn't love her, I'd slap her for drawing attention to my tired eyes. "It took me a while to fall asleep. I had a lot on my mind."

"Now, that doesn't surprise me. Sit down," she replies.

Unable to ignore Liam any longer I take the seat opposite him and look him straight in the eye. He's looking directly towards me, studying me.

"I hope you slept well," I say.

"Best sleep I've had in years," he replies. "How is your head this afternoon, Miss… Amelia?"

"I don't suffer from hangovers if that's what you're implying…" I lie.

"Amelia, the young man isn't implying anything," Izzy scolds me as she hands me a cup of coffee.

"Of course, he wasn't," I respond with a note of sarcasm in my tone.

He nods his head and stretches his shoulders towards me over the table and whispers, "I was." Then sits back in his chair.

Shaking my head, I grab one of the daily newspapers from the pile on the table. Unfolding the first one, the main picture grabs my attention, and I can't help the frustrated sigh that escapes me. This picture is from yesterday; Harry has his hand on my upper arm and is smiling. No, he's not just smiling. The soft gaze in his eyes along with the intimate touch appears to imply affection. It's an image that tells the world a romantic story; it's a fictitious account of who we are to one another, and he's certainly not someone I want to be associated with in this way.

"What the hell am I going to do about this?" I say, tossing the paper across the table, trying to ignore the beaming smile on Harry's face, from a slightly different angle, in the picture of the next paper on the pile. Lottie's right, from the way he's looking at me in the photograph Harry Donaldson thinks he stands a chance with me."

"I think the pressing question should be, what are you going to do about Prince James?" Izzy asks with concern. "He shouldn't have come, and if Queen Sofia or Effie find out he's come all this way here to see you…"

"Izzy, do you think I want him here? I'd be much happier if he were back in London with his very dreary fiancée."

Liam sits sipping on his coffee, paying attention to our conversation.

"What did he want?" Izzy asks.

I shrug, no point in making her anxious until Liam and I talk, and he tells me his plan. "You know James, just another of his impulse decisions about something," I say. I shake my head a little to indicate this isn't a conversation I want to have with her. But I don't trust the Palace anymore since James' visit. Him coming here means they think they have something to lose if Harry wins the vote.

I know that wasn't the last I'll see of Prince James. He said forty-eight hours, then I know he'll be back. I can hear the conversation before we've even had it. He'll tell me the future of a united monarchy rule for the UK is in my hands. Which of course it's not. I can't believe he'd happily condemn me to a marriage of convenience; an alliance made out of duty to the Crown. I'm sure he'll dress it up differently and say we'll be a powerful couple the nation will love. Instinct tells me the Palace and politicians would put up a united front.

I know from his previous visit James has agreed to this.

In a situation like this, no one would care what I want.

Where is Lottie when I need her? Probably tucked snuggly in her bed, oblivious as to what I've been through.

"Izzy what are you cooking?" I ask. "Whatever it is smells delicious."

"Soup. Although I should ask if you require a special menu for this evening?"

I shake my head. "No, there will be no special dinner guests."

"I see," she says flatly, and I hope she does. Prince James hasn't been invited back.

Izzy continues to make her soup and my stomach rumbles with the aroma in the kitchen, but for now this cup of coffee will do. Liam doesn't say anything further and his lack of conversation is unnerving. Izzy goes into the utility room and closes the door behind her.

"Do you have any plans for today that I should know about?" Liam finally asks.

"None that involve me needing security," I state, confidently holding his gaze.

"Amelia, you and I need to have a talk. If I'm working for you, it's important you follow what I tell you to do without question. You're hiring me for a reason—"

"Are you going to tell Harry you're working for me now?"

"He did have a valid reason for hiring me, but it was a self-serving one. From the letters and Prince James' visit I believe there's some risk to you."

"And what does that mean?" I ask curiously.

"I'm not sure." He stares straight at me. "Do you have an engagement for this evening?" he asks nodding toward the newspapers, and I know he's read that I have.

"I won't be attending," I snap. "After seeing today's headlines in the newspapers, I don't want to be seen with Harry again tonight. I think there's enough speculation linking the two of us together, which, might I add, is never going to happen. Not even in his wildest dreams."

Liam sniggers and I raise a brow, so his smirk disappears. "I think he's trying to show his close association to you rather than anything romantic, but like you, after seeing these pictures, I can see he's mesmerised by your presence."

"I think it's a wise decision not to go," Izzy says coming back into the kitchen and looking over her shoulder as she stirs the soup again.

I wonder how much she has heard, not all of it, I'm sure, because she would have freaked out if she'd heard all of the conversation between Liam and myself. Liam is frowning, his gaze fixed on me while I think.

"That man is delusional," I say, shoving the newspaper pile away in frustration. "I know I'll be letting people down by not going, but I have to distance myself from this wretched referendum.

"What about Prince James?" Izzy probes, as if I need reminding about his visit.

"Well, I've made it clear, I don't want what *he's* offering either.

"Which was? You still haven't told me," she probes.

"I need to be totally briefed of your schedule," Liam says, interrupting the conversation. It gives me space from Izzy, and I'm thankful for it. She knows my family lineage, but if she thought my life was at risk it could push her over the edge, and I don't need a hysterical woman around me while I think.

Liam's mobile phone beeps in his pocket. After reading a text, he messages back before laying his phone on the table. "My colleague, Ross is bringing your friend over, and I've arranged for your car to be brought back from the hospital to the garage here. Is there anything else you need me to do?"

I chew on the inside of my cheek. There are lots of things he could do for me. Although none he could do with an audience, especially not Izzy. If she could read my lusty thoughts about Liam, I fear she'd have a heart attack.

"No," I say.

His phone buzzes again and he stands. He leaves my kitchen area and wanders over to the living space to take a call. "Mr Donaldson…" I hear Liam say, but the clever acoustics make his voice mute two steps further away. My heart pounds as I watch his mouth moving and wonder what they're saying. He looks at me and his eyes soften, they tell me he's not going to disclose what we've spoken about. Without being able to hear the conversation my eyes are drawn to his suit. It looks as immaculate as it did yesterday. *Has Izzy pressed out the creases for him? I'm betting she has.*

Of course Harry would call to check in. I wonder, again, if my trust is misplaced, but I quickly decide the genuine look of concern in Liam's eyes when he speaks to me, tells me it isn't.

"Amelia, are you okay?" Izzy asks coming and sitting down beside me.

"Truthfully, I'm not that sure."

"The way Prince James showed up here was astonishing."

"I know."

"Am I to presume the First Minister knows your family background?" she asks in a hushed tone. She nods at the letter that lies open on the small coffee table near the sofa. I should have known she'd figure it out. She heard Liam was guarding me and her ability to join the dots on my life amazes me.

"I've had a less than romantic proposal from one man, and another who's trying to make the world believe we're a couple."

"Prince James proposed?"

"He did… but no, I'm not marrying him."

Izzy frowns. "This has to do with Harry?"

"Yes," I say, and chuckle. "Harry wants to use me to question the validity of the monarchy in Scotland."

Izzy's eyes open wide, but she doesn't crumple in a heap like I had suspected she would. "That's absurd."

I nod and flash a nervous smile. "Right? But worrying because James wouldn't have made a visit like this off his own back. He was pushed into it, I suspect. Why can't people leave me alone to live a normal life?" I mumble quietly.

"Sweetie, you would be bored with a normal life," she says with a warm smile, and of course she's correct. "Now, if you're serious about not going out tonight, what would you like for dinner?"

I blink, her ability to switch direction makes my head whirl. "You were up half the night, you're not cooking. We can get a takeout and relax. Both of us."

"And what about me?" Lottie asks popping her head up from the stairs, closely followed by Ross. She's the only other person in the world, apart from Izzy and me, who has keyed access to my home. "Oh my gosh, Amelia you look rough, did you have a busy night?" Her eyes flit to Liam and she smirks wickedly. "Was he good?"

"Lottie!" Izzy barks at her innuendo, and glares in my friend's direction.

"I'm only asking," she says innocently. "My night was fun," she says, laughing at Izzy's reaction. Ross rubs the back of his neck and his gaze darts between Lottie and Liam.

"Of course, it was," I drawl, well aware of my friend's sexual conquests. "But I'm sorry to say our nights were completely different. I arrived home and found Prince James here."

Ross walks over to Liam who makes eye contact with him and then me but continues with his phone call. I figure Liam will already have shared the information with his colleague. As long as it is on a need-to-know basis, I think I can cope with this.

Lottie pulls out the chair Liam was sitting in and drops heavily into it. "What? Why?"

"He came to propose," I mutter, shuddering visibly.

Her eyes widen and she gulps like she's swallowed her tongue for a few seconds. "As in marriage?" I nod. "Wow, this is insane. You've never even dated," she shrieked echoing my sentiment exactly. "What happened to Effie?"

"Keep your voice down," I warn, glancing over to Ross.

"If you need me, I'll be doing laundry," Izzy informs us as she wanders toward the utility room. My guess is she wants to skip the recap.

I nod, acknowledging Izzy before she leaves us alone. Liam has finished his call and is now conversing with Ross. I can hear their murmuring voices, but not what they're saying. I sense Liam is bringing his colleague up to speed on the latest events after the call. I'm not sure I'm happy with yet another person knowing something so sensitive, but the secret is out there, and people I don't know have opinions of what should happen now that they are aware of my connection to Mary Queen of Scots.

"So many fun things happen to you," Lottie says, distracting me from the men's conversation.

"Your idea of fun is completely different to mine," I tell her, my eyes darting back to where the men are standing.

"Did I hear you tell Izzy we're not going tonight?" Lottie asks. "If not, what are we doing?"

I'm just about to answer her when Liam and Ross walk back over to the kitchen.

Liam stops beside me and drops my car key on the table. "Your car is safely parked in the garage. That was Donaldson calling."

"I know. What did you tell him?" Liam glances toward Lottie and I nod. "You can say whatever in front of Lottie, we have no secrets," I say.

"Nothing of the prince's visit if that's what you're asking. I also didn't tell him I'm not working for him, as yet. For the moment we're going to let him assume our position hasn't changed, until we figure this out." He wags his finger between him and his colleague. "As we're now working for you, our presence will be just the same, and when the time comes to enlighten Mr Donaldson, I simply won't bill him."

"Will someone tell me what all this is about?" Lottie pleads.

We ignore her and Liam reaches into his pocket. He pulls out a black and gold embossed business card and places it in front of me. "This is my mobile phone number," he says stabbing it with his index finger. "Add it to your contacts and make me your number one speed dial. Then, give your mobile phone to Ross. He'll place tracking software on it so that we can find you, should we become separated for any reason. If you see anything that makes you in the least uncomfortable, don't hesitate to call me. I need to know."

"Separated?" I vaguely hear Lottie question.

On closer inspection of the card, there's no information, not even his name, only a phone number. "Thank you," I say holding out my hand to him which he takes with a handshake, sealing his contract with me. His gaze holds mine and a spark ignites in my stomach. The connection I feel tells me what I already know; that I want him and unless I am wrong, Liam feels this connection as well... which is ridiculous given the circumstances.

"Don't worry, Donaldson knows nothing of what I've learned while I've been here."

Lottie heaves a deep, exasperated sigh. "Donaldson? Will someone tell me what the fuck has happened since I left Amelia last night?"

"Thank you," I say, my tone genuinely grateful for his discretion. I know Lottie is freaking out in the same way I'd expected Izzy to. "One minute, Lottie," I say, still staring at Liam.

"In light of a potential risk to you, I think the best course of action would be for me to move in for the time being, if possible. The apartment is secure for now, but my risk assessment so far is that your security should be twenty-four hours a day. This is a fluid situation, you understand, and things may change. However, with this arrangement, I'll have to drop by my home and pick up some extra clothing."

Knowing he's leaving fills me with a sense of panic, but I swallow it down.

"I'll need a key card or a code to come back up here," he says. "Please instruct the lobby that no one, not even Jesus in a second coming, is to be allowed up to this apartment. No visitors at all until I am back here. Do you understand?"

"Will someone tell me what's going on?" Lottie pleads.

I hold up my finger to tell her to wait again. "You think I'll be safe here?"

"I hope so," he replies seriously.

"Who threatened you?" Lottie asks.

"I'll explain everything to you in a minute," I tell her.

Lottie stands and hugs herself. "All right. You've got my number, Ross. Give me a call sometime," she says as the men walk towards the stairs. It's as if she can't get rid of them fast enough, to find out what's going on. I stay seated and watch them go downstairs.

There's an ache in my chest as I watch Liam leave, but until I can figure my way out of this mess, he'll be living with me. My gut feeling is he's worried they could do anything necessary to secure Queen Sofia's reign.

CHAPTER 11

$\mathscr{L}$iam
18th July

"You look fucked, Liam, and not in a good way," Ross laughs as we ride down in the lift.

Story of my life.

"You seriously went and tapped that? Must you always think with your dick?" I reply about his night with Lottie.

"That's a low blow. I rarely let pleasure get in the way, but you saw her, Liam, can you blame me?" he asks with a smug grin. "She was worth it. That girl was dynamite in the sack. Anyway, you can talk. You can't tell me there wasn't a spark of something between you and posh totty, Miss Campbell, I saw it. But one look at you this morning tells me you've kept the relationship strictly professional."

The lift doors open, and we walk toward the exit. "I never mix business with pleasure, you know me," I say, hoping my words are enough to end our conversation. If Ross thinks there's something else there, he'll keep on nagging. He can be like a dog with a bone once he gets his teeth into something.

I'd never admit I had almost dropped my guard and was close to kissing her. The moment I knew Amelia wanted me it would've been easy to take advantage of what I also wanted. However, in hindsight, I'm glad we were interrupted because something tells me with her, it would've ruined my professional reputation and my current change of roles to keep her safe.

"I just thought…"

"You can't afford to let personal feelings cloud your thoughts. Anything that isn't specifically work related takes your eye off the ball. Distractions don't keep the principle safe," I state firmly, because we both know the consequences could be life or death.

"She's your client now, so what are you going to tell Donaldson?"

The doors to the building open and we walk towards my car.

Great, I have a parking ticket. "I'm not sure yet," I say shaking my head and peeling the ticket off the windscreen. "But not the truth. He can't know that we know what he's up to. No one can."

"This situation is more fucked up than either of us," Ross suggests as we both stop. I turn and lean back against my car. I glance up toward the penthouse we just came from.

"Our Mr Donaldson believes Amelia will help him win the referendum and after Prince James' late-night visit, I've no doubt, Amelia's in some kind of risk."

I'd already given Ross a brief rundown of what happened when I brought Amelia home. Prince James may have proposed, but I fear the moment Amelia turned him down, a plan B to protect the current monarchy was put into action. What that is bothers me, and Ross knows it.

"I've seen that look on your face before," he says wide-eyed.

"I think... no I *believe* she could be in danger. Not while she's up there, they wouldn't be so stupid as to harm her at home, but..." I didn't need to fill in the blanks, Ross nodded; he understood.

"First off," Ross says, "you need to shower and nap. I'm staying. I'll grab my stuff when you get back here. When you wake up, we can regroup and discuss this mess again."

"There's definitely something fishy cooking, and it doesn't smell fresh to me," I tell him as I turn and open my car door. "How long until the vote?"

"What? Oh, the referendum, fifteen days."

"They're going to be long ones. Go on, get the fuck out of here," he says, closing the door and taps on the roof of my car once I'm seated.

* * *

I'M IN MY APARTMENT, hair still wet from the shower, when I begin to pack up my clothes; three suits, a dozen freshly laundered shirts, and a few sets of casual clothes into garment bags. I make myself some tea before I open my laptop. I search the three people involved in this equation. I wonder who I should start with and decide to type Harry Donaldson and Amelia Campbell into the search bar. Instantly, the images appear on the screen and I lean back in my chair to study them. There's only a handful of them together, until the latest pictures where Harry is staring doe-eyed at Amelia where she stands beside him.

My focus narrows in on the few pictures from yesterday's event, and they do look happy together, but they had reason to smile, the opening of the unit was quite an achievement. One thing that strikes me in the news is that every article speculates on whether they are together. On closer inspection of her body language, I see nothing that suggests Amelia even likes the man. This is in keeping with my personal assessment from the interactions I witnessed between them at the hospital opening.

I close my eyes momentarily as the vision of her in the taxi comes to mind again. I could hardly mistake the look of want in her eyes, or the way her tongue traced her lips. There is too much chemistry between us, and we've only just met, I didn't get that vibe from her towards Donaldson.

I close my eyes and shake my head. "Stupid man, you need to stop fantasising, and fucking concentrate," I say aloud, opening my eyes and I begin to click through the articles again.

I concentrate on the referendum campaign and notice that Amelia hasn't voiced her opinions or given Donaldson her backing. That wasn't the impression he gave me; indeed, he implied her involvement with him and the referendum could be the reason for hiring me. He's a typical politician; a liar.

Next, I type in HRH Prince James and Amelia's name together. "That's interesting," I say aloud again. There's plenty of pictures of the two of them together from various functions they've both attended. I read that there is some speculation from a few years ago linking the two romantically. When I search this further, I can find no firm evidence to back this up.

"Oh, man," I say to myself when I focus on the picture I've just clicked on and enlarge it on my screen. From the way Prince James is looking at her, I'd say the Prince was lovestruck back then. *Interesting.* I wonder if he still holds a torch for her, and this is the reason for his offer of marriage, which is another piece of the puzzle. Again, from Amelia's reaction, it was a one-sided affair for him too.

I'm not entirely sure what I'm searching for, but I continue researching the prince and Amelia. I can't find anything else that I haven't read about either of them already. Drawing blanks doesn't sit well with me. My instinct is telling me there is danger for Amelia from all sides.

"Oh, fuck off," I say when my phone buzzes, and I see the name on the screen. I know I need to talk to him and sigh when I pick it up. "Mr Donaldson," I say.

"Do you have anything else to report?" he asks cutting straight to the chase. We spoke less than three hours ago.

"Well, actually, yes, I do."

"And?"

"Miss Campbell has dismissed me," I say, deciding on impulse that he should know, and I listen to how he reacts. I'm hoping he'll disclose something specific that would help me do my job better.

"She's done what?" he shouts before he falls mute while he thinks, and I wait. "How did she know you were following her?"

"I guess she's not as naïve as we thought. She spotted us," I say, which is probably true.

"I'll speak to her. She needs protection," he assures me.

"Okay, she's at her apartment at the moment," I say, not giving anything else away. "I can be ready at a moment's notice if you resolve your differences."

"Thank you. I'll call you soon." He abruptly ends our call.

I lean back in the chair and run my hands over my face and through my hair. I'm drained from a lack of sleep, and I could do with another couple more hours of it. It would help me sharpen my wits and make me focus better.

I click the mouse and a new image of Amelia pops up on the screen, one I wasn't prepared for. *Holy crap.*

I feel my cock stir and grow in my jeans. I squeeze it through the material because my arousal isn't welcome if my involvement is to continue with Amelia, going forward. In the picture she's posing in a tiny string bikini; her slim figure and tanned skin look flawless. Amelia has an amazing body of gentle curves, long shapely legs and a perfect cleavage, just as I had imagined. My heart pumps faster when I focus on her smile and refocus on her long, dark, shiny hair cascading over her shoulders.

There are no clues as to where this picture was taken or who she is with. She appears happy and relaxed. I immediately wonder if she's smiling at someone special behind the camera lens. I really hope not.

A low groan leaves my throat when I realise I'm still staring, and I snap closed my screen. "So much for remaining professional," I mutter as I stand and adjust my jeans.

Stretching my arms above my head, I make my way to my bathroom. Quickly, I stuff my toiletry bag with what I will need, and, after checking around for any items I may have missed, I leave my home, close and lock my door, pack my car, and head back to Amelia's apartment.

CHAPTER 12

melia
18th July

LIAM HAS BEEN BACK an hour when the buzzer to my intercom shrills through my apartment.

"It's Prince James," he says after the lobby security informs him.

"I can't refuse to see him," I say with a shrug.

"Neither Ross nor I are leaving the room," he tells me. "He could pose a threat."

I roll my eyes. "James isn't going to kill me or anything." It sounds absurd I'm even having this conversation about our future monarch. This situation feels like an episode of the dramatisation of the Tudors and Stuarts I watched on TV a long time ago.

"Send him up," Liam says. Then, "Ross, you head upstairs." He then heads for the entrance. Lottie, now up to speed on Harry's plot and the Prince's previous visit, makes herself scarce in my bedroom.

A couple of minutes later I hear the lift stop downstairs,

but there's a pause before Izzy tuts her tongue and goes over to see what the hold-up is. Just as she reaches the staircase Prince James' head comes into view.

"Amelia, you have a visitor," she says, as if I could possibly have missed the whole charade. I plaster on a professional smile. In spite of him saying he would give me forty-eight hours, I had hoped his previous visit was the last I would've seen of him. What I didn't expect was for him to give me even less time. "His Royal Highness, Prince James," Izzy finishes, curtseying.

I stand. "James," I say. Izzy curtsies again and shakes her head in annoyance at my clipped tone. "Two visits in less than twenty-four hours, to what do I owe the pleasure this time?"

"It's always a pleasure seeing you," he says, which sounds disingenuous. He walks towards me.

So much for my relaxing evening.

"Izzy, if you would make some refreshments and maybe fetch Frazier something to eat?" I ask.

"Of course," she says gesturing for Frazier to stay at the kitchen counter. Liam hangs back with him, he thinks the Prince is no threat, but the jury's still out on Frazier. He's loyal to the Crown and as such he'd be well placed to take a pot shot at me. *How crazy do I sound? No one's going to kill me.*

"May I?" James asks pointing towards the sofa.

"Yes, please sit down." I wait until he's sitting and then I sit on the opposite sofa, maintaining a safe distance between us.

"Amelia, have you thought about my proposal?"

"James… Your Highness, the answer is still no," I state firmly.

"Do you realise what Donaldson will do if he wins his referendum?"

"I don't think for one minute he couldn't table a motion

and raise the question about our Queen. This all seems so incredulous."

His nostrils flare. "It might appear far-fetched, but the nationalists could make a last push to cause disruption to further their cause.

James continues, "The problem for the monarchy is real if Harry succeeds at the vote. His argument could give him the most disruption there has been for centuries. With your family lineage, it would provide a solid argument. The bottom-line is, they could force a split whether you want that to happen or not."

I know what he's saying but it's still a shock to hear it. There's no way either Queen Sofia or the British Prime Minister would accept this lying down. *Hence the threat to me.*

"I have no desire to interfere."

"That may be so, but if they win the vote and the media get this story, there will be nothing you can do about it. You won't be able to hide, Amelia. Your family connection to the Scottish throne will be out in the open."

"Does your mother know you're here?" I ask.

"She does and she's, shall we say, somewhat disappointed at the timing of this intelligence, considering the Palace is meant to be announcing a royal engagement."

"Yes, I can see how she would be displeased. However, dear Effie is very compliant and will do whatever is best for you. I can only presume she is the Queen's choice of wife for you?"

He smiles. "See, you know me so well. You would make a far better choice, hence my offer to you."

I swallow roughly because I'm not convinced he's made the decision to come and do this on his own merit; not that it would have made any difference if he had. "I'm deeply honoured by your confession, but I'm afraid I don't feel the same, James. You ought to know that by now."

He stands and runs his fingers through his hair. "I'm acutely aware how you've spurned my advances over the years, Amelia." He walks toward the windows. "I could make you happy, and I think you could grow to love me," he implores. "You won't do better than me," he says with all the arrogance of a someone used to having his way. "We could have fun together. As my wife you would have the lifestyle you're accustomed to. Nothing would have to change…"

I sigh. "James, please stop, of course it would change. I wouldn't be free to pick and choose how my diary worked. I'd be told what to think. My life would belong to the country. Besides, I won't marry someone I don't love. With you being heir to the throne, marriage for you is vastly different from that of a normal, loving relationship. I can understand the match the Queen has picked for you in Effie. She won't rock the boat and will carry the role by your side with grace. You're in a position where the crown matters more than your heart. Fortunately, I'm not, and I can't understand how you'd think I could contemplate an arranged marriage."

He turns around and I can see the flash of disappointment in his eyes. Even I know my words are hurtful but every one is true.

"Is that your final decision?"

I realise his question is loud and aggressive and Liam and Frazier turn to look at us. They've obviously heard his tone if not what he said.

"Yes, I'm sorry."

"I hope you live to regret this," James states, his eyes boring holes into mine as he clenches his fists by his sides.

"Is that a threat, James?" I ask. My body is physically vibrating because I now don't feel safe in his presence. As if Liam notes my discomfort, he starts to walk towards me.

When James sees him coming, Frazier quickly on his heels, the prince's gaze falls to the floor and for the first time in all the years we've known each other, his body slouches in defeat.

"I should go," he states. I stand and he walks towards me and places his hands on my shoulders. "Amelia, be careful," he warns. "You have my direct number if you change your mind…"

"James, careful of what?" I ask. When he doesn't answer I shake my head. "I won't change my mind."

"A man can hope," he replies, but I can see in his eyes that he knows I mean what I say.

"Frazier, we're leaving," James calls out as Liam stands slightly blocking my view. Frazier immediately falls into line and stands by his prince. "Goodbye Amelia," James says as he kisses me on the cheek, before reluctantly taking his leave with Frazier two paces behind him. Liam follows them down the stairs and I flop down on the sofa.

"Fuck me, that was intense," Ross says from the top of the stairs where I realise he's been listening just out of sight.

I should feel relieved the prince has gone, but instead I feel more troubled by his second visit and his, *'I hope you live to regret this'*, comment.

My parents used to say drama followed me, but it would appear I don't even have to leave the house now to be involved in one scene or another.

"Amelia, you have several messages on the answerphone from Harry," Izzy reminds me. I know this, the phone hasn't stopped ringing since a few hours after Liam went home to get his clothes.

"I won't be returning any of his calls," I tell her, opening my eyes to see her standing before me.

"Is that wise?"

"Is any decision I make wise?" The corners of her mouth tug into a smile. "Maybe don't answer that."

"You may have to talk with him sometime," Liam says, sounding like the voice of reason.

"I know, but I'm a bad liar.

"So, I noticed," he says, and I feel my face flush when I remember our little flirtatious moment.

Lottie returns to the room. "Izzy, can we order takeout for everyone?"

Izzy nods. "Sure, I'll get the menus out of the kitchen drawer, I'll be right back."

* * *

19TH JULY

I haven't felt good since I woke this morning. In fact, I've felt better after a long night out, partying. I wish I had been on this occasion, then I could put how I feel down to a hang-over. There's a horrible rumbling in the pit of my stomach and it's not because I'm ill. It's a nervous feeling of dread that's unsettling me.

Throwing the covers off, I make myself get out of bed. I don't see the point in staying there any longer when I've struggled to sleep for the last few hours. My head is spinning from the events of the previous two days. Regardless of the cloud of fear I'm under, I'm still drawn to the man with piercing blue eyes who has sworn to protect me. I can't shake the impression he's made on me as he continues to invade my thoughts.

Why he consumes my mind when I have more pressing issues to deal with confuses me. Is it because my need for someone safe has been heightened, or is it something else? I stare at myself in the bathroom mirror. My reflection hasn't got answers and that frustrates me. *Time to move on with my day.*

Izzy is in the kitchen. "Good morning," she says without

turning around, and she puts the kettle on. "Ross took Lottie home earlier," she informs me. "She had an errand to run with her father, something to do with her trust fund."

"Where's Liam?" I ask. I sound needy and I hate that I do, but I guess fear does that to a person.

"In the shower. He and Ross have been up half the night talking. When Ross left, he thought he'd have time to freshen up because we didn't think you'd be up yet," Izzy replies.

I look at the clock and It's barely eight a.m. I sit down and put my hand on the pile of newspapers on the table.

"Ah, Amelia… I should warn you about those," she says quickly, startling me. She turns to look at me, her eyes darting back and forth between me and the newspapers.

"What the devil is it now? Should I be worried?" I ask picking up the first tabloid and turning it over to see the front page. "Shit!" I gasp. "What the hell! When was this taken?"

"Well with what Prince James is wearing I can only presume it was when he came here again yesterday."

My gaze stays on the image. James is in the passenger seat of his car which is parked beside my well-publicised vintage Mercedes convertible.

The headline reads:

Prince James visits the home of Amelia Campbell.

The question beneath reads: ***Is this the reason Miss Campbell failed to round off her charity obligations at the Summer Ball, with First Minister, Harold Donaldson as guest of honour?***

I shiver. *This is getting out of hand. Is someone watching my movements? Or is this just some opportunist looking for their five minutes of fame?*

I don't want my name linked to either man and yet there it is, in black and white, sandwiched neatly between them. We make an awful threesome. Izzy puts a cup of tea on the table before me and continues to stand behind me as I read the story in its entirety. Once I finish with the first newspaper, I pick up the others. Each front page reads with a similar account of his visit.

"Oh well, I assume I won't be leaving my apartment today," I say, scooping them all up and dumping them in the utility room near the door. "Take that bunch of trashy BS to the rubbish chute, Izzy."

Liam enters the room. "No, I'd advise you not to. The lobby security has already sent a voicemail to my mobile to say he's requested extra security," he says as he comes to stand by the table. He looks appealingly fresh, smells divinely clean, and his smoothed back, dark brown hair is still wet. "Apparently, there is quite a presence of news reporters outside. I believe a few of your neighbours in the building have complained about being harassed as they've tried to leave, according to a text I received from Ross."

"How does he know?"

"He's set up his own surveillance across the road."

I digest the enormity of this information but don't comment on it, focusing instead on how the intrusion of the press must feel to others. "I'll have to ensure I apologise to everyone," I say, looking at Izzy to remind me to do this, and thinking about how nice my neighbours are but how they value their privacy. My face is in newspapers and magazines at times, but I don't usually attract paparazzi to my home.

"Now…" Izzy frowns and it isn't something she does very often.

"What?"

"Despite the early hour, Harry has called several times again this morning, demanding to speak to you. My guess is, he's seen those articles. I told him you weren't awake yet but would get back to him."

I sigh before I sip my tea and think what I'm going to do.

"Before I do anything, I know I need to speak with James. The Palace will be furious that his trip up north didn't go under the radar."

"Of course. I'll leave you to make the call." Izzy grabs her mug and heads for the lounge upstairs. Liam slides into the seat across from me, it's clear he's going nowhere.

"Thank you," I say at the same time as I hear my apartment intercom buzz. I ignore this and leave Liam to deal with it.

I exit the kitchen area to look for my phone and find it on the sofa in the open plan lounge. Quickly, I scroll through my contacts until I find James' personal number and press call.

"Well, I was wondering when I would hear from you," he says, answering almost instantly. Two clicks on the line instantly alert me he's not the only person on the call.

"Good morning, James," I say, cautious of the other listener.

"Now, it would be wishful thinking on my behalf, that the reason behind your call is to tell me you've changed your mind. But I suspect it has to do with what we can spin to the media."

"I will have to give a statement at some point, if only to keep the reporters away from my neighbours," I admit.

"What do you suggest?" he asks.

"I'm not sure. I don't want to say anything that will upset the Palace."

"But you don't mind upsetting me?"

I sigh. "James, that's not fair."

"You can't blame me for feeling disappointed," he says, sounding sad that I rejected his proposal.

"I don't, but... I can only speak honestly. Can we get back to these articles? In my statement, I'd like to say that while you were north of the border you thought it would be nice to catch up with some close friends? I mean Lottie was here too yesterday, although you didn't see her. That's not an implausible excuse, since we move in the same circles and do socialise."

"I'll get my press secretary on that now and send you a copy of the statement. Anything else?"

"No… and thank you." I end our call because there is nothing more to say.

With my phone still in my hand, I sit down and throw my head back. Staring at the ceiling, I sigh and try to clear all thoughts from my mind.

Ross comes up the stairs and I realise who had been announced on the intercom to Liam. I'm not sure my poor heart can take anymore unwanted visitors.

"Okay, with that circus downstairs I think we need to bring forward that plan Liam and I formulated during the night. We think it's time to consider alternate living arrangements," Ross says.

CHAPTER 13

*L*iam
    19th July

IN MY OPINION, the newspaper articles of Prince James' visit to Amelia have escalated her problem, both in terms of the images *and* the story they've run with. As her protector, I won't have her coerced into something by a feud involving two powerful men. The prince reaching out to her is an indication of how desperately the monarchy wants this issue quashed.

I keep telling myself to just do my job, but I've realised this isn't an assignment like any other. I need to help find a solution to the dilemma Amelia has found herself in and in doing so I feel Ross and I will end up being dragged into the politics of this situation.

Amelia looks tired and frustrated when I observe her, and the fact that she so readily trusts me suggests she doesn't think she's safe around many she knows, which is a frightening feeling I imagine. But it's the right instinct to have in her case, and unusually for me, I fight an urge to hug her and offer her reassurance that everything will be okay. However, experience tells me if she remains here, I can't guarantee someone won't get to her. The roof terraces in this apartment are weak spots, security-wise. Without moving her to a place of safety where no one can find her, at least until after the vote, she remains vulnerable.

Amelia's talking to Ross and I take another opportunity to study her features. She's a beautiful woman. Full cherry red lips cover her amazing, straight white teeth, and with her little nose and huge hazel eyes, the combination brings a certain purity to her appearance. I realise I'm staring and scoff. I'm supposed to be her bodyguard, not marking her out of ten for how attractive she is. My interest has grown from that of a professional bodyguard to something more protective, yet less defined. *Who's going to protect her from me?*

For all we know, there is already another surveillance team primed to watch Amelia's every move. And although I know Ross and I are more than capable of working counter-surveillance and can make Amelia disappear at a moment's notice, to execute this smoothly we've had to enlist the help of a couple more trusted people to ensure this happens quickly. Still, we know it will take most of the day to have all of the elements we need in place for us to move her safely.

Although I'm not working for Harry anymore, we still have ways of finding out what he knows. If he really does have a plan for Amelia, he'll make his move sooner or later, and when he does, we'll know… Ross will see to this.

CHAPTER 14

*𝒜*melia
    19th July

ROSS AND LIAM are talking at the table and I feel I need a break. All this skulduggery is making me feel sick. Yet, despite the whole situation that's been going on around me, I've been aware that I'm attracted to this man. My breath hitches when he looks across the room and his piercing blue eyes meet mine. His gaze is steady, and he bites his bottom lip as he watches me. I suppose he's thinking what to do next.

Ross stands and shrugs into his jacket, without speaking to me. I see he's leaving when he heads for the stairs.

Liam walks over to where I'm sitting. "I think we should talk," he says in his deep husky voice. My mouth feels dry, and my heart flutters at how intense his eyes are on me.

Izzy comes from the upstairs lounge. "Can I get you anything before I do laundry?" she asks, her narrowed eyes curiously darting between me and the man commanding the space in my living area.

How much laundry do we have? Is there more laundry, or is this a pretend task she uses for dismissing herself?

"No, thank you Izzy," I say without breaking Liam's stare.

"Very well," she says, and she scurries away, leaving me alone with him. He's standing in front of me; so close I have to tilt my head back to look up at him. His eyes darken from sky to midnight blue in colour as he studies me. The concentration in his gaze detonates a series of goosebumps over my skin. *He's taller than I remember.*

Dressed in his dark blue suit, with a crisp white shirt and a navy silk tie, he's immaculately turned out and in this powerful attire Liam is strikingly appealing.

"Take a seat," I finally say, finding my tongue, but still holding eye contact with him. I'm taking slow steady breaths in an attempt to remain composed. Liam sits down crossing one leg over his knee, looking somewhat relaxed despite the formal meeting.

"So, talk," I say, facing him. "Have you spoken to Harry again? Did he say anything more? I'm surprised he hasn't tried to come here himself considering he's been phoning all morning, and because of the news that the prince has been here."

"We haven't spoken again. However, I told him, yesterday, you had dismissed me. I suspect that's what all the phone calls are about. I told him if he resolved his issue of me protecting you, he should get back to me. However, I may still need to talk to him in the future."

His answer makes me anxious. "What does that mean?" I'd rather he didn't talk to Harry at all now that I know the man planned to use me.

"Donaldson was the one who told me about you, and Prince James' visit here confirmed a risk. Donaldson has no idea that Ross and I know what the prince came here for. I'm sure Ross can find out everything we need to know without

Donaldson, but just in case we need him, I'm letting him think we're all on good terms."

"So, if he sees me with you, he'll think you're still doing as *he* asked and not me?"

"No, I don't want you around Donaldson either. I know you won't want to hear this, but we need to move you from here." He leans forward in the chair. "I think there's a credible risk to you, that they could try to take you out of the equation," he says decisively, in a low, flat tone that gives me chills. His eyes hold me hostage, and his admission takes my breath away. "Your ancestral history makes you a target on all sides. Donaldson hired someone to keep you safe; namely us, but he's the person at the centre of this and the man who is putting you most at risk."

"I don't understand."

"He's willing to call you out no matter what that means for your safety." Liam didn't have to say any more.

Scotland and the rest of the United Kingdom would be at odds. And my family secret that's been buried for centuries, a secret my ancestors didn't draw attention to, would be out in the open.

"It's a ridiculous predicament I'm in, don't you agree? Not to mention the oddest threesome," I add.

"Maybe it is, maybe it isn't. Someone is obviously spooked by this. On the surface both men appear to want to protect you. That's a quality many women would find attractive."

"They aren't doing it out of a sense of chivalry though, are they? I'm sorry but growing up in those circles you gain a natural sense of suspicion."

"I want to know what the prince said when came back the second time to see you."

I shrug. "Same pressure as before, that I should marry him."

Liam shakes his head and uncrosses his leg. When his eyes flare, I realise my comment has provoked a thought in him. He sits forward in his seat and clears his throat but doesn't speak.

"On Friday, I received an official invitation from Queen Sofia to Prince James' engagement party. The Palace will most probably make an announcement this week about his engagement to Lady Effie since I've refused."

"I wouldn't bank on that," Liam says, but I'm not sure what he means, and I frown. He sees my confusion. "If the vote is yes, you could find the prince back again with some kind of ultimatum."

"If I'm still alive by then," I joke, and I hate how my voice quivers when I speak. "I couldn't actually die because of this, could I?"

"I doubt we are there, but there is a possibility you could be taken somewhere against your will to save Donaldson from raising the question at all.

"Kidnap me you mean?"

"Sounds crazy but who knows. It won't happen though, not with Ross and me taking care of you.

My heart pounds at the thought and a mixture of fear and anger streaks through me. "You're right. Harry has much to answer for. I don't see how the Palace can possibly announce an engagement straight away after this. If they do, poor Lady Effie will be wandering around pretending she's fine with the prince's scandalous behaviour, of going behind her back and visiting me."

"I bet Donaldson isn't taking the news very well either, about the prince's visit here."

"Well, you're still guarding me, just not at his request anymore. But strangely enough, I do have to thank him for hiring you in the first place. Thank God you were here when the prince visited me on both occasions. I should kiss you for insisting on seeing me home."

Liam sits quietly and stares at me for a long moment.

"What?" I ask.

"Nothing. I'm just curious. I'm trying to figure you out."

I hold my arms out. "What you see is what you get."

"But is it?" He cocks his head to the side, studying my face. "The media seem focused on your love and party life. But in the short time I've been around you, I've seen a different side to you. I'm guessing a side very few choose to see. And as for Donaldson being romantically linked to you, that man would have *no idea* what do with you."

His comment intrigues me. It's borderline opinion without stating what he means, so I ask, "And you would?"

He chuckles. "Perhaps… yes." His eyes narrow in on mine. "I think you're a complex woman, and I suspect you'd require firm handling, but challenges can ultimately be far more rewarding than something that's easily managed. I think you need someone who is confident enough to allow you to take the reins sometimes. That's not Donaldson. He's weak…selfish; a man that can barely meet his own needs, never mind those of a beautiful ballbreaker like you."

"Ballbreaker, huh?" I say, laughing. "Compliment accepted." The skin on the back of my neck prickles in response to his assessment of me, and the slow reluctant smile he gives makes my core pulse with need. Of course, Liam is right about Harry… and the rest? Well, I'm enthralled by his words. Harry is totally not my type. And the fact that Liam thinks *he, himself,* is, although not in so many words, makes my heart skip a beat.

I'm resting my chin on my hands while we talk, but the heat in his gaze suddenly floods my body and I sit upright. My protector is watching me intently, but there's a glint in his eyes that screams his attraction towards me, and I can't take my eyes off him.

A heavy silence hangs between us in the connection we're sharing, and I'm struggling to keep my breaths even as I drink him in. I've never felt so enticed by any man the way I am by him. Yet there's a line I feel he won't cross. My body is almost ablaze from the sexual chemistry we share, it's such a desperate reaction within me and I don't recognise it. I lick my lips, I'm parched, in need of water, or my tea which is growing colder by the minute on the kitchen table. I feel my skin burn under his gaze and for the first time that I can remember, I feel excitedly nervous just being in the company of this man.

I break eye contact with him, turn away and take several deep breaths while trying to compose myself.

"Amelia we're going to do everything we can to keep you safe," he says again. His voice is low and gruff, and I nod.

"But safe from what, or whom?" I sigh. "Oh my God."

"What?"

"The car."

He shakes his head, clearly confused. "What car?"

"I thought it was nothing, but now…"

"What? Tell me exactly what happened," he says shifting closer to me, and taking my hand. I have his full attention and he looks concerned again.

I go on to explain about the two men in the black saloon car that almost hit me and Lottie the other day, and how I thought it was a near miss.

He rubs his hands roughly over his face. "Shit, you *were* going to be taken. And this happened *before* Prince James came to see you? If so, then *his proposal* was the Crown's plan B."

"Now what?" I ask, hoping that he will be able to shed a tiny sliver of relief in all of this.

"Now, I definitely feel the safe house is the right choice. Ross's contact is identifying somewhere we can... hide you, at least until we know the result of the referendum. If Donaldson loses the vote, I guess the threat to you goes away, if we do it right."

"But I'm safe here." Although I sound quite terse at the prospect of moving out of my home, I feel quietly excited at the prospect of spending time with Liam, providing I'm safe. I digress to wonder if the connection we have will dwindle the more we're around one another, or whether it'll grow?

He shakes his head. "I disagree. Today was the second time someone from the Palace has been into your home at your, or your housekeeper's, invitation."

I begin to feel flustered. "I have three meetings tomorrow, that I need to conclude for my charity work. After those there are no more until after the summer. If I don't turn up for the first meeting, they'll know... I don't know *what* they'll know... I need to finish those meetings or monies don't get released."

Liam thinks for a few minutes before he takes a different phone out of his pocket; it's one of those that are sized between a phone and a tablet. "It's too risky, Amelia," he says.

"Please, it's one day, and there will be eight other people in the room at each meeting. You can stay with me."

"I don't like it, but if you share your schedule for those meetings to my email address, and I can assess they have reasonable escape routes, I'll agree. I'll need the length of the meetings too. This way Ross and I can plan your movements safely. But, again, I'll have to ask Ross if his contacts can mark us until your meetings are finished. If we do this, Amelia, you won't be coming back here tomorrow."

"Mark us?"

"Watch us," he clarifies.

I sit up straight and grab my phone, then pull up my

calendar and read. I ask Liam for his email address and forward the schedule to him.

"I spoke to Izzy when I came in and warned her I may be staying. She's said I can have the same guest bedroom I slept in before. As you will be staying here today, I'd like to go and change my clothes, if that's okay with you?" Liam says.

"Sure," I reply, slightly thrown by his request. The thought of spending time doing nothing with this man should unsettle me, but instead, I'm intrigued by him. "Feel free to go and make yourself comfortable." My thoughts drift to wonder what he's going to change into, now he won't be wearing his suit. *Will he wear jeans or slacks? T-shirt or sweater?*

He stands with his eyes still on me and gives me a subtle nod before he heads for the stairs, and I'm left sitting alone. I feel his loss from the room, and this unnerves me. Izzy seems to have disappeared just when I need her fussing around to distract me.

I shouldn't want this intrusion, yet I find myself eager for him to stay near, he makes me feel less afraid just by talking to me.

Despite his role I find Liam charismatic, and I know I shouldn't. He's going to be in my life for at least two weeks, until after the referendum. I've decided I'm not going to fight whatever they tell me to do, and instead I'll let Liam and Ross take care of me. I also intend to make the most of getting to know more about Liam.

CHAPTER 15

Liam
19th July

THIS HOME IS as beautiful as the woman who lives here. I've never slept in a bedroom as elegant as the one I've been given. I didn't take much notice of it last night when I stayed, but now that I'm here again I can appreciate the quality of everything in it. As soon as I brought my luggage upstairs, Izzy took my three suits from the carriers and hung them in the vast walk-in wardrobe.

Glancing around the spacious room makes me consider that I should move from my small apartment and find myself a proper house, somewhere I can call home. Since my protection work has shifted from military to a civilian role of protecting VIP public figures, politicians and dignitaries, my current living needs have changed. Up until recently my studio has been sufficiently comfortable as somewhere to sleep whenever I come back into the country. Now most of my work is on home turf, so I think it's time to make changes and put down some permanent roots.

Having changed into jeans and a T-shirt I head back upstairs. Izzy is in the kitchen by the stove, and whatever she's cooking smells mouth-watering.

"Roast beef with all the trimmings. I hope that's okay with you?" Izzy asks turning her head.

"Sounds perfect to me." A smile spreads on my face, and my stomach groans in anticipation of the delicious lunch to come.

"Amelia's in the sitting room."

As it's an open plan lay out so I can see this for myself, but I smile, nod and take this as my cue to leave her to get back to cooking.

Amelia is sitting exactly where I left her, her eyes are closed, and she looks so peaceful as she rests. I stand, using the opportunity to take in all the small details about her that I've been dying to absorb but couldn't until now. She has a freckle just to the right of her mouth; they're perfect, kissable lips. These personal thoughts are not ones I should have about her, yet they're stacking up inside my head, and the picture of my attraction towards her is clearer than ever. My mind is making a silent list of her attributes; all the reasons why I find her as beautiful as she is. What I should be doing is marking up negatives and helping find things about her that turn me off.

Amelia Campbell is the perfect image of sophistication, elegance, and natural beauty. It's no wonder she brings would-be kings and powerful men to their knees. I consider wandering back to the kitchen to see if I can help Izzy with anything before my infatuation takes hold, or I'm caught objectifying her while she's vulnerable in sleep and totally unaware.

"Are you just going to stand there, Mr McKenna?"

Fuck. Her voice startles me, causing me to jump. I glance towards her and she tries but fails miserably to hide to a smug smirk on her face.

"I didn't want to disturb you," I say walking further into the room and taking a seat on the sofa opposite her. I feel awkward that she caught me staring.

"I wasn't sleeping." She rubs her forehead as though she's got something on her mind, or she has a headache.

"What's wrong?" I ask, knowing my question is a likely intrusion, but in the scheme of things, plenty in her world must feel intrusive right now.

"I was just thinking, trying to piece everything together."

"And did you find any answers or solutions?"

"If only." She sighs heavily and now she looks as though she's carrying the weight of the world on her shoulders.

I move to the edge of the sofa. "I might be here to ensure your safety, but I'm also good at connecting the dots in situations." Solving problems has got me out of many tricky settings.

"Of course, you are, I imagine you would need an analytical mind in your job."

Her eyes study me carefully as they slowly sweep over my body. It's my turn to smirk a little more wickedly than I'd have liked, when her eyes linger on my broad chest for a few moments longer than anywhere else. In jeans and a fitted T-shirt, I look somewhat normal, certainly less intimidating than in my suit.

Eventually, I ask, "What are the plans for the rest of the day?"

Her eyes hold mine before she quickly looks away. "After Sunday roast I have some work to catch up on in my office. Meanwhile, you are free to do as you please. Izzy mentioned earlier that she wanted to watch a movie."

"If you're certain you won't be leaving the apartment tonight, maybe I'll go out for a run," I say.

"Oh, I should've mentioned there's a gym and swimming pool in the basement of the building, for all residents."

"Now, that sounds perfect and it's okay for me to use both?" I ask.

"Yes, I'll get Izzy to call down and put your name on the list. That reminds me, although you have a key card and code to come to the apartment, I should give you the codes for the main security system."

"Thank you," I say, appreciating her trust and knowing how big a deal this must feel for her.

"Lunch is ready," Izzy calls over to us.

Amelia stands immediately. "Come on, let's eat, I'm starving." The fact she has an appetite despite what's happening to her, says a lot about her resilience in the current circumstances.

The table is formally set for the three of us. Sliced roast beef is plated in the centre of the table. I can't remember the last time I tucked into a Sunday lunch with all the trimmings: roast potatoes, a selection of vegetables, Yorkshire puddings and a delicious beef stock gravy. From the mouthwatering aroma in the air, I know I'm going to enjoy every mouthful of this home-cooked meal.

"Izzy this looks incredible," I say waiting to see where Amelia is sitting, before I take a seat.

"You look like a man that enjoys a home-cooked meal, tuck in."

She doesn't need to tell me twice, but I do have manners and I wait until Amelia puts food on her plate first. There's a bottle of red wine opened on the table along with three glasses. I want to do some training so I'm not sure having a glass of wine is a good idea for me.

"Where are the glasses kept?" I ask rising from my seat.

"What's wrong?" Izzy asks.

"Nothing is wrong, I'll just have water with my meal."

Izzy smiles but I catch the subtle shake of Amelia's head. Izzy points me in the right direction of the glasses, and I fill one with ice and water before I sit back down.

Amelia tilts her head. "You're allowed to drink on the job, unless you have an alcohol problem."

Izzy gasps at what Amelia has just said.

I shake my head. "No, I don't have a drinking problem. I want to train sometime later today."

I can see Izzy almost sigh with relief at my answer. I don't add that drinking and being attracted to the woman I'm here to protect isn't the best idea.

"Well, that's good, at least I don't have to ask Izzy to hide all the alcohol," Amelia says dryly, with a grin as she lifts her cutlery and starts eating.

After the initial awkwardness at the table, lunch is enjoyable. Izzy's a fantastic cook and I note this will be one of the benefits to guarding Amelia. Usually, I live off fast food, microwave meals or sandwiches because I find no enjoyment cooking for one.

"Thank you for lunch, Izzy," I say as she stands to clear the dishes. I rise to my feet and start helping.

"There's no need to thank me or to help," she says sweetly.

"Nonsense. What kind of gentleman would I be if I just sat there?"

"You're a charmer," Izzy says, rubbing my arm.

"I try," I reply, flashing her a smile before turning my attention to Amelia, who is still sitting at the table. I raise my eyebrows silently, questioning if she agrees. I can see Izzy has amused her by flirting with me. It's safe to flirt with an elderly woman who feeds me well.

As soon as we're finished washing up, Izzy darts off, she has some programme or movie she wants to watch on

TV. She goes to the lounge upstairs, taking her unfinished glass of wine with her.

Amelia stands hugging herself as she looks around her kitchen, and I can see she finds her situation awkward. She turns her back to me and I see her body sag. My presence is affecting her, and although she's doing her best to hide it, I still know. She tips her head back and drains the last of her wine, brings the glass down to the sink, and just stands there. I sense something is off and suddenly she's not the confident party woman the world knows and loves.

She glances towards me and I see a vulnerable look in her eyes. I step towards her and reach out – knowing I shouldn't – and place my hand on her shoulder. *Fuck.* All I want to do is pull her into my arms and hug her. After this past couple of days, I bet she could do with one. Surprisingly she doesn't flinch when I touch her and appears to relax instead. She looks over her shoulder, then turns around to face me. We're standing closer now and there's an electric connection between us again. From the darkened look in her eyes, I can see she feels it too.

"What's troubling you?" I ask quietly.

She doesn't answer, and I give her whatever time she needs. With a heart-felt sigh she looks up at me through her lashes. I inhale the sweet fragrance of her perfume. When I do I immediately know I've found my favourite scent in the world; the intoxicating mix of Amelia Campbell, and whatever the fuck she's wearing.

My thoughts and reactions are starting to betray me. She's so near that I can feel her breath faintly on me.

"This is all so outrageous," she says with hesitation.

"You know I'm here for you… for whatever you need." Despite my words, my hand has found its way to her back.

"I'm attracted to you," she says, boldly.

My heart speeds up with her confirmation. "I know, but

that doesn't have to be a problem. I don't mix business with pleasure," I tell her. My hand says different, yet I can't bring myself to remove it at this moment in time.

"Usually, I don't either." She takes a small step closer until our feet are touching. My eyes are on her and there's something unsure in her gaze. She's questioning my motives, and so she should.

When she places her hand against my chest, her lips part and her fingers splay over my pectoral muscles.

I dip my head but turn it away. "I'm sorry," I mutter shaking my head. "We can't do this. I'm here to keep you safe. You're vulnerable, Amelia. I won't confuse your situation further, and I need to focus all of my attention on your safety."

Amelia sidesteps and walks away from me and my gaze follows her. She stops at the fridge and takes a bottle of dessert wine, grabs a clean glass, and heads in the direction of the living area, leaving me standing in the kitchen alone. I'm boiling with frustration at my own near miss of giving in to my feelings. *What now*? Time to go and let off some steam in the gym. Refocus my attention on why I'm here, and not who I'd like to seduce. If I can.

CHAPTER 16

 melia
20th July

I'm NOT sure locking myself away in my office for all of last night was the right thing to do, and especially not drinking wine in there, alone.

What did I think I was doing, hitting on a man I've hired to protect me? Today I feel sick to my stomach with nerves, but I have a busy schedule ahead. It's my last three charity board meetings before the summer break, and according to Liam, when they're done, I won't be coming back here.

I can excuse my avoidance of Liam, as me pretending to work, but I couldn't stay around him because our connection keeps drawing me in. The frustration that has built within me since he refused to act on what I know we *both* wanted, has left me wondering if my heightened emotions are due to what I've learned. I shake my head, dismissing this thought.

Yesterday, from the moment I saw him in jeans and his clean white T-shirt, I was done for, and after lunch when his huge, strong hand landed firmly on my shoulder, the heat from it scorched through my cotton top. An instant thrill ran down my spine. When I turned and saw him standing so close, I felt sure he was going to kiss me. When he didn't our connection felt even more complicated. Of course, hiding away meant I didn't have to deal with those feelings in front of him, but my action only delayed coming face-to-face with him again now. And not only do I have to deal with being around Liam all day, I also have a slight hangover from the wine to contend with. Not a great start to a Monday morning.

My chest feels tight when I hear Liam and Izzy talking in the kitchen as I climb the stairs, and I inhale, filling my lungs with some much-needed air. I'm conflicted, because as much as I want to see him, I dread feeling awkward because of this magnetic pull that persists between us.

Despite a pep talk about playing it cool, I've taken extra time over my appearance today. I'd like to say I didn't do this for him, but that would be a lie. Growing up, my mother used to say, *"A Campbell must always dress one's best whenever she feels anxious about facing any given situation."* And as I'm dressed to the nines, my attire is evidence that anxiety is slowly killing me. My anguish is two-fold: the ridiculous threat aimed towards me, and resisting my hot bodyguard. I've taken an age over my long, dark hair, but it's been worth it. It's in a half up, half down Grecian style. My makeup isn't too heavy, and my straight black skirt and red silk blouse are the perfect choice for the meetings I'm attending today.

Lottie and I are booked in for lunch between meetings. I hope Liam lets this take place. I feel I should at least explain to my best friend that I won't be around for a while. I've texted her saying she must not look surprised when Liam accompanies me. I'm not sure how the other attendees at the charity meetings will feel about me having a bodyguard with me. The thought of him trailing along to them feels absurd.

Like a good actress, I paste a warm smile on my face as I climb the stairs from the lower floor and turn into the kitchen. My breath hitches when I see Liam, handsome and freshly showered. Once again, he's sitting at the table holding an espresso cup, which looks so tiny in his hand.

Again, his shirt is crisp, pristine and white, no signs of any wrinkles, and his perfectly knotted, dark grey, silk tie matches his dark grey suit. His jacket hangs over the back of the chair where he sits, the waistcoat over his shirt still unbuttoned. He's a sight for sore eyes on a Monday morning… he would be on *any* morning come to that.

"Started without me?" I ask cheerily.

Izzy turns from the stove and I give her a kiss on the cheek. "Good morning Amelia, you sound chirpy," she says with a wide smile, her cheeks glowing as she casts her approving gaze over me.

"I thought I was always chirpy," I say. "It's Monday, the start of a new week, and I have a busy day ahead."

"Ah, last appointments of the season," she says. "Please let me know if there are any changes to mealtimes that we haven't already discussed. Am I cooking for one extra every night?" she asks. I frown, narrowing my eyes at Izzy.

Liam coughs to clear his throat. "Actually, Izzy, we may be decamping to different accommodation for a while."

"When?" I look sharply at Liam and know whatever he and Ross have planned must already be in place. "Don't worry, Izzy, if I'm leaving here, you're coming with me," I say and glance to Liam for confirmation of this.

He looks at Izzy and nods. "Of course, but not a word to anyone, Izzy."

"Morning," I say, acknowledging him formally as I take a seat opposite where he's sitting. "You really think this is necessary?"

"Affirmative," he says with a nod. "The press aren't going

away, and as long as they're following you, all interested parties will know exactly where you are. We won't have Ross driving us today," he says, and then slowly takes a drink with his gaze still focused on me. "He's involved in the planning of our alternate living arrangements."

"So, it will just be the two of us?"

"Yes. I've assessed your meetings, and they're in public places so I've come to the conclusion that none of them pose any threats. Who knows you are going to them?"

"Just the members of the board, Lottie, and the secretarial minute taker," I reply.

"Lottie?"

I nod. "Yes, she makes personal notes for my actions, and carries them out with me. We have lunch booked, but it's also a very public place, so we should be fine there, right?"

Liam shakes his head slowly as he considers what I've said then nods. "Normal routine until it's not," he mutters, and I wonder what this means.

Izzy hands me a cup of tea and even she raises her eyebrows, silently questioning the conversation we're having.

I fix Liam with a stern gaze. "I've worked with these charities for a number of years, I'm sure everyone, at each of the meetings, is trustworthy."

"No one else has information regarding your diary?"

"Lottie, she makes my appointments for me."

"Well, that's good to know," he muses.

"I can't believe I've found myself in this surreal position. I've never been interested in this referendum. And now that I've met Harry Donaldson I don't believe he has the best interests of our country at the forefront of his campaign. He's out for himself. It's outrageous that he's dragged me into this, I won't play a part in his crazy plot. Look, this is all too heavy for a Monday morning." I rub my head. "Oh, come on, taking on the monarchy? It sounds insane."

Liam sighs. "If someone really has tried to abduct you, and the prince has come to see you, then they're taking all of this seriously."

"That stupid man has no idea what he's doing," Izzy mumbles, as she hands me a plate of toast.

She's right. Harry would create havoc if this were to be put to the people. "Thank you," I say to her. "He's putting me between those who want the union and those that wish for the monarchy to continue."

"That's why we need to rehouse you for a while. You're a sitting duck here. After today, you'll be a prisoner in this apartment until the result from the referendum is known. And the risk to you only diminishes if the result of that is to the monarchy's satisfaction. I can only guarantee your safety if no one knows where you are."

"Life has no guarantees," I retort.

We both sit quietly while I eat my toast, the atmosphere in the room feels highly charged. I'm not sure if this is because of the conversation we've just had or if it's the chemistry that constantly arcs between us. If Izzy notices the shift in our mood, she doesn't let on, or ask any questions, but I can see her observing us both with narrowed eyes. Liam takes a large bite of toast and chews for a moment. His tongue darts out and he slowly licks his lips. In reaction to this I grow warm with desire, wondering what that tongue would feel like on my skin.

"We should get going," I say, taking a last sip from my tea as I stand. Glancing down at my clothes, I smooth down my skirt, ensuring there are no crumbs on it.

"I, or rather *we*," I correct myself, looking at Liam, "shouldn't be late." I turn to Izzy. "As we're moving somewhere else, would you please pack outfits and toiletries for me, while I'm out?"

"We won't be coming back here this evening," Liam tells us. "And we'll be gone from here until after the referendum. Ross will be back to help you at some point, Izzy. He'll bring you to us. Meanwhile, I suggest you don't answer the phone today, or take any messages. Don't tell anyone we're leaving here. When Ross collects you, please leave any internet devices and phones – anything that can be tracked – in the apartment, he'll advise and explain why."

"This all sounds a bit like a spy action movie," I suggest.

He turns to glare at me. "Good, keep thinking like that. Now, leave all your electronic devices here before we go this morning… your phone too," he says, and his expression tells me not to argue.

"You will keep Izzy safe?" I ask.

"That's Ross's job. Don't worry, Izzy, you'll be in expert hands. Moving Amelia is just a precaution, I don't believe this is a life and death situation, you're not in any danger." He turns his attention back to me. "Meanwhile, today is going to go as you've planned. Everything you do must be as stated in your diary. After the last meeting, life will change for a short while."

I leave the kitchen without waiting for him, but I hear his footsteps following quickly behind me as I walk downstairs towards the lift.

"Don't talk about anything except charity work in the car on the way to the meetings."

I immediately wonder if he thinks our transport has been bugged. This intrusion of my privacy makes me furious, but I say nothing because I've been told not to question him, so I won't.

If we don't need Ross today does that mean Liam intends to drive?

The lift doors open and I step inside, Liam joins me, shrugging on his jacket and doing up the top button before he drops back to my left. Goosebumps spread over my skin when I hear his deep, steady breathing, and note mine has grown fast and shallow. I nervously chew on the inside of my mouth, acutely aware of him standing close to my shoulder and I fight the urge to turn around.

I'm going to have to figure out a way of spending time with him without allowing the effect he has on me to show.

I inhale deeply but quietly to slow my body down, and when the doors open, I march out, my high heels clipping on the floor of the underground car park. I stop by my cars and look around for him. The lights flash on my Range Rover and I turn, widening my eyes as I see him with the key fob to it in his hand.

"Miss Campbell," he says, sounding formal, and opening the back door of my car.

"We're taking mine?" I ask, almost in a whisper.

"We are. I'm insured to drive anything." He pulls me away from the car door and whispers, "We're leaving it at the last meeting, and it will give us a few hours advantage to head where we are going before anyone knows you've gone."

I consider what he says for a moment, and he gestures toward the back seat again.

"Thank you," I reply, offering him a smile as I slide, graciously in. He closes the door, rounds the car, and gets in behind the wheel.

As he starts the engine, he pulls his seat belt on, adjusts the side and rearview mirrors, and looks back over his shoulder. As he reverses, I sit back and keep my eyes on him because… I *can*. He's too busy manoeuvring in the garage to notice me watching.

It feels strange sitting in the back of my own car, and I survey the view from my window. The sun is shining, and the cloudless sky is blue; those two things help briefly to lift my mood. A few minutes into the journey silence grows and fills the air. It makes the atmosphere feel awkward. Every now and then, I catch him glancing over his shoulder; it's as if he's checking I'm still here. With each tiny glance my heart races and my train of thought drifts. I'm not so sure the connection we share won't spill over regardless of what he said before. If he's feeling half the allure I have towards him, I sense that, despite his best efforts and his professional stance, this spark between us will somehow ignite and catch fire.

"Can you put the radio on?" I ask, needing a distraction from my thoughts.

"What channel?" he asks.

"I don't care."

He huffs at my response, but presses the button for the radio, and I chuckle when he flinches, because the volume is louder than he'd expected when we hear, 'I Should Be So Lucky' by Kylie Minogue, disrupting the quiet of our shared space. He immediately switches station and, 'Born to Run' by Bruce Springsteen blares out instead. I can't hide the smirk that takes over my face because I feel the gods are sending me a message within the lyrics of these songs. What it is, I have yet to determine.

* * *

"OH MY GOSH!" Lottie squeals as she rushes forward and hugs me after my first meeting. "You weren't joking when you said you were bringing him with you," she whispers into my ear as she kisses my cheeks.

"No," I say, flatly. I want to tell her what's happening, but I'm mindful of what I can say. "I'm glad we're having lunch together," I say, because I'm not sure when I'll see her again.

A lump of emotion grows in my throat at the thought of going away.

She links her arm with mine as we are led to our usual table in *Divino Enoteca Italian Restaurant & Wine Bar* by the maître d'. This is one of our favourite places to eat and drink because we get privacy at the back, good food, delicious cocktails and wine; everything we could want.

"Amelia Campbell you're hiding something, you need to spill the beans," Lottie says, leaning close as we approach our table. When we're seated the maître d' looks at Liam who has followed us and is standing near a table for two situated close to ours.

"I'll have this seat," Liam tells her. The hostess looks flustered, and I guess it's a combination of the reserved marker on the table, and how imposingly handsome he is. She hesitates for a moment, unsure what to do with the man who commands the space and the air around him.

I'd know what to do with him.

I fight a smile at my thought and see her nod and lift the reserved marker from the table before Liam sits down. Lottie is sitting with the drinks menu in her hand but is looking past it with her eyes on him too.

"Earth to Lottie! I thought you were here to see me, not spend your time day-dreaming about my bodyguard," I tease.

She lifts her head and sits back in her seat. "I'm just trying to figure out what the hell is going on with him. I don't get any of it."

"What don't you get, him or Harry?" I ask her.

"Both, to be honest. This is all a bit crazy," she whispers with her eyes darting around conspiratorially. "I'm a little perturbed by the game Harry's playing."

I quickly fill her in on the part of my saga that she's missed and tell her in a cryptic way I'm going away to live somewhere else for a while.

"We should order some champagne," she says, looking sad that I can't take her with me. I can't even tell her where I'm going.

I shrug and reply, "Why not, I don't have to drive anywhere." I'm acting like my usual self, but I've already decided drinking today isn't a good idea.

Lottie grabs a waiter's attention and orders a bottle of our favourite Dom Perignon, and she also orders a non-alcoholic cocktail and a sandwich for Liam. I only order a few nibbles because I'm too nervous to eat.

"So, what is your plan for the next two meetings?" she asks, injecting a little normality into our lunch, and we discuss the final outstanding charity items I need to resolve.

"What if…" Her eyes widen when she suddenly thinks of something, and I'm actually fearful of what she's about to say. "What if, James hopes to change your mind, and that's why they're holding off on a public announcement?" she whispers in the same hushed tone as earlier.

I shrug because it's a problem for Queen Sofia, not me.

Lottie takes a drink, then tilts her head to the side, her gaze drifting past me and straight to Liam, who I sense, without turning to look over my shoulder, is staring directly towards our table.

"I see someone else has their sights set on you, even if his work keeps getting in the way."

Could she be any more obvious?

"Stop it," I snap, not finding her usual immature teasing funny.

"I see the way he looks at you."

"He's paid to do that, he's my bodyguard."

"But he's not looking at you like he wants to fend off anyone who comes near you. He looks like he wants to devour you. I can see it in his eyes, you fire him up and I bet he's a filthy lover. I wonder what his kinks are?"

"You're unbelievable," I mutter, wiping my mouth with my napkin and placing it on the table.

"If you find he has some, will you share them with me?"

"No. Liam," I call over, breaking up our conversation. "We need to make a move if I'm to be on time for the next meeting.

"Spoilsport," she goads.

"Yes, ma'am," Liam says pushing his glass away from him and rising to his feet. I glare at him for his use of the word 'ma'am' it makes me feel much older than my twenty-eight years.

"The two of you could have so much fun together," Lottie whispers in my ear as we say our goodbyes.

"You're so immature. Can you at least try to be good until I see you again?" I tease her.

"Where is the fun in that?" she asks, laughing.

Lottie's perception is spot on, and the question I need to ask myself is, can Liam and I keep our relationship professional?

CHAPTER 17

$\mathscr{L}$iam
20th July

AFTER WARNING Lottie not to talk about Amelia's situation whilst in the car, I open the Range Rover door and both women climb in the back seat.

I take the driver's seat, with the words of Amelia and Lottie's conversation playing over in my head. I didn't hear what Lottie whispered in Amelia's ear, but I can hazard a guess after hearing a small part of their quiet exchange. Lottie is not as discreet as I need her to be. Ross will need to talk to her. I'm contemplating whether we need to take her with us, and if there's anything she could disclose that would enhance the threat to Amelia's safety. I decide against this, she's another person I'd have to hide.

The one thing I did hear Lottie suggest clearly to Amelia was that I might be a filthy lover.

Kinks? I have plenty. But right now, I'd take vanilla sex with the woman I'm commissioned to protect, just to be inside her.

I shake my head as I try to change the direction of my thoughts. I'm taking Amelia to her last two meetings, and I've already decided Lottie is making her own way home.

Being with them today, has given me a good insight into the kind of women each of them are. I've sat in the background and watched their interactions, both in and out of the meetings. And as I thought, there's a lot more to Amelia Campbell, famed for her partying, than the media portrays. I listened with interest as she discussed one of the charities that she is patron of. The confident and intelligent way she conducted her business made her the central player in the room. I can tell she's proud of the causes she champions. Hearing the way in which she believes she can help others, demonstrates her devotion to make lives better. Something that strikes me is, even if she didn't lead the life she does, I believe she'd still choose to get involved in the needs of others.

I wonder why her lawyer was in attendance at the last meeting with Amelia when he wasn't present during the others. But then I hear what she wants to do for a young couple she met at the hospital; she wants to clear off their mortgage and put an emergency allowance in an account for them. The chairman is far less charitable when he advises her that she has already given more than enough with her donation towards the hospital. I sit and listen; even Lottie has a tear in her eye when Amelia retells the plight of the young family she'd met, and what they've already gone through. It makes me want to help them myself. When she's done talking, she instructs her lawyer to start the ball rolling to deliver the funds.

When the last meeting finishes, Amelia excuses herself and goes to use the restroom. Lottie is deep in conversation with the chairman of the foundation and Amelia's lawyer. I swipe Amelia's jacket off the back of the chair and slip out of the room without being noticed.

I stand by the restroom door, and as soon as Amelia comes out, I grab her by the wrist.

"We need to leave now," I tell her, and begin walking purposefully towards the fire exit.

"But Lottie?" It's not a complete protest, more of a pointed question.

I shake my head. "Sorry, she's a liability to travel with us right now. But I'll ask Ross to contact her later if he can."

I'm surprised when she doesn't argue, and instead lets me lead her out to the car park at the back of the building. I glance around and see a mid-sized Ford Mondeo, a popular, modest car, with slightly tinted windows that is unlikely to draw attention. Amelia looks hesitant when we pass her luxury model, but soon picks up her stride when I keep going. Our 'getaway' car is the last on the lot, nearest the back gates of the building we've just left. I know it's the correct vehicle because the regular number plates have been swapped out for ours.

Dropping her wrist, I make my way to the rear and grab a set of keys from on top of the back wheel. Pressing the fob, I quickly open the door and tell her, "Get in." I quickly close the door after her and climb into the driver's seat.

"Why can't we just take my car?"

"It may already have a tracker installed."

"Is this car yours?"

"No. It's a rental. By now all the vehicles I use, my telephone numbers, email addresses and all other forms of my normal communications could be compromised by my involvement with you." She looks worried and I know I need to reassure her. "Don't worry we've got this."

"Then how do you know where we're going? Has Ross already told you?"

I sigh. "Look let's just get out of here and drive until I think you're safe, and I'll answer all your questions." All the while we've been talking, I've driven out of the back gates knowing the car park was secure and it couldn't be over-looked. I have no idea how Ross got the car in there, but whoever delivered it knew what he was doing.

For a few miles I drive around the city, taking round-abouts twice and dipping down narrow streets to counter any surveillance I may have missed. Only when I'm sure we're home free, do I head for the M8 towards Glasgow.

"Okay, I'm confident we're not being followed," I inform her.

"Can I sit in the front?" she asks.

"I'm not stopping, maybe when we get to our next pitstop," I say.

"Are you going to answer my questions now?" she asks, unbuckling her seatbelt and climbing over between the seats. She sits beside me and fastens the seatbelt.

I glance at her and the air crackles, until I shake my head and look out the window again. "Crack on, what do you need to know?"

"The car…"

"It's a rental, like I said. Ross has contacts in very obscure places. I can't even begin to explain this to you. Whoever hired it has no connection to me, and Donaldson thinks Ross is merely a driver. The elite intelligence community he has access to means it would take a hell of a lot of work to connect anyone other than Ross to me. Don't worry, we're ditching it long before we get to where we're going, and it'll be returned with the clock turned back and the original registration plates in place, so it'll look like it's only been driven locally, in Edinburgh."

"Where are you taking me?"

"We're not discussing anything right now. I'd rather you

were silent and let me concentrate on my job." I know my tone sounds clipped, but I can't chance that someone has found, or tampered with, the car. Ross always says I'm paranoid when I think like this, but if paranoia is what it takes to keep Amelia safe, I'm happy to own that label.

melia
20th July

Two car changes later, it's dull and blustery when we arrive at the secluded house in the desolate back hills of Glencoe. Here, there's no CCTV; in fact, there's very little apart from dramatic rolling mountains, rich grass and rough bracken as far as the eye can see. I feel exhausted from all the cloak and dagger moves of the day.

Pushing the door open, I climb out of the back of the latest bumpy ride we've swapped into – an olive-green Land Rover Defender. Liam drove it with confidence through the windy pass for the last sixty miles of our journey and the vehicle blends in well with the surroundings.

I stretch and a shiver runs through me.

I walk around to the boot and see Liam and Ross have thought of everything. It's packed with things it would never occur to me to take if I ran away.

From the boot of each car, Liam has taken items left inside, and transferred them into the next. In the glove compartments of each vehicle he's found cheap mobile phones filled with texts giving instructions for each subsequent part of our journey. After reading each instruction, Liam confirmed receipt, then destroyed and discarded the phone before we drove to the next car change. The last of these texts had led us here, to our final destination.

"This looks…isolated," I say, wrapping my arms around myself. The temperature has fallen on this shady side of the foothill, but it's still daylight at eight in the evening here in the Highlands of Scotland.

Liam goes to the back passenger side of the car, grabs a heavy, dark Barbour jacket and comes beside me to place it over my shoulders. I feel grateful for the weight and hold the sides together tightly because I'm shivering all over now.

He goes back to the boot of the car and takes out the two padded bags of devices and a large box of groceries that must have been preloaded into this vehicle.

"Let's get you inside," he says, gesturing towards the substantial grey farmhouse Ross has found.

He did well. One road in, one road out, and a thick brush of rough bracken surrounding the house.

"How do you know they won't find us here?" I ask as I glance around.

"I don't," he replies in an even tone. "But I know this house has been rented by one of the many shell companies in foreign third-party names Ross has set up for jobs we've done in the past. He's never let me down yet."

When I reach the porch, I'm surprised the door isn't locked. "So much for security," I say.

"Yeah." He appears to agree as he places the bags of electronic devices on the floor. He leans forward and pulls a bench full of Wellington boots away from the dwarf wall to one side and I see a locked key box situated behind it. Kneeling, Liam punches in a code from the final text Ross sent.

Pulling the key from the box, he shoves the bench back in place and hands it to me. "Give me a few minutes," he says.

I'm surprised when he takes a drone, wrapped in grey jersey cloth, from the larger of the two bags, steps outside and places it on the ground, along with a laptop. Next, he uses elastic bands to fix the phone containing the instructions onto it.

I step out of the porch to get a better view and watch him setting up a small satellite dish on a tripod. After a minute or two he fires up the laptop. He appears to get a camera signal and the screen shows a grainy view. Taking a remote control, Liam presses some buttons, and it seems to synchronise both pieces of equipment.

The drone launches and I realise it was the gravel on the driveway the laptop had picked up from the drone's camera when it was on the ground. The images of the view it sees as it soars in the sky are showing up on the laptop screen. It's a serious piece of equipment and it's fast. Within seconds it's a dot in the sky, disappearing over the hill to our left. Liam's gaze switches from where the drone has disappeared to the laptop.

"What are you doing?"

"Just throwing anyone off the scent who may be sniffing around," he says, concentrating on the flying the drone on the screen. It swoops down a valley at least three hills over and Liam crashes it into a fast-flowing river.

"Right," he says, like its loss is nothing. "I'm freezing my arse off out here, let's get inside."

The house feels like a refrigerator when we walk in, and although there's electricity, the oil filled radiators in the hallway are stone cold. It smells musty like no one has been here in a while.

"Fuck, I think its warmer outside than it is in here," Liam grumbles, as he takes out a tiny torch from his pocket and shines it in a dark pantry-style cupboard in the kitchen where the strip lighting doesn't quite reach. I hear a switch flick, and a small electrical buzz lets us know the heating is working. "It's going to take some time for the place to heat up," he warns me as he leaves the room.

I sit in the kitchen and huddle inside his jacket; waiting for him to come back.

Two minutes later he pokes his head around the door. "We're in luck there's a wood burner in the living room. It was already stacked so I've set it alight. I've pulled a duvet off the bed in the master suite, and I'm warming it up in front of the fire. Come, sit and get warm in a chair while I get changed and make us a hot drink and something to eat."

"Changed?" I ask. "What are you changing into, a rabbit?" I've found my sense of humour. "Where are you getting more clothes? We don't have anything here."

"That grey thing you saw the drone wrapped in is a sweatshirt, the other is wrapped in sweatpants. I have a vest underneath my shirt. The outfit will do until Ross gets here, but that may not be until the morning.

"How do you know all this stuff… what to do in this situation? Did you go to spy school or something?" I ask, half joking.

"Both Ross and I were in the military together. We were selected for our specialist skills; his in cyber and communication intelligence, and mine in combat skills. Our role with a few others was to formulate and execute plans for hostage situations."

His care and attention to detail in keeping me safe, along with his resourcefulness, only makes him more appealing, and hearing that Ross and Izzy may not be here until tomorrow sparks an element of excitement in me. I want him and he knows it. The more he's around me, the harder it's getting for me not to show how drawn I am towards him. I know it's unbecoming, but I can't help my feelings.

I need to pull myself together.

Rising to my feet, I follow him into the living room. The seating is antique, high backed, with deep cushions. I sink into the sumptuous, red velvet, tapestry cushions and the tension leaves my back. It's luxury compared to the hard bench seats of the Land Rover.

Liam picks the duvet up from the rug and places it over me. The heat seeps into my cold bones in an instant, and I smile like it's the best thing I've felt in years.

"Give me twenty minutes and I'll rustle something up for us to eat.

"AMELIA, wake up you should eat something." Liam's raspy, Scottish brogue drags me from sleep and my eyes flutter open. I stretch lazily and notice it's dark outside now, but Liam has lit both lamps at each side of the long sofa I've been resting on. The smell of lobster makes my stomach rumble.

"Tinned soup," he informs me. "It's not much but it's warm and hearty," he says placing a bowl of lobster bisque soup and a chunk of crusty bread and butter in front of me. "There's some shortbread, teabags, milk, and a packet of porridge oats, as well as eggs, bacon and potato scones for the morning. If this soup doesn't fill us, I'll do us some eggs and bacon," he says, placing a tray on the floor and sitting in front of the fire.

I take a spoonful of the soup, it's nice, not the best I've had, but I don't think I've ever had soup from a tin before.

"It's lovely," I say, and he grins.

"You're only saying that because your relative made it." I

stare at him puzzled until he explains, "It's Campbell's soup." I chuckle at his wit despite the long day we've had.

"There's a bottle of red wine in the supplies," he informs me.

I finish my soup and bread, and take our bowls back to the kitchen. I see the wine and grab two glasses from a kitchen cabinet.

"Do you want to share?" I ask.

"Not for me, I'm on duty," he replies, as I place a glass before him.

"You can't let me drink on my own. What could possibly happen here? I know your security is tight. No one can find us, unless they have a crystal ball, after all your planning to get here. *I* can't even find me. Please…" I cringe when I hear the desperation in my voice.

Maybe opening a bottle of wine isn't one of my better ideas. I fear if I'm going to be alone with Liam, I'm going to need something to knock me out, and help me get through the night. The dark, brooding look he gives me tells me I could easily end up an alcoholic with all the wine it would take to cool my libido. I shudder at the thought.

Liam reaches for the wine and opens the bottle effortlessly. He pours some into my glass.

"Just fill it up," I say, not caring what it tastes like.

He does, and then pours a lesser amount of wine for himself. I see this as a small, but not insignificant, victory.

A silence falls between us, and it's charged. I take a sip of my wine and watch him watching me. The air has thickened a little around us, and I fear it will be impossible to have him so close around the clock and not try to seduce him. I drop my gaze to my glass, looking at him makes me want him.

"You think too much." His statement catches me by surprise, and I look up through my long lashes at his perfect face.

"What?" I ask.

"You drift a lot, like your mind is somewhere else."

I frown. "And how would you possibly know that?"

"Because I've watched you. You've done it numerous times since we met."

"I have many things to think about," I say, slightly unnerved by his observation. I sip my wine and tilt my head. "What do you do to pass the time, any hobbies?" I ask, hoping to change the subject.

"I don't have time for hobbies. My life revolves around my work. Fitness training is about as near to a hobby as I get."

"So, there's definitely no *Mrs* Bodyguard?" He chuckles and shakes his head, so I continue, "What did you do before you were in the military and doing this?"

"Not much," he says, shaking his head slowly and reaches for his wine. He sips it, and I can tell my question has unsettled him.

This arouses my curiosity. "Well?" I ask, waiting for him to feed me more information. I take another drink and realise my glass is almost empty. *Slow down.*

"My employment history isn't up for discussion. I'm sorry," he says with a sigh.

"Okay, I understand, if you tell me, you'll have to kill me, right?"

His head tilts to the side, and I realise what I've said. Despite my situation, I'm still allowed to joke. The mystery surrounding this man suits him.

"What about you, Amelia? You have a law degree, but you choose not to use it."

"I needed something to focus on, and law seemed the perfect way for me to do that. Although I have chosen not to make it my profession, I still use what I learned from my studies to help others."

A hint of a smile plays on his lips. "See, this is the side of you the media should be reporting on." He takes another drink, and I note his glass is now empty.

"What side?" I ask, lifting the bottle of wine. I pour myself another glass, and before he can reject it, I pour some into his glass as well.

He ignores my action and continues. "The passion that runs through your veins to help others. You'd make a good politician if you ever wanted to think of that."

I laugh. "Lottie has said that in the past."

"Well then, I can't be wrong." He smirks, and suddenly the tension in the room disappears... although this could be due to the rapid injection of wine flowing through me. We sit in a comfortable silence finishing the rest of the bottle.

"Do want to go to bed?" I ask, as he lifts his hands above his head and stretches.

"I'm not sure that's a good idea," he replies.

"That wasn't an offer," I say, smiling at his flirty tone.

"Pity," he says, and shakes his head. He looks startled at what he's said. "Excuse me, you make it too easy to flirt."

"I fear you're giving me mixed signals, Liam."

He scrunches his nose. "I do, don't I?" he admits, casually. "It's not intentional, I assure you." He stands, and I also rise to my feet, but it's all too quick and I'm not expecting the stumble I take. *Shoot.* Liam catches me and prevents me from falling over.

Firm, muscular arms wrap around my waist, and he holds me up with his body. His dazzling blue eyes show concern as he gazes down at me. His body feels warm, hard and powerful pressed against mine. My heartrate is skipping like a spring lamb inside my chest, and it's making me feel giddy.

The sensible voice inside me is telling me I should wriggle free from his hold. But instead, I freeze the moment and look up at his handsome face. My gaze skims his jawline;

the five o'clock shadow that's appeared only makes him hotter. I note a small muscle flex in his jaw. It's a hint of the irritation within him, on an otherwise stoic appearance, but I take this as confirmation Liam is fighting his attraction too.

My lips are so close to his and I feel a flush in my cheeks, as the heat we're generating between us burns deep within my core. I tell myself this is due to the wine, when deep down I know, wine or not, my attraction is too strong to ignore.

The pause in his action stuns me and I hold my breath while I wait. His pupils are dilated, his breathing sounds deliberate, and I sense the conflict within him whether or not to act upon what he clearly wants.

Kiss me, I think, hoping by some telepathic means he hears what I've said.

Internally I scream the words again, and as though he can read my mind, with a torn expression on his face, he inches closer to me. I feel his warm breath against my skin, smell the wine on it, and know – mistake or not – I want everything he has to offer.

My eyes flutter closed, and I wait in anticipation of the moment when his plump lips collide with mine. Seconds later, I open my eyes, searching his… but I can see his will is much stronger than mine, and he stares with renewed determination in his gaze.

The arms that held me possessively fall away, as Liam shakes his head. A deep frown between his eyes shows me how angry he is with himself that he had almost crossed a line.

He quietly takes a step back making space between us. "Are you okay?" he asks with a tinge of regret in his voice, as he inspects me since I nearly fell over.

I want to scream at him that no, I'm not okay, but instead I nod without saying a word. I'm disappointed again and he knows it. He takes a further step back, subtly shakes his head, turns back and picks up his glass. He makes his way into the kitchen and I follow. Turning on the water, he begins to rinse the soup bowls like he's at home and has lived in this house all his life.

I pretend to yawn, and he jumps on this. "Did the wine make you tired?" he asks, giving me a way out and I take it.

I nod and bow my head, swallowing rapidly at the burning sensation in my throat as tears well in my eyes.

"Go to bed. You take the master suite; I'll sleep on the chair. I'll do one last security check of the house and I think I'll catch some sleep myself."

I pull myself together and walk away without uttering a word, but by the time I reach the bedroom my blood boils when the full impact of another rejection from him takes hold.

Who the hell does he think he is, testing my emotions? I know he wants me, and he won't give in. The feeling inside is torture. I slam the master bedroom door closed, ensuring the bang can be heard from wherever he is.

Frantically, I pull at the buttons on my expensive red silk blouse, and I end up ripping half of them off. "Fuck!" I scream out as I watch them fall to the floor, and tears finally trickle down my face. I should go for a shower and wash away the day, but I can't be bothered. Instead, I pace my bedroom floor, replaying what just happened as I try to piece together why my reaction is so strong. I glance towards the bed and notice the duvet is missing.

Shit, it's still in the living room and my buttons are ripped off.

I feel exhausted trying to figure him out, and I'm beginning to think Liam McKenna is going to be bad for my emotional health.

There's a gentle knock on my door and Liam steps in without waiting for permission from me. "You forgot to take the duvet," he says, walking past me and shaking it out over the bed.

When he turns our eyes meet and his gaze falls from my face to my blouse where my bra covered breasts are exposed. He runs his hand through his hair, and I stand frozen as he leaves and I hear him groan and utter, "Fuck", as he closes the door.

Frustrated as I am, his curse brings a smile to my lips before I turn and strip out of my clothing to my underwear and climb into the huge four poster bed.

CHAPTER 19

*L*iam
        21st July

"LIAM?"

I hesitate in the living room doorway when I hear Amelia's voice. It's the early hours of the morning, and the room is in darkness apart from the glowing embers of the fire.

Since Amelia went to bed, I've sat on the chair nearest to the fire and tried to catch some sleep before the sunrise which is still early this far north during the third week in July.

"Amelia?" I respond, the sound of my voice a question, like hers. "It's Ross on the phone," I advise her. "Let me finish this call." I turn back towards the fire. It's then I remember I'm in fitted boxers, and look towards my sweatpants lying over the opposite chair. Quietly I conclude my call and rise to my feet. Grabbing my sweatpants, I pull them on and walk towards her.

"Everything okay?" I ask, as I fix my waistband into place. Despite the darkness I can see she's concerned.

She's hugging a pillow to her chest. "What did he say?"

"It's all good. He'll be here in the morning," I say, placing my hands on her upper arms and immediately wish I hadn't done this. "He's taking the convoluted route to ensure there's no one following them. They've stopped in Pitlochry for the night. He and Izzy will leave around seven. It should only take them a couple of hours to get here at the most from there."

"I can't sleep," she confesses. "Would you think I was a wuss if I said I'm a little shaken?"

"Not at all, I've been thinking how brave you've been. If someone had threatened my life, I don't know that I would have handled it with the grace you are."

"Thank you," she says, and my chest tightens because I can hear she means it.

"You should at least try again to get some sleep," I advise her.

"I can't. The bed is huge and there's a whistling noise in the window. It's like an episode of Ghost Hunters in there. Every time it happens, I freak out," she tells me. Her eyes search my face and I know her fear is genuine.

"Do you want me to sit in your room?" I ask.

"I can't ask that of you. You need to sleep more than me, after all it's you who's keeping me safe."

"Right now, the only thing we're both at risk of is hypothermia," I say, and she laughs. I glance at the pillow she's holding, and I'm reminded of the missing buttons on her blouse when I took the duvet to her room earlier.

"Will you lie with me?"

"Amelia," I say, my voice going soft because it kills me to reject her again. "I don't think that's a good idea," I tell her, honestly.

"I know, but it's the only one I have right now. I'm tired and cold and..." She sighs. "Just get into my bed and let me sleep, please?"

When I hear the defeat in her tone, I turn slowly, and we walk towards the master suite. The lamp by the bed gives off a soft pink light, and I inwardly curse at the romantic ambience in the room. Between that and the four-poster bed I'm in agony. My change of heart is against my own advice and I'm acutely aware of this.

Amelia plumps up the pillow she's been holding and puts it back at the top of the bed.

I swallow and my throat feels rough. She leans over to lift the duvet in her underwear, and I instantly fight an urge to grip her curvy hips, which look perfect wrapped in white lace boy shorts. My heart sinks and my dick moves in the opposite direction. In fact, it feels so tense it could have probably held up the Titanic until help arrived.

Amelia climbs into bed, and I'm determined not to take advantage of the situation, so I get under the covers without taking a stitch of my clothing off. She's facing me when she gathers her hair at both sides and flicks it behind her shoulders. My gaze drops from her hands to her cleavage, her breasts held in place by the cups of her white satin and lace bra.

Jesus save me.

I wait for her to speak; she opens her mouth to say something, but nothing comes out. She doesn't need to talk; I already know what she's thinking. She's distracted by me. One of the many things I know how to do well in my line of work, is read people.

Her eyes appear heavy from lack of sleep and I'm sure she can see I'm tired too. I've been awake most of the night thinking of her, in one way or another. Mostly the other. I'm careful not to touch her.

"I'm not sure I want this," she says quietly.

"Good," I say, "because that dirty thought you're thinking isn't going to happen. Go to sleep," I snap because my cock is bursting out of its skin, and I need to let out my frustration somehow.

She adjusts herself in the bed, her eyes still holding my gaze. "I will," she tells me, before she turns away and turns the light out.

* * *

A WARM, soft hand glides leisurely over my torso, and I smile for a second in contentment before I freeze. When I open my eyes, I see Amelia's head on my chest and her special scent is all around me.

I consider whether she knows she's doing this, but her soft, even breaths inform me she's still asleep. Knowing this lets me enjoy the warmth and feel of her semi-naked body lying next to mine. Or rather, not *next* to it, more half on top of me.

She begins to stir, and I pretend to sleep. When she realises what she's doing her breath hitches, and she holds it for a second. When she exhales, it sounds like a long sigh. Her head moves and I can feel her watching me. I don't move and I continue to pretend I'm asleep. Eventually dawn breaks and my leg has gone numb. The second I move it she pretends to be asleep. I can't suppress the chuckle that escapes my lips, and she scurries over the bed like I've bitten her.

"You were awake?" she questions, alarmed.

"For a minute," I lie. "I didn't want to disturb you."

She goes quiet. "That wasn't fair," she complains.

"What wasn't? You objectifying me or me waking up before you were done?"

She considers my question and grins. "Both," she says and laughs. We fall silent and I lay with my hand over my chest where her head has recently been. I can still feel the ghost of her there.

"Tell me what you're thinking?" I ask tenderly, as I inch closer to her on the bed. I take her hand in mine, rubbing my thumb across her soft skin. It's out of character for me to cross a line like this. But in my eyes, it's already done now, so I may as well enjoy the moment. She closes her eyes.

"Open your eyes and talk to me." It takes her a moment but when she finally does… I'm done for. Her eyes burn with desire and my heart reacts by racing so out of control, that I can barely breathe. The physical pull towards her is like nothing I've experienced before. "You look perfect in the morning," I say stroking her hair and smoothing a few tresses away from her face.

Her smile makes my heart clench and in a moment of weakness I throw my arm around her waist and pull her against me. As I do so, my hand brushes her silky skin at the small of her back.

Her reaction to my move is instantaneous. Pulling her hand free of mine, she throws her arms around my neck and draws my face toward hers. I take a deep breath and restrain myself from losing control because Amelia Campbell deserves better than that.

"I don't want to talk, not now," she whispers tracing her fingers across the scruff on my jawline. "I just… need you."

I look into her honest gaze and see she has no doubts. She's expressing how she feels again, and this time I'm powerless to resist her. With all barriers down, I slowly inch my lips closer to hers, giving her precious time to change her mind, because once I kiss her, I know there's no going back.

She silently questions me, her eyes ticking back and forth

over mine. Her silent plea is all I need to know, and I won't make her wait any longer. I hold her gaze and I've never felt more certain of what she needs from me. Something that I thought so wrong has never felt so right. The gasp that escapes her mouth as our lips meet tells me we both need this. I wait a moment enjoying an almost innocent peck against her silky soft lips before I press mine firmer against hers.

Fuck!

The sexual chemistry we share is toying with all my senses, and I know this isn't just a physical attraction to Amelia, it's a visceral connection which affects me down to my soul. At the back of my mind, somewhere in the distance, I know I've put my job on the line.

Fuck it! I don't care anymore. The only thing that matters right now is showing her I want her just as much as she wants me.

Seconds later, her lips part, and her tongue traces along my bottom lip, teasing me. I look into her eyes and she nods gently before her eyelids flutter closed. I'm not sure why, but I expected this kiss to be frantic between us, it isn't. This kiss is slow and tender as I follow her lead until our need grows. She moans quietly into my mouth when I push her onto her back and press my torso against her. I need to feel her, *all* of her.

My eyes close and I hold her tight as our tongues continue to dance together. I savour the sweet taste of her as my mine gently explores hers. I feel a slight tremor in her body, and I fight the urge rushing through me to speed things up between us. I'm determined, if I am only allowed to have her once, I'm going to do everything I can to make every moment last.

I pull back, reluctantly, because I need to control these

raw carnal feelings surging through my body. She opens her eyes and narrows them, silently questioning me.

Climbing out of the bed I strip out of my sweats. I watch her shoulders sag when she releases a breath; she's relieved I'm not leaving. Her eyes gleam as she takes me in and her slight smile tells me she approves of my actions. Amelia pushes back the bed sheets and I regard her again in the underwear she has on. Her dark, pebbled nipples are hard against the flimsy, transparent fabric. With a smile on her lips, she draws her hands over the silk, and pays attention to her breasts.

It's that time between night and day where the dim dawn is breaking. The shadowy light accentuates her curves, and she's the sexiest sight I've ever seen. Her confidence tells me she's not afraid to take matters into her own hands for her pleasure.

I slide my hand down and squeeze my erection; it aches for her and strains in desperation, begging for a release. When her eyes widen and a soft gasp escapes, I know my size pleases her.

I'm mesmerised as I watch Amelia's hands gliding lower down her front, and I take a deep breath to calm the nerves vibrating within me that's fuelling my need to lay my hands on her. Her fingertips toy with the waistband of her delicate lace panties before she sits up in the bed. Leaning towards me she unclips her bra then tosses it to the floor as she lowers back onto the mattress.

If I had any lingering reservations about what I'm going to do, they've completely vanished when my desperation grows at the sight of her almost naked body. I already knew she had a perfect figure from the photo on the internet of her in that bikini, but seeing her like this, in the flesh, Amelia is so much more. My breaths are ragged, and it feels like an age since either of us has spoken. I could cut through the sexual tension with a knife.

"Surely you're not just going to stand there," she says, teasing me as I'm transfixed beside the bed. She pats the bed beside her now I'm naked, but she's not ready for what I have in mind.

A squeal of delight leaves her throat when I drag her to the edge of the bed and spread her legs wide. I drop to my knees and settle myself between them. She giggles and wriggles when I lightly trace my fingers up and down her inner thighs. I continue to do this until her body stops tensing under my touch and she relaxes.

Her soft moans spur me on.

A slight dip of my head has me exactly where I want to be. I gaze up through my lashes, looking for any sign that she's uncomfortable with my current position. I allow my fingers to glide tenderly over her bare, sensitive skin and watch her eyes close before she throws her head back.

I lean into her and inhale her intimate scent. With the first swipe of my tongue through her glistening folds her back arches and I'm in heaven. Her juice is hot, slick, and sweet. Delicious, like I'd imagined it would be.

I slide my hands under her tight arse, squeezing gently, and guiding her closer to me.

"Oh, God!" she cries, and a tortured groan escapes her as my tongue tastes, explores and teases. She moves beneath me, pushing, yet pulling back. Her fingers claw at the bedsheets and I feel her body buckle underneath me. I continue teasing her with my tongue and I lift my eyes to focus on her and watch. "Liam!" she screams my name as her orgasm rips through her, but I don't stop. I continue lapping and sucking through her climax as her body quivers and bucks in my hands. She lifts her head, and our eyes meet, and I swear she's the sexiest woman I've ever seen. "Liam, please," she pleads through her whispered words.

"Please what?" I ask, finally stopping and licking my lips.

"I don't know," she replies breathless. She looks restless.

Climbing onto the bed with her I shift her to where I need her to be. Where *I* need to be is balls deep, I decide.

"Condom?" I sound desperate because I don't have one. I'm not happy. I've come this close to having her, *God, I don't know what I'll do if I have to stop now.*

"I'm on the pill and I'm clean. I've never been with a man without a condom," she says wriggling beneath me, getting herself into a much better position. I know I'm clean, I had a physical two weeks ago, and I haven't slept with anyone since. Hell, I haven't slept with anyone without a condom since high school. I lean down placing my elbows on either side of her head and I hover over her. She wraps her arms around me, pulling my body closer.

My erection is lined up exactly where I want to be, and I wait. I drop my forehead to hers and I stare. "Are you absolutely sure you want this? There's no going back if we do," I whisper.

Her eyes search mine and right now she knows the decision is still hers. As soon as she nods my lips meet hers and I mask her gasp when I push, steadily, deep inside her. Our mouths meld together, our kiss deepens and our tongues tangle. I move slowly wanting to make this last, but I moan loud with raw carnal need when her fingernails dig deep into my back, urging me forwards.

Every nerve in my body is screaming for me to take her how I need, but I want this to be slow and sensual. Although I can sense that's not what she wants either. I move my hands from the bedsheets, and I take her face in my palms trying to slow down our passionate kiss, but she's determined, and fights me on this.

When I pull back and plunge deep inside her again, she wraps her legs around me holding me exactly where she wants me. Her fingers clawing at my back. "Ride me," she mumbles, her eyes dark with desire.

Small spasms ripple within her, and I feel her muscles tighten around me, telling me she's close. In response to feeling her changes I pick up my pace and ride her hard, just like she asked. Sweat beads erupt on her upper lips when my mouth leaves hers.

I rest my forehead against hers and say, "Do it," as I push us both towards the edge. Her eyes close and I gently cup her jaw. "I need to see you," I say, and her focus is back on me.

My need builds with each thrust, my body wired for the release I know is coming. Suddenly Amelia's pussy walls grip me tight, and she screams and jerks rhythmically beneath me.

"Oh my God!" she cries out, the words rushed as they're followed by another scream and I feel my myself coming when her climax clenches through her whole body. A guttural groan leaves my throat and I pull out as pulses of pleasure make my head swim and ribbons of my orgasm coat her stomach. The sight is physical evidence of the effect she has on me.

CHAPTER 20

$\mathcal{A}$melia
21st July

THE ONLY NOISE filling the room is our deep, laboured breaths that eventually even out, leaving a calm, quiet atmosphere. There's nothing uncomfortable about it, as we both come back down to earth from our bliss.

Liam strips one of the pillows of its slip and cleans my stomach before he pulls the duvet up over us.

"What now?" I ask rolling over to look at him. I take a moment to fully appreciate the naked, muscular body of the man commanding most of the space in the bed. *He's beautiful.* I think to myself that I would never tire of waking up to him every day.

He tilts his head, our eyes connect, and his fingers brush over my cheek. "Now, I suggest we put this behind us; at least until we know your safety is assured. We both had an itch and we've scratched it. Looking at you lying here with me, I can't have any regrets about it. I've never crossed a line like this before. It's not something I'm proud of, but I can't, nor would I change it." He lets out a sad sigh. "However, I can't allow myself to have feelings that will cloud me from doing my job. That would be dangerous, and with a sexual distraction I fear I'd miss something. If anything happened to you because…"

I place my fingertips on his lips to silence him because I get it. He's not rejecting me now that he's had his fun; his serious expression shows me how a slip in my security would pain him.

I'm not sure I have had my fill of him, but I'm not about to open my mouth and tell him that. I know where we stand for now. But as I look at him, his mouth tugs at each side until he's smiling at me; he knows what I'm thinking.

How is a woman supposed to have secrets from a man like him that's always one step ahead? I don't know, but that's something I'm going to have to figure out, and quickly.

He reaches out tracing his fingers along my cheek before he brushes the pad of his thumb over my lips; lips that are bruised but missing his hungry kisses.

How is it possible to have been drawn so rapidly, and to have placed my total trust in him the way I have done?

I lay my hand on his hard, warm chest, watching it rise and fall with each breath. He rests his hand on my shoulder, and I'm fighting the deep urge to snuggle into the safety and warmth of his strong embrace.

Who is this crazy woman and when will the real Amelia return?

"I suppose we should get up, as we're awake?" I suggest, trying not to sound weak. It's daylight and now that he's spelled out how he feels, I've got to play my part in all of this.

"We should. It's still early, but I'll clean out the fire and reset it for this evening." I remember my torn top and I frown. "What's wrong?" he asks on seeing my worried expression.

I cringe. "I ripped my blouse last night, and I have nothing to wear."

"No problem, you can have my sweatshirt or my shirt to wear until Izzy and Ross get here." The thought of wearing his shirt thrills me and a smile tugs at my lips.

"Don't," he chastises like he's read my mind again. "The thought of seeing you wearing my clothes is killing me already. Do you mind if I grab a shower first?" He climbs to his feet and stands at the side of the bed, naked.

"Sure, be my guest."

I watch him head to the en-suite bathroom, and when he looks over his shoulder he laughs when he catches me staring at his delicious, hard arse.

"Amelia," he warns.

I laugh and let out a sigh. It's not going to be easy going back to him being the professional here to save me, not when I know I'll be revisiting our time in this bed in my mind. He may not want any distractions, but for me, in truth it was a welcome one from all the insanity I'm facing right now.

He turns on the shower and it doesn't take long for the steam to filter into the room. I get out of bed because I can't think straight with him so nearby. I need space to clear my head and refocus my direction. I go upstairs in search of his shirt and find it neatly laid out on top of his suit in the first of the upstairs bedrooms.

I pick up the shirt and pull it on to cover my naked body. Despite my resolve to behave platonically around him, I find myself pulling the collar to my nose and sniffing the woodsy cologne left behind on it. It was that fragrance that attracted me to him in the first place.

Five minutes later, I'm back in the downstairs master bedroom, dressed in his shirt. I hear the water stop running and Liam walks back into the bedroom, still naked, drying the back of his neck with a hand towel. This man is testing my willpower and I'm definitely not immune to his charms; I'm weakening by the second.

His footsteps come closer, and I pretend to be busy, but I can smell fruity shower gel on his skin, and I know that he's right next to me. This feels like a form of torture, and I only have myself to blame.

I steal a glance and see water droplets from his hair coursing down his pecs. Apart from the back of his neck, he's made no other attempt to get dried. He has a folded bath sheet tucked under his arm.

I tilt my head and say, "I think, don't quote me on this, but you're supposed to wrap that around yourself, not carry it."

"Sorry, force of habit, I'm used to living alone," he remarks drily and it's uncharacteristic of the professional Liam I know.

"Oh please, I've seen enough for one morning," I reply, when in all fairness I could be tempted to take up drawing if he was the naked model. In reality, I'm horrible at art, it would take too many sessions to create a piece that did him justice.

Directing my eyes towards the floor I walk towards the bathroom. I can sense his eyes burning into my back, but I don't glance over my shoulder. I make it to the bathroom and close the door quietly as I enter. I hear him chuckle as I lean against it.

How the hell am I going to live with this man for a couple of weeks and not want more of what I've already had?

A smile comes easily to my mouth when I remember exactly what we did, and I chuckle as I peel off his shirt and step into the shower.

The lines are blurred now between Liam and me, whether he wanted them to be or not.

* * *

IT'S JUST after nine in the morning when we hear a car driving over the gravel. Liam doesn't move and I think this is odd considering he's hypersensitive about my safety.

"Ross is here," he states.

"And you know it's him, *how*?"

He glances toward me and his lips tug up in a smile. "He said just after nine, and it's just after nine."

"Right." My tone is sarcastic thanks to the smug expression on his face, and I stand to look out of the window.

"Relax, I doubt anyone knows you're missing yet. Trust me." Liam stands and heads for the door and I hear Ross and Izzy's voices outside. A mixture of relief they've made it, and a small thrill at what Liam and I did in their absence runs through me.

Izzy knows me better than anyone and I'm not good at hiding my thoughts or feelings. Even as a child I was never a good liar, I always got caught when I was up to mischief. Instead of going to the door I head for the kitchen and put on the kettle, I'm sure Izzy and Ross will want tea after their journey. I know I'm thirsty after the morning I've had.

As the kettle boils, I hear their voices move as they go into the living room, and when I turn, I catch a glimpse of Ross as he follows the others. I put tea in the pot, find a tray and load it with cups and the carton of milk we brought with us. I can't find any sugar so if anyone takes it in their tea, they're clean out of luck.

Entering the living room, I note Izzy sitting in the chair nearest the window, she still has her jacket on, and I can see by the smile on her face when she sees me, she's relieved I'm unharmed.

I place the tray on the coffee table and Izzy talks about their journey like she's been on a wild adventure with a younger man, but she looks happy to finally be here. I notice the tension in both Liam *and* Ross' postures as they stand in the far side of the room talking. Their voices are low, and I sense they're talking about what happens next.

"What's wrong?" I ask when I take in the scene, and dread fills my stomach.

Silence fills the room and all three sets of eyes land on me.

"Liam?" I lift my eyes to his.

"We can deal with this," he says softly.

My eyes dart to Ross, who is looking between Liam and me. Liam turns away.

"Ah, I see it now," Ross yells, wagging his finger at Liam and then glancing back at me.

Ross knows we've been intimate but how can he? I'm certain Liam wouldn't have shared this information. He strikes me as being discreet.

Do I really look as guilty as I feel?

"Not now," Liam snaps turning back to face him. "We have more important things to attend to."

I huff. "Can someone please tell me what's going on?"

Liam clenches his jaw. "Nothing as yet, like I told you, no one appears to have noticed you've gone."

"And you'd know this how?" I query.

"Because Ross here is a technical genius, so too is an old buddy of his brother-in-law's."

"I'll have to meet this brother-in-law sometime, Ross knows some very interesting people," I remark.

Ross chuckles. "That I do, you don't know how right you are."

"Let's just say, Ross' relative is a ghost, he's one of those people that watch those watching us," Liam says after a quiet exchange between him and his partner, which gives him permission to explain.

"God, I'm lost," I say, and sigh.

Liam smiles and wanders over to the tray. "That's exactly how we want it."

I lift the teapot and fill a cup for him. We exchange a lingering look, and then he averts his gaze.

"How will we know when I'm safe? Will I ever be safe again?" I can't help the worry that laces my voice.

"Of course, you will. We just need to ensure you're out of the frame while the politics play out," Liam says. I frown and he continues, "Donaldson can't raise the question about your lineage if he can't find you. And leading up to the vote, the Crown or Palace can't get to you if they don't know where you are either. If Scotland doesn't get independence, you should be free to do what you want, and the problem should fade away."

"And if it's a yes vote?"

"You could always marry Prince James," Liam states, but his tone alone smacks of his distaste for his words. "Or you could just disappear. It's not as if Scotland would relish the expense of a constitutional challenge, and I'm sure nothing can happen in retrospect regarding your lineage anyway. Scottish people are shrewd, they wouldn't want money diverted from the heart of where it's needed. I'm sure the Scottish Government, sans Harry Donaldson, would far rather have full control over the decisions they make, in respect of the people they're elected to govern, without resorting to spending taxpayer's money on a whim. But this is only my personal take on the matter," Liam admits.

"How close is this race?" Izzy asks, and I'm surprised this hasn't occurred to me.

Ross tells me, "Neck-and-neck right now. The 'Nos' lead by about three percent."

My chest tightens. "Okay, so Harry is going to use any tactics he can to win this vote."

"It would appear so," Liam finally says. "And as far as the

monarchy is concerned, he'll make as much noise as possible to bring the question of rightful heir back to the table. They're so desperate for this not to be discussed they're willing to do whatever it takes to ensure there's nothing *to* discuss."

"You mean they'll get rid of me?"

"That's not what I'm saying. James' offer would have let them control Donaldson better. I guess perhaps they would have maybe taken you and tried to coach you on the official phrasing they'd want you to use in case the question arose."

I nod. "It all makes sense. When I was in Edinburgh everything was moving too fast for me to think."

"And you're thoughts now?" Liam's gaze pierces mine, and he waits.

I shake my head. "My brain is numb... no I'm petrified, I don't know what to think or do."

Liam places a hand on my shoulder; his simple action soothes me. "We're not expecting you to do anything. You should be safe here. We'll let the drama play out, but I'm confident with Ross and his brother in law's contacts we'll be one step ahead all the way."

I lift my head to look at Ross, and Izzy pours him some tea. I'm glad she's taken over because my hands are shaking now.

Ross nods in agreement at Liam's comment. "As this all sounded so incredulous, and out of the general terms of what you hired us for, I did some digging of my own." I frown but let him carry on talking. "Downing Street and the Palace were both aware of the issue for the monarchy if Scotland gains independence before they knew about Donaldson's intentions. I'm surprised it's taken this long to act on their information."

I sigh and stare, helpless, at Liam before Ross continues. "From what I've read, information regarding James II of

England, James VII of Scotland and his Catholic heir, James Francis Edward, after the King's deposition in 1688 has been held in a vault at the royal court. Nothing much was known about Prince James, the deposed King's son after he was defeated during several attempts to claim the throne. His claim was eventually eradicated by Queen Anne with the introduction of the Settlement Act of 1701 which stated no Roman Catholic, or anyone married to a Catholic could hold the crown.

"Only the monarch's sovereign secretary, and a few other closely vetted advisors, have ever had sight of James Francis Edward's lineage as he lived his life in exile near Rome. God knows how Donaldson stumbled upon your connection."

"But I'm Roman Catholic."

"Yes, and the faith part of the Settlement Act was amended in 2015 to reinstate the inclusion regardless of faith. Hence Donaldson's interest."

Ross continues to talk but I'm no longer listening as Izzy continues to rub my back. I know all of this. A letter left to me by my parents, to be read in the event of their deaths, explained the presence of an ancient parchment paper bearing a seal with a coat of arms which was left with their other important papers in their safety deposit box at the bank. The parchment is the genogram of my lineage. Apparently, it's a second coded copy of one held in the vault somewhere that Ross mentioned already. According to my parents, anything to do with James Francis Edward that isn't already public has been sealed there for hundreds of years. The one they left me has been passed down through the generations since James Francis Edward's death.

"Okay, I need to explain something that generations of my family have kept hidden from public knowledge. To date, I am the last direct descendant of Mary Queen of Scots as my lineage goes back to her direct descendant James Francis Edward.

"Fuck, this is mind-blowing," Ross says, and he looks quizzical in thought. I can see his brain is ticking. "Nothing can happen retrospectively in regard to the Crown, but I can see going forward how Donaldson thinks he can open a dialogue that would gain favour with the Scots. Not so much for a new queen, but perhaps to get rid of the question of Scotland as a sovereign nation at all."

"That sounds a pretty incredulous story," Liam states, yet the look on his face shows me he knows I speak the truth.

I nod at Liam's assessment. "It is, but it's true. I don't think Harry would ever be successful in getting rid of the monarchy, but he could create havoc, even religious unrest in the process of people reaching that conclusion.

Everyone in the room is stunned into silence, and I can see the impact of the full implication of my words.

"Right, Breakfast?" I ask needing to push the attention away from me. Everyone is looking at me as if I'm in denial, Ross and Liam exchange a look but say nothing. I know they're both grappling with what this could mean.

"Did you eat already?" I ask my housekeeper and Ross, because I need to shift the focus away from the reason why we're all here. If I don't, I feel I'll cry. "We have bacon, eggs and some other goodies, although I don't know what else there is." I suddenly wonder how we're going to stay stocked up living in the middle of nowhere.

"Leave breakfast to me.," Izzy says. "Cooking will keep me occupied. It won't stop me worrying about you, though."

"If we're going to be here for some time, what are we going to do for food?" I enquire, eventually speaking my mind.

"There are plenty of supplies in the back of the van," Ross replies.

At that we all stand and go outside to the slate grey van that he's driven himself and Izzy here in.

Turning the handle, Ross opens the back door, and my eyes widen at what I see. A sack of flour, bags of root vegetables, and a sack of potatoes sit at the forefront, but there is a side of beef, one of pig and a lamb, all vacuum packed. There are tins of salmon and tuna, soups and jars of sauces, as well as trays of water and juice, wine, cheese, butter and two trays of eggs. Whoever did the shopping has thought of everything. We even have cereals, pulses, oats and even tinned biscuits of various brands. The van has been carefully stacked and it's packed to the roof. There's enough food to feed an army for a few days, or four people for more than two weeks.

"How the heck did you manage this?"

"Don't ask," he replies with a wink. "Thing is, now that we're here we can't risk leaving again, unless we can't help it."

With more confidence in my appearance than I feel inside, I nod and smile, but seeing the amount of effort both men have gone to in their preparation before bringing me here, makes the danger they think I'm in, much clearer.

CHAPTER 21

*L*iam
　　21st July

WE WATCH as Amelia and Izzy go back into the house; the elderly housekeeper is carrying the trays of eggs, and Amelia two cartons of orange juice and a bag of dried oats. When they've gone, both Ross and I drive the vehicles into the barn at the side of the house and shift all the supplies into the sunroom at the back door. From there Izzy directs where she wants everything unpacked as she stands at the stove and cooks. And by the time breakfast is ready, all that's left to be done is the meat sectioned off and all the items she wants stored in the freezer.

We eat breakfast, and the conversation turns to normal reflections as Izzy and Amelia tell us stories about Lottie and the prince, which make Ross and me laugh. But when break-fast is over, we excuse ourselves from the table and head to a bedroom upstairs. We begin setting up our equipment and sit down ready to work. Ross goes outside and angles our matt green coloured mobile satellite dish at the back of the house, while I check the internet connection; the signal is good.

When Ross returns he mutters, "I can't believe you actually did it." He's shaking his head and

I immediately know what 'it' he's talking about. He's not looking at me because, as a technical nerd, he's in cable heaven, connecting computers to sockets and a tablet and satellite phone into docks he's invented himself.

"Don't," I warn, not wanting to be reminded of how weak I was, giving in to my feelings for Amelia.

"I thought you were smarter than me." He's running his hands through his hair. "I'm…" He shrugs, "speechless, man. What were you thinking?"

"Probably the same thing you were thinking when you tapped Charlotte," I reply. "I'm just not as quick with my dick." I shrug. "What can I say? She wore me down."

"There's a difference here and you know it."

I stare at him because I don't have a comeback. There's nothing I can say that justifies my actions, but I don't regret what we did.

Ross sighs heavily, and I know he's frustrated with himself as much as he is with me. "Okay, so we have what we know… can you fucking believe all that by the way? It's… I have no words for what it is."

I change the subject and hold up a cable. "What do we do with this?"

He takes it and inserts the jack into the back of one of the docks. "This job isn't like the usual stuff we've dealt with in the past," Ross mumbles.

"I'll admit, Amelia's story's a mindfuck but we'll do what we always do: watch and wait. Can you run me through what's been set up and the tech resources we have?"

"Covert cameras at her place as per usual, covering all floors, the stairs, lift, and the terraces. In the garage there are cameras watching her cars. I've also got the entrance to the building, and whole inside of the garage covered. Trackers have been embedded in her vehicles and in all the devices left behind. We already have a tracker on the mobile phone of yours that you left there. Amelia and Izzy's phones, tablets and laptops have spyware installed, so that we can see who these fuckers are. These," he points to the docks, "have encryption software installed prior to being switched on. IP changers and scramblers are also working on these docks. Nothing can be traced back because I've built in constant automatic interruptions to connections every thirty seconds. This will act as a failsafe addition to the comms, should anyone think they can fuck with how clever I am." He smirks because he knows he's a genius.

Ross finishes setting everything up and opens the military grade computer, connecting the mobile phone on the dock to it. Firing it up, he surfs for a few seconds and Amelia's sitting room appears on the screen. He clicks and a series of stills fill the displays, followed by images from all the other cameras he's set up. From his laptop we can see small screens for every camera.

"If there is movement, the camera image will enlarge," he informs me, pointing at the screen. "Looking good. No one has been in the apartment yet, if they're watching – and we know they are since the car incident you told me about – they'll realise sooner rather than later she's gone."

We hear the two women come upstairs and Ross steps out of the door and into the hallway to check on them. "Let me get that," I hear him say, and all three go into the bedroom next to the one I'm in. Ross and I are sharing a room, Izzy is upstairs with us, but as the master suite is on the ground floor, I won't be sleeping in our shared bedroom at night; I'll sleep downstairs near to Amelia. I'd rather keep her downstairs anyway, as there's plenty of ways to get her out if necessary.

* * *

IN THE AFTERNOON we talk strategy, and as Ross has everything under control I go downstairs and sit with Amelia. The smell of fresh baking is making my stomach rumble.

"Lunch!" Izzy calls out.

We both stand and head to the kitchen.

"What can I do to help?" I ask Izzy as she places a fresh, homemade quiche on the table, along with two large bowls of potato salad, and one of coleslaw. The woman's amazing; she can make a banquet out of a few ingredients.

"Help?" She sounds surprised at my offer.

I shrug. "Yes, I'm feeling pretty useless. Ross has everything under control upstairs and Amelia's as safe as houses."

"I am?" Amelia asks as she sits at the table. Izzy places a slice of quiche on her plate.

I nod. "From the looks of things no one knows you've left Edinburgh, yet."

She frowns. "How can you know that?"

"Because Ross has cameras in place. The first place they'd go is your apartment. If anyone had been in there they would have been captured on screen by now."

Her eyebrows lift. "He bugged my home?"

Izzy interjects. "Well, he doesn't call it bugging, Amelia, he calls them security cameras. I was surprised at the day-to-day things those tiny things can be hidden in."

Amelia stares at her housekeeper. She looks stunned because Izzy's taking everything in her stride.

Izzy turns the radio on low, and we eat our delicious lunch to the sound of Katherine Jenkins followed by a catchy classic by The Bangles, and once again the conversation is normal. When I finish, I excuse myself immediately, and swap places with Ross.

The second computer he's set up is constantly refreshing, and views of Amelia's home flash constantly on the screen. A bird flies past the front door and the screen immediately swaps over to the outside of the front of the house where we are. My partner really does think of everything. It's almost an hour later when Ross comes back upstairs yawning and rubbing his stomach.

"That old woman has some serious cooking skills."

"Go catch a nap, there's no point in us both being bored," I say, but just as I do I see Ross's expression change and he's leaning in, grabbing the computer mouse and he begins clicking away.

One screen switches to Amelia's apartment when it detects movement and the lens zooms in on a guy in work-men's clothes shinning down the wall from the roof to land on Amelia's outside terrace. He has no idea we're watching him as he takes out a pocket toolkit and in seconds, opens the door to her upper floor. The screens change as Ross follows him inside and downstairs. The intruder moves hurriedly to the entrance of the apartment, just inside the door. He places a small electronic device on the alarm which gives him the disable code.

"I think we can say they know Amelia has left the build-ing," Ross advises me in a mock stage announcer's voice.

"Not bad, almost a full day's head start," I reply, checking the time which states it's nearly three p.m.

Ross grins. "With something this big, I can't believe our domestic intelligence operatives have been a tad slow, don't you think?"

We watch the intruder stalking from room to room until he eventually stops in the living area and lifts Amelia's laptop from the coffee table where I had her leave it. He sits, opens the laptop, and immediately our window flickers and his face appears on our screen.

"Know him?" Ross asks, making a screenshot, before we go back to watching him live from Amelia's living room.

I shake my head. "Never seen him before." My eyes tick over his face while I wait for a spark of recognition.

"Time for some fun, I think," Ross says as he presses a button, and an alarm shrills through the apartment. The guy on the screen looks like he may shit his pants as he squints left and right when his ears are assaulted by the sudden noise. He leans closer and snaps the laptop shut. Both Ross and I chuckle at the guy's reaction, and Amelia pops her head around the door.

"Did an alarm go off?" she asks. She looks skittish and her cloudy hazel eyes are as wide as saucers.

I stand and move to reassure her. "Ah, it's just a programme that Ross was uploading." I know it's a lie, but I think she's been spooked enough in the last day or so. There's no need to add to her anguish by telling her there's a creepy intelligence guy from the dark side mooching around in her apartment.

"Why were you laughing?"

"Because old 'Balls of Steel' here almost jumped out of his skin," Ross says, adding to the previous lie I told her.

She appears to accept our joint explanation, smiles and heads back downstairs. Ross watches from the doorway to ensure she has gone, then comes back inside the room and closes the door.

"Now we wait."

"Again," I reply, sarcastically.

"These guys are so predictable. He'll have stashed that laptop and taken it with him. We don't know who he's working for yet, but we'll get his exact location.

* * *

THE REST of the day passes uneventfully apart from Izzy's pork dinner, which is an event in itself. It's wholesome and tastes delicious and now I've finished, I'm feeling sleepy.

Ross is back at his post, having had a nap and gone first for dinner.

"I'm going to grab a couple of hours in bed before I head downstairs for the night," I tell him from the door of the makeshift command centre.

He nods and continues watching the screen, lying on one of the twin beds in the room like a teenager. "Go, I'm riveted by the action on my screen," he drawls, but nothing at all is happening.

I turn and head into the bedroom straight across from the one we're working in. Closing the door, I climb onto the bed, and because of all the events of the past day and a half I lie down and crash out.

CHAPTER 22

*A*melia
24th July

FOR THE FIRST three days in this farmhouse, I felt jittery, reacting to the slightest movement outside, and suspicious of the quiet conversations that took place between Liam and Ross. Occasionally, the amount of time they spent in the room upstairs made me wonder what they were doing that took up so much of their days.

A few times, I went upstairs to be nosey and heard them talking, but not necessarily about me. A lot of their conversations appeared to be them reminiscing about people they knew, or funny events that had happened to them. Liam spoke about his school days in the North East of Scotland, and Ross mainly recalled date nights with some of the women he'd gone out with in the past.

We're at day five now, and my emotional state is more settled. My reasoning for this is, the longer it has been since we left Edinburgh and haven't been found, the more confident I am that no one *can* actually find me. I've taken to documenting my journey through this in my diary.

For the past two hours Izzy's had me baking, we haven't done that together since I was a small child. I think I'm going to be much fatter when we leave here as we have plenty of sponge cakes, flapjacks and cookies, since that's all we've done today.

The house has begun to feel lived in now, instead of somewhere borrowed for the night, like it did when we first arrived. And now, instead of the musty smell that greeted us when we arrived, I think the brickwork has taken on some of our heat and the fabrics now smell of the delicious food Izzy makes.

The weather has been changeable all day, not unusual for Scotland, but it was sunny this morning, then we had scattered showers and now a thick mist is rolling in fast.

"What are you seeing out there that's keeping you so enthralled?" Liam asks.

I'm standing back in the shadows from the window like he's told me, to ensure I can't be seen from outside.

"Thinking," I mumble as I continue to stare ahead. Since I've been standing here, the lower part of the hillside beneath the house has disappeared, shrouded in a heavy blanket of mist.

"About?" he asks.

"This is a stunning, peaceful place, yet I can't help thinking how such a beautiful glen was the scene of so much carnage." Liam looks at me frowning, and I know he'll have been taught about the Massacre of Glencoe in school. It's where so many from the Clan MacDonald met their demise at the hands of Clan Campbell, when over one hundred Campbells, the Duke of Argyll's army, slayed the MacDonald's clan chief, and so many others.

"I was thinking how quickly the mist has come down, and

I can imagine it wouldn't have looked much different during the massacre. Did you know those that managed to flee hid in the fog from their attackers? It was this that spared them," I say, nodding out at the cloud below us.

"I suppose some would say it was God's divine intervention that saved them," Liam says as his hand lightly touches my shoulder and he smooths it down my back. I think he means it as a comforting gesture, but I tremble involuntarily when a thrill of pleasure runs through me, and he stops.

I turn to face him, my eyes connecting to his gaze and he holds me captive. "If God had a hand in it, those Campbells wouldn't have turned on their hosts in the first place." For a moment I feel emotionally connected to the fate of the MacDonalds on that day. Like the survivors, I feel betrayed as the reason they were attacked was because they were seen as a threat to the Crown.

I turn back and stare out at the glen again, because I know Liam wants to remain professional. I expect him to walk away but he doesn't.

We both stand in silence for a few more minutes, and I can feel his breath on my neck as the pretty, dramatic view I see looks less than inviting than it has in the previous four days we've been here.

"I only came to tell you that Ross got a message to Lottie," Liam eventually says. "She has no idea where you are, but she wants you to know she's thinking of you, and missing her party partner." He sniggers. "Oh, and she wanted to know where the tickets are kept for some concert you were both going to next week?"

* * *

I SETTLE in front of the jigsaw Izzy's found, and has been cursing at for the previous forty-five minutes. It's been amusing watching her because I think it's the first time I've ever heard her swear.

"Geez, it's all blues, greens, and browns, what the heck does this make?" I ask. She holds up the box and I peer under at the picture and laugh. "Izzy, how do you expect to make the picture when the jigsaw pieces are stored inside the box and you can't see the picture you're piecing together?"

"This is going to take a while. I've still only found two corner pieces," she mumbles, ignoring me, with her eyebrows knitted in concentration.

"Want some help?" I ask, giving into my boredom. I figure anything is better than moping around with the minutes feeling like hours. Every day in this house feels like a week. By next week I bet they'll feel like a month.

An hour later we've made very little progress, and a frustrated Izzy excuses herself to put our dinner in the oven. As she leaves the room Liam turns up in the hallway, drops onto his front and starts doing push-ups. *I swear the man's trying to torture me.* I feel like I'm dying a slow death as I drag my heavy chair across the faded carpet in my quest for a clearer view of him.

Ten whole minutes later I'm squeezing my thighs together after watching him doing a combination of one and two-handed push-ups, abdominal crunches, thigh squats and lunges.

If he's noticed me watching he doesn't let on. Now he's perfectly balanced in a handstand pose doing push-ups from this position. When he dips, his chin almost touches the floor each time, but he's completely poised and in control. His strength is incredible and although he looks effortless doing it, I know he's working hard. I'm mesmerized by the darker sweat patches visible in interesting places on his light grey sweatpants and vest.

"Come here," he says, and I'm out of my chair before he's

even finished his command, like I've used starting blocks in a sprint race. "Don't get any dirty ideas, I just want to use you," he says.

"I'm up for that," I counter, with a wicked grin, and his eyes meet mine and turn dark. He scowls and I know my words have affected him.

"Not like that…" he grinds out almost in a groan, and he shakes his head a little too slowly. "Do you want to help me or not?" he asks, sternly.

"Let me see," I say, tapping my lips with my index finger. "Help a hot guy hone his muscles and listen to him grunt? Duh, yeah," I reply, and he can't help but crack a smile.

"Okay, come closer," he says, as he lies flat on his back. He opens his legs. "Closer," he coaxes again, and I walk into the space between his outstretched legs and stare down at him. He looks amazing lying beneath me.

"Would this exercise require me to get horizontal at all?" I ask with a straight expression on my face.

"Vertical will be just fine," he replies. "Now, hold my ankles," he says lifting his feet up to my hips and holds them there until I take one in each hand. "Okay, I'm going to do five repetitions of fifteen, of this exercise. Plant your feet wide and make sure you don't fall over."

"What does this exercise do?"

"It'll make my quads and glutes burn." Immediately he finishes talking and begins his workout again. Lifting his butt off the floor and lowering in a controlled manner.

I don't know about his quads, but I do know the man sets *me* on fire. I'm not prepared for my body's reaction to the upward groin thrusts that he starts to do. What's playing out in front of me as he tightens his muscles, feels like a form of erotic foreplay on the one hand, and an exercise in abstinence on the other.

He straightens his body from his shoulders to his feet,

and I watch as my hot bodyguard's hips piston back and forth. My core clenches in reaction to this. After one repetition he rests for a minute and repositions his vest top that had shown just a slither of his fabulous six-pack. He starts again and keeps his breathing controlled, inhaling and exhaling steadily. His eyes are fixed over my shoulder, maybe at something on the wall.

Again, he stops, stretches his arms above his head, and when he does this, his package bulges provocatively in his sweatpants. A groan escapes my lips and I quickly look away from him. I hear a chuckle, but before I can meet his gaze his hips are thrusting up and down again. This time the torn concentration on his face reminds me of the time we spent in bed. Heat rises to my cheeks and sweat coats my palms.

Somehow, I make it through the last three repetitions of the exercise, and I drop his ankles to the floor. I'm turned on almost to the point of pouncing on him. As I step backwards to escape his attention, he catches my legs between his and my eyes meet his gaze. He's flushed and slightly breathless, but the smile he gives me tells me the past fifteen minutes of my life were well spent.

"Thanks Amelia, that was a huge help."

"For you maybe," I mumble. "For me, it felt like hell." I spin on my heels to head for the kitchen and the safety of my housekeeper.

* * *

IT'S ALMOST seven in the evening by the time dinner is ready. Liam is freshly showered, and I swear it's getting harder to maintain this barrier he's put between us. Izzy eats her food like she's in a race, then places her plate in the sink and tells us she's going to wash out the shower in the upstairs bathroom. I hardly register her talking because I'm staring at every forkful of food Liam eats with his very talented mouth, and eventually he looks self-conscious, and presses his lips into a line because he's caught me watching.

"Here," he says, holding up a forkful of squished up mashed potato, steak pie and peas. My eyes widen because I've been rumbled, and he smirks. "You obviously think mine tastes better than yours, open," he says.

"I don't know what you're talking about," I say, looking at my plate and realising I've barely touched mine.

"Come on, open," he says again. His arm is stretched fully across the table and his fork is an inch from my face. I take his offering into my mouth, close my lips and he slides his fork out from between them, painfully slowly, watching the prongs lengthen as he does.

"There, good right?" he says, turning the silverware over and smoothing it clean between his lips. There's a moment where we're lost in one another. Then, as if drawn by magnets, each of us bends forward until our faces are so close I know we're going to kiss.

Suddenly a thundering roar shakes the house once, closely followed by another and we both jump back in our seats. My hands fly to my chest and adrenaline invades in a rush and floods my body. My heart is pumping erratically, and I'm frozen in my chair, temporarily petrified by the noise.

"Fuck, they almost frightened the shit out of me," Liam says, but he starts laughing. When he sees how unravelled I am, his smile drops, his eyes soften and fill with concern. He places a hand over mine and squeezes it. I feel something warm and look down at myself. My top is covered in food from when I must have caught the plate when I was startled.

"It's okay, Amelia, is only fighter jets. They do low flying training here in the hills sometimes."

Before he can say anything else, Ross comes into the

kitchen shaking his head. "Well, that woke us up. Still, it's the most excitement I've had in days," he says, taking his plate out of the oven. "Nothing new to report," he tells Liam.

Liam stands and scrapes his plate into the waste bin. "I'd better get upstairs, I'll catch you later."

iam
28th July

It's been four days since the fighter jets flew overhead and since then I've watched Amelia's mood sink more with each day that has passed. The noise really scared her, and I suppose it tipped the balance between her feeling brave and showing her vulnerabilities. It's day nine and she's been sleeping a lot during the day. I think she's depressed because she's quiet and not really interacting as much as she usually does. I know it would help if she could go for a walk, feel the wind in her hair and blow some of the cobwebs away. I've been tempted to suggest this, but we've come this far and it's only three more days until the referendum takes place. We're over the halfway mark, and this is something to be celebrated.

The news from Ross's contacts is that the monarchy and government are getting desperate. He said heads will roll for

Amelia being allowed to disappear the way she has, but so long as it's not Amelia's head I'm perfectly fine with that.

After a conversation with Ross, I've taken to exercising with Amelia each day. The first day I just let her watch, but since then I've encouraged her to take part. It at least gives her another thing to add to her routine, and it helps pass the time.

It's nearly midday and Amelia still isn't up yet. She's missed breakfast and I could sense from her mood last night she wasn't coping as well. When Izzy tells me lunch is ready I have an excuse to get her out of bed.

I knock on her door, and when I get no answer I open it and go in. "Amelia?" I say, softly. "Are you okay?"

She stirs in the bed and pulls the duvet down from over her head. "Actually, I'm not. What if the vote is yes?" she asks. She's asked this before, and I know it's worrying her. She'd be a fool if she wasn't concerned about this attention. Yes she could just refuse to have anything to do with a debate, but this could also have the potential to make her look unpatriotic by some fanatical nationalists.

I sigh. "I honestly think it won't be, but I've told you before, Ross and I can make you safe, sweetheart. If you don't want to go back to Edinburgh, we'll ensure your safety somewhere else. It may not be in this country, but I swear to you, we have the knowledge and skills to make sure no one will find you." She looks alarmed and I wander over to the bed and sit down. Finding her hand, I hold it in mine and give it a gentle squeeze. "Look, I know you're frightened. If I were in your shoes, I don't know that I'd have handled all this with such grace, like you have. But you've trusted us this far and you're still here, right?" I say, hoping I sound convincing.

"I do trust you, it's them, whoever they are out there, I don't trust," she replies, her eyes dull with worry.

"Come here," I say, pulling her up to a sitting position and wrapping my arms around her. I don't care in this moment that I'm her protector; I'm a man who can see the woman he cares about needs to be comforted.

She leans in close, her warm body melding into my chest, and the door flies open.

"Someone is coming up the path," Ross says in a rush before he leaves the room again. We've had a plan for if this happens during the day. I glance out at the bottom of the drive, which is about a hundred and fifty metres from the road. I can see a couple, and they look like hikers, but then again, as Ross and I know well from our past, looks can be deceiving. The back of the house is secure, no one has been about out there.

We won't answer the door. Ross has gone back to monitor, and Izzy has already been primed to turn everything off and stand in the pantry once she has locked the sunroom door at the back behind us. From the outside looking in, the downstairs appears empty, if we have enough notice. There are only the living room and dining room windows to the front, and the front porch. The door into the hallway is solid wood and doesn't have a letterbox. I thank my stars it's been a warm day and we haven't started the log burner.

My heart starts pumping and my mind begins executing the plan we've practiced verbally daily since we've been here. Amelia is out of bed in two seconds, the duvet smoothed back as if no one has been in there, and I can see she's focused on me. I grab the clothes she took off last night and lead her quickly into the kitchen. We sneak out the back and into a side door in the metal barn.

"Lie down on the floor," I say, shoving her clothes into the Land Rover Defender before her and then lifting her into the back still in her satin pyjamas. The keys are in the ignition and I'm ready to drive away at any second. If the main barn door opens anyone in my way will be run over.

"You're okay," I say in reassurance. "We've got this. Hopefully it's just a couple of hikers, but better to be safe than sorry."

For several minutes we sit quietly until I hear a quiet sniff, but I won't break my silence, because if I do and it really is a covert operation to take her, I could bring them straight to us. Another ten minutes pass and I start to fear something's wrong, but still, I can't compromise her by going to find out if Ross and Izzy are alright. It's nearly twenty minutes before Ross comes and finds us. Relief washes through me and I turn to see Amelia whose eyes are red raw, but she's barely made a sound.

"It's okay, sweetheart, they've gone," I say, quickly climbing down from the vehicle. I run and open the back door, and she still hasn't moved. "Come on, Amelia, let's get you inside. I scoop her out of the back, close the door, and I carry her from the barn to the house. When Izzy turns the key in the door, locking us back in the kitchen, Amelia bursts into tears.

"Hey," I say, "you were so brave just now, but it's over and you're still okay."

I lead her by the hand and follow Ross upstairs to talk to him.

"I'm highly confident they were only a couple of hikers," he tells us. The benign look in his face tells me he speaks the truth.

"How could you possibly know this? Isn't that what they do, send couples so that they look like ordinary people?"

"Oh, yeah, they do, but look." He turns and rewinds the CCTV footage from outside, and seconds later when it begins to play, we see the female crouch by a tree on the righthand side of the house. She's on the opposite side to the barn where we were hiding.

"See, it's not only bears that shit in the woods," he says

and grins. "She's just a hiker relieving herself." His crude comment makes me chuckle as we watch the couple sit down at the end of the property, back beside the road, and take out a picnic. The video footage lasts another five minutes before they repack their rucksacks and leave.

CHAPTER 24

*𝒶*melia
   29th July

"CAN'T YOU SLEEP?" Liam asks when I wander from my bedroom in the dark. The weather was hot for a change yesterday, but now, in the early hours of the morning, the temperature in this old house has dropped considerably. I haven't been sleeping at night at all.

Liam is sitting in a chair by the fire with his feet up on an old wooden footstool he found in the kitchen. The fire has gone out, and it's raining outside.

"No, I was just listening to the rain. My head's too full of this," I say waving my hand in the air. "Besides, apart from my current anxiety, I find it hard to fall asleep when my mind hasn't been taxed in the right way during the day," I say.

"I guess. But your usual work is finished for the summer, so what would you usually be doing?"

"Partying," I say with a chuckle. "Getting sloshed and dancing the night away with Lottie and some of my other friends."

194

"All summer?" he asks, shifting from his slouched position, and straightening up in the chair.

"Not all of it," I reply. "We had some rock concerts booked… and a couple of plays I wanted to take in. The rest of the time I think I'd maybe have gone for a week or two to my villa in St. Lucia."

"How the other half live." The way he responded wasn't with malice; it was more like a statement of fact. Nevertheless, his comment has made me feel awkward.

"Tea?" I ask, when what I really want is to sink into his lap and take a hug.

"Tea would be amazing."

I tilt my head. "Ah, do I detect a hint of boredom in your tone?"

"Not if it keeps you safe."

"I've never thanked you properly for all you're doing, have I?" I say, as he stands and walks with me into the kitchen.

A smile plays on his lips. "It's thanks enough that you're doing all that I'm asking of you. It can't be easy to place your trust in someone you hardly know."

"I know you're a good man."

"I've done bad things in my life." His comment makes me pause as I go to fill the kettle.

"A good man who's done bad things," I state, and turn the tap on. When he doesn't protest, I know I've assessed him right. He has that hint of danger to his aura, but from the way he's looked out for me from the start, I think he has a good heart.

As the kettle comes to the boil, Liam pulls out two mugs. "Earl Grey tea tastes like perfume," he says, as he drops a tea bag for me into one mug.

"It's a real tea drinker's tea," I argue.

"No ma'am, Yorkshire tea's the real deal."

"Commoner," I tease, and he chuckles.

"You got that right," he says, as he pulls milk from the fridge and pours a little into each cup. We're on long life milk because we've been here so long, but Izzy still insists it tastes better straight from the fridge.

I sit down at the kitchen table and Liam leaves the room. Moments later he comes back with a small fan heater he's found. He crouches down, plugs it in, and warm air billows out.

"Not long now," he says, encouraging me that my plight will soon be over.

"I can't wait for this to be done." It's day ten and the nearer we get to the vote the more anxious I feel. I'm trying not to let it control me, but sometimes it's been hard.

"Maybe next month we'll be sitting having dinner somewhere with a lesser view, but with the freedom to make stupid decisions," Liam replies with a note of want in his tone.

"Yeah? Who'll be having that dinner? You and me? Or the four of us in general?"

Bending towards me in his chair, he brushes hair from my face, slides his fingers down the length of it and slips it over my shoulder. His hand cups my chin, and for a moment I think he's going to kiss me, but he doesn't. The desire in his eyes is almost as good as a kiss, but not quite.

"That would depend on you, Amelia. I'm a common man with far less to offer, and a job that means I'm in high demand."

"So, you're not entirely immune now?" I ask, having spent all these days like platonic friends, since we gave ourselves over to the one night we spent together.

Liam has been careful ever since. The sexual tension has been there, but we've tried to keep our appropriate distance.

However, if I'm honest, the chemistry between us has, at times, slowly been killing me.

"I never have been. However, I'm fortunate enough that I can compartmentalise my feelings for most of the time. If I hadn't been able to do this it could have put you at greater risk. I won't screw with your safety for a quick release."

As hard as it is when he pulls his hand away, I don't object. It's honourable that he puts my life before his carnal desires. When he sits back, the moment of temptation recedes, and I quietly sip my tea.

"You should take that to bed," he suggests, and I immediately sense he needs help to maintain his distance.

I want to protest but I don't, instead I stand, nodding. "Good idea. Thanks again for keeping me safe," I say, as I leave the kitchen and make my way back to bed.

CHAPTER 25

$\mathcal{L}$iam
    29th July

IT'S THE MORNING, and if anyone heard Amelia and I having tea in the night no one mentions it. Ross got fed up sitting upstairs all day; the view from the back bedroom window is of one large hill. He's taking a risk by coming downstairs, and has set everything up in the dining room at the front. We haven't been using the room anyway, and the scenery out of the picture window in there is spectacular. He's made a black out screen for night-time from some material he brought with him.

* * *

I'VE JUST COME out of the shower and it's almost lunchtime. After Ross got up this morning, I crawled into bed, and fell fast asleep upstairs. I'd intended on forty winks, but that turned into almost three hours; boredom will do that to a man.

We're all a bit stir crazy here in the house after the excitement, because after ten days of counting each white imprint on the blood-red, flock wallpaper, we're all desperate for this to end. The referendum is only two days away and the thought of another game of gin rummy with the dog-eared pack of cards that we found, or the Scrabble game with the missing letter K, makes me want to strip naked and run screaming into the hills. I'm a patient man, but I'm just about done. Watching Amelia and Izzy pore for hours over a three-thousand-piece jigsaw is making me slightly insane.

I glance at Ross who is studious and precise in all that he does, and watch him check his equipment. I've always admired his technological mind and I'm so thankful he's with me on this particular assignment.

Thanks to his expertise we know who we're up against, and as we suspected, the guy with the laptop is an MI5 field agent working for the government. It took less than a day for him to turn up with the laptop again. It was taken to a location we both know is a security services premises, located on a run-down industrial estate. It's a disused storage warehouse they use as one of their many hidden bases. From the satellite images on the outside, it looks pretty derelict, but we can imagine there's some serious analytical equipment inside. What it doesn't have is Ross's genius.

I think back to the moment when the laptop opened again, and Ross identified where it had led us. The second the machine was switched on Ross tracked where it was. It's a bonus because we now have the name of Amelia's intruder, Graham Boxley, thanks to the generic looking security badge hanging from the breast pocket of his jacket that had been displayed on the screen. It obviously didn't announce which company he belongs to, but the fact that it didn't, allowed us to make an educated guess.

As we watched, another guy came into view on the screen and the two men quickly swapped places. We watched him get comfortable and he immediately began to type. Ross sat watching him like he was enthralled in an action movie. Amelia's password is lame; it's her initials and date of birth backwards. The computer guy was inside her home screen in less than two minutes, and ready to access her content, when Ross tapped a sequencing code on his machine and closed out the screen.

"Okay, back to what I was doing," he said, nonchalantly and my silent look asked what I had missed.

Ross chuckled when he looked up and saw me. "Amelia's computer is going back to factory settings right now. After that there's a whole pile of shit waiting to upload. It'll keep him busy for days. Oh, and it also wipes the software I've installed."

I glanced in awe at Ross, who never complains, and I thought about how lucky I was to have him.

Back to today and I can see he's looking at emails. He's currently hacked into not only Harry Donaldson's personal email accounts – a personal one in his real name and one in the name *celtic dot warrior*, but he's also in the First Minister's official government ones as well. I'm wondering where he gets his patience from. He's the smarter of the two of us on the analytical side, but my skills of perception in the field outshine his. We each compliment the other, and as a friend, no one is more loyal to me than Ross.

"Look!" he says, and I shrug because I'm already looking.

"What am I looking at?" I ask, staring at the screen.

"The government emails are as clean as a whistle, which, considering everything going on in Scotland at the moment, looks odd. I would expect to find something about the referendum." I shake my head not following. Ross continues, "Well, it looks as though Harry thinks he's been covering his tracks."

I frown. "And has he not?"

Ross grins. "No, he's not done a very good job of clearing his trail. It's been too easy for me to get into the server and pull up his deleted emails." I watch as he scrolls through email after email.

"There's a lot to look through," I say.

"Not really. I can narrow it down by just looking for keywords, namely words connected to Amelia or the Crown." He types *debate, crown, and monarchy* into the email tab for his government account. "Bingo, looks like we have more than enough to analyse."

We spend a few hours going through each email, and it seems there's only one that could vaguely be a possible connection.

When the same word search is applied to his personal *celtic dot warrior* account it reveals an entirely different story.

"Our dirty Harry's been having an affair with Lisa Hood, the Parliamentary Private Secretary to the Home Secretary, whenever he's been in London. She's his source. Who'd have thought Donaldson had it in him? I would never have guessed him capable of sneaking around in hotel rooms, screwing some poor deluded woman for information to further his cause. But he's a politician," Ross says like it cancels out that thought. "And do you know what else I've learned?" The way he flashes a demonic grin tells me whatever he knows is good. "Lisa Hood is *Mrs* Lisa Hood, she's married," he discloses wiggling his brows. "I wonder how her husband and the Scottish people will take to the news the First Minister is porking a married woman, if I was to leak it?"

"Interesting." I'm grinning because this is information we can use. It's exactly the break we wanted.

Ross goes on, "It would appear Donaldson has been planning this move for quite some time. He's been sitting on Amelia's connection to the Scottish throne for over a year, just waiting on the right time to use it. Apparently, the PM was informed about this just after he'd given the go-ahead for the Scottish referendum. Obviously, he couldn't recant his decision, but the PM then had a discussion with the Home Office Minister that this subject had been identified as a potential constitutional issue and Lisa was the minute taker of that meeting."

He holds up his hand and I high five him. "We have more than enough material here to sway the faithful, and shake the numbers up before the referendum takes place," Ross says leaning back in the chair and stretching his arms above his head.

He clicks out of the deleted column of emails after screenshotting each one he needs. When he resets the email to the inbox there's a new email that's just arrived.

"What's that one?" I ask, pointing towards it.

"It's Harry's source, *cassie dot snoup.*"

"Well?" I'm eager to see what she says.

"I can't read it until he opens it," Ross says, but as he does the highlight goes off, and both he and Harry are in. The email has an encryption, the stupid code is 1234 and the contents of the email open on the screen.

From: cassie.snoup
To: celtic.warrior
Subject: Where's Wally
Story... Royal flush in the works.
BG/LM connected.

"Well, we don't need a MENSA membership to work this one out, do we?" Ross scoffs. "Someone needs to take this guy aside and teach him something about coding and encryption for his communications. Looks like the powers that be are going to use the public to find us. Good luck with that one. By the way, BG/LM is laughable, if no one can work out Bodyguard Liam McKenna is going to be the fall guy."

* * *

AMELIA IS SITTING in the kitchen, with her feet perched up on the chair, and hugging her knees. She's dressed in black slacks and a red fitted top, and her long dark hair is in a simple ponytail. She looks pale, but elegantly composed. After the last scare of the hikers, she's been holding up well.

"Wow, Izzy something smells good," I say.

"Oatcakes made with maple syrup," Izzy informs me as she opens the glass oven door and takes another tray full of the goodies out. My mouth waters at the delicious, sweet aroma.

I pass Amelia and I can't help squeezing her shoulder. "You okay?" I ask, concerned at how quiet she's been today.

"Yeah, I'm fine, just feeling a little morose," she replies.

"I get it. We've been here for nearly two weeks and apart from what Ross and I tell you, you have no real idea what's going on out there in the world."

Her head bobs from side to side as she considers my assumption. "I suppose, but it isn't just that, today would have been my mother's birthday."

I sit down at the table and cover her hand with mine. "I'm sorry." If our situation were different, I'd stand and pull her in for a hug, but it isn't, and I know now, more than ever, our circumstances here in the farmhouse could change at any minute. I choose to say nothing else on the matter and focus my attention on Izzy and the biscuits. "These are making me hungry. How soon will it be before I can eat one?"

"As soon as the kettle boils, I'm making afternoon tea," she replies.

Ross pokes his head around the kitchen door. "I think you might want to see this."

I stand but before I can get out of the kitchen Amelia is out of her chair and is following Ross in front of me.

He shows me the Reuters breaking news ticker scrolling across a screen and it reads: *Socialite Amelia Campbell kidnapped by Liam McKenna, the man hired to protect her.* The screen refreshes and I know it's the failsafe internet disrupter Ross has installed. He pulls up the news channel, and a well-known, middle-aged newscaster is reporting from a studio with a picture of Amelia on display over his left shoulder. And, just as the email to Harry Donaldson hints at, I'm involved in Amelia's disappearance. The screen refreshes again and my picture, the one on file from my passport, stares back at me in place of Amelia. What the news report is broadcasting amounts to an appeal from the public to help find us, with a reward for information leading to the safe return of the woman standing next to me.

A Crime stoppers number flashes up on the screen and my eyes flit to Amelia and see she immediately hugs herself. Without thinking I wrap my arms around her and pull her into my chest. The feel of her soft body against mine immediately makes me hard and I clear my throat.

"Don't worry; we expected this, and it's good news."

"It is?" she shrieks lifting her head from my chest. She pulls away slightly to search my face for honesty.

"Definitely. The fact they've had to go public tells us they have no idea where to look, and confirms the hikers were just that... hikers." She allows herself a small smile at this.

Ross clears his throat and stands. "To be honest, I'm

delighted by this turn of events. We've been sitting in this house for a long time, and apart from growing hair, we've done very little. It's time I had some fun. I'm going to fuck with everyone out there that thinks they're dealing with a couple of amateurs. With what I've found with this little baby, everyone involved will wonder what's hit them," he says, patting the lid of his computer.

Watching Ross talk makes Amelia's smile wider.

Dropping my hands from her, I take a step back and make space. My body is cool now, feeling the loss of her heat. "So… those biscuits?" I shove my hands in my pockets, partly to hide my erection, and to stop myself from reaching out to Amelia again.

"Yeah… I really need one of those biscuits," she replies, as she lowers her eyes, turns and leaves the room.

CHAPTER 26

AT DINNER, Liam appears distant, and I feel like he's annoyed that he hugged me after I'd seen the news article. However, the fact that he did, gives me hope that he cares for me, not just as someone he's been commissioned to keep safe, but because his feelings are growing deeper.

Long pauses during dinner suggest both men are avoiding discussing something in my presence, and I wonder if they've found something else out. From their lack of conversation, I know they're being careful what they say. Perhaps they think talking about what they're doing scares me too much.

As usual Izzy's food is delicious, and since we've been here, I've noticed she has a glow about her. I think she secretly likes having more people to look after. She must get bored when it's just the two of us at home.

After dinner the men are as complimentary as ever of her

efforts, then excuse themselves back to the dining table where they have their computers set up.

Once everything is neatly tidied away after dinner, Izzy and I take a bottle of wine and settle back in the sitting room in front of the three-thousand-piece jigsaw we've been making. I've never seen so many blue pieces of a puzzle that make up the sky in my life. It doesn't help that when the jigsaw is complete it will form a picture of Glencoe.

After one glass of wine, Izzy is fighting to stay awake and when I look at the time it's barely eight o'clock.

She excuses herself and goes upstairs to bed, leaving me in the sitting room with a half-bottle of wine and no company to share it. I pour myself another glass and drink it faster than I should, while I stare through the window at the dramatic landscape surrounding us. From day to day nothing much changes outside, apart from the sky, clouds, sun and the rain. The highlight of our time here so far has been the day we saw a herd of deer running through the glen, the low points have been the fighter jets and the hikers.

As I pour the last of the wine from the bottle, I hear Liam and Ross laughing and go to see what they've found that's so funny.

Liam smiles when he sees me at the door. "Come and see this, Amelia. I bet this cheers you up."

Ross has multiple tabs open on his laptop: Instagram, Facebook and Twitter. When I begin to read, I realise it appears there have been hundreds of sightings of me all over the UK, as well as parts of Western France, a couple in the Canary Islands, some on the Isle of Wight, and also the Isle of Man.

"Are all these people saying they've seen me?" I ask in disbelief.

"Yeah, although they don't know they're doing it.

Although these accounts are still current, none have made a post in over a month.

I stare at Liam's smiling face and mimic his expression, but I'm still clueless. He gestures for me to take a seat and points at the screen.

"So far, how many have you done, Ross?"

"Eight hundred and thirty-seven," he replies, but can barely speak for laughing.

Liam tells me, "He's hacked all these accounts and posted sightings of you everywhere. Some are in clusters which will have people running around like chickens trying to follow up on the leads. It'll keep them busy for the rest of the week, and until after the vote, when we'll bring you out of hiding."

"This is incredible," I reply.

"Yeah, like me," Ross says and laughs.

"No, you really are," Liam tells him, in praise of his work.

"I can only come out of hiding if the vote is no, and even then, I'll be worried. What if someone harms me anyway?"

Liam's eyes soften. "They won't. Thanks to this, everyone will be looking out for your welfare. You're too high profile now for them to try anything, thanks to the whole country trying to find you. If anything were to happen to you, someone with knowledge of those that have done this would likely grass them up. Besides, the vote isn't going to be yes. Not by the time Ross is finished with Harry Donaldson's PR."

I frown. "His public relations?"

"Yeah, let's just say the First Minister has been using his position to get laid, isn't that correct Ross? I can't see how else he's managed to attract a woman." Both men laugh. Liam continues, "I won't go into it now, but by the time Ross is finished with the First Minister's reputation he'll be lucky to get a job in government at all."

I widen my eyes. "Why? What do you have that could be so damaging?"

"We're waiting for something to back up evidence we've found. I'll let you know when we've got confirmed proof. Go get some rest. Things will look brighter tomorrow.

I want to talk to Liam alone, to feel close to him at least, but I know he doesn't want that, so I head to bed.

* * *

30TH JULY

I've been staring at my bedroom ceiling since coming to bed over an hour ago. It's past midnight and so we're barely into day eleven. Spending twenty-four hours a day with a man I crave intimately, yet I'm not allowed to touch, could pass for a slow form of torture. Part of me thinks our time spent here could have been so different had he allowed what I know we both feel to blossom.

These past ten days in this bubble have felt some of the loneliest of my life; living in close proximity isn't the same as having company when you want it. I miss Lottie and her frivolous banter, with her light heartedness, which would be welcomed right about now. It's not been easy containing some of the thoughts that have been running through my mind and appearing brave all the time.

During all this time there have been two common threads I've focused upon: the threat to my life, and whether there could be a future with Liam in it, should everything turn out fine. I won't allow myself to think of alternative endings to my ordeal. To do this would be like saying I have no trust in Liam and Ross's abilities to keep danger away from me. I do trust them; I have put my whole faith in these two men that I had no knowledge of before all of this happened.

* * *

THE FAINT SOUND of a car in the road below immediately pulls me out of sleep. It's so quiet here any noise at all is magnified. Shockwaves course through me one after another as my heart thunders in my chest. I'm lying here with my eyes searching blindly in the pitch dark.

In my panic I forget to listen, until I realise either the car has stopped, or I can't hear it for the loud noise of blood roaring in my ears. I try to listen harder, my body now moving freely after the initial shock recedes. I turn in the direction of the bedroom door and look at the crack beneath it; there's no light at all.

Did Liam hear what I heard? What if he's asleep?

Quietly, I climb out of bed and open the bedroom door, the hinge squeaks and I freeze, pulling a face and swearing silently because this isn't the life I've been used to, I've never been taught to sneak around. I stop and listen again but hear nothing. I realise I've been holding my breath, and I exhale shakily, as quietly as I can.

After listening again, I believe I could hear a pin drop, and make my way along the hallway to the living room. I freeze when I hear a shuffling movement. My heart rate spikes, and I pray it's Liam, not some ninja that has stolen his way into the farmhouse and has slit his throat.

Finally, I brave a peep and see that it really is Liam. He's standing back from the window looking out, and I know instinctively he's watching someone outside.

"Liam?" I whisper, and he turns sharply in my direction. The moonlight streaks over his face before he moves back into the shadow.

"It's okay, go back to bed, it's poachers." He's already focusing his attention through his night scope as he scans the outside.

"Are you sure? Can't I stay here with you? I'm terrified lying alone in bed."

"Sit on the chair and don't talk. I'm ninety-nine percent sure it's deer stalkers breaking the law, but there's always that one percent."

His open-ended *one percent* doesn't inspire confidence in me. I climb onto the chair, slide under his duvet and pull it up under my chin. As scared as I am my eyes start to droop after the adrenaline rush wears off.

An hour or so later I awake with a start.

"Fuck me," Ross hisses. He makes me jump as he's crept down the stairs without me knowing.

"Poachers, they've just shot a stag," Liam informs him in a murmured tone.

Ross moves behind him and stares out of the window over his shoulder. "You should have woken me."

"No need. Look, there you go, they've bled it out and loaded it up on the back of their pickup." We hear the diesel engine on the four-wheel drive vehicle idle a few seconds longer before it speeds away. Ross leaves the living room and goes back upstairs without even noticing I'm there.

Liam walks over and lifts his duvet off me. "Come on, let's get you back to bed. You're safe." Taking me by my wrist, he pulls me out of the chair and leads me back to my bedroom.

"Please stay with me," I say, grabbing his arm. "Lying here will be a waste of time if you don't."

"Amelia…" The pain in his voice tells me he wants to, but he keeps his eyes on the bed.

"Please… clothes on, I promise. I just want to feel safe."

For a long moment Liam closes his eyes, and I know he's debating what I've asked.

"Clothes on," he agrees, and pulls back the duvet for me to get into bed. Climbing on after me, he turns me away from him and pulls me back into his chest.

CHAPTER 27

$\mathcal{L}$iam
        30th July

FOR MOST OF the night I only nap because lying with the sweet smell of Amelia under my nose is only half the battle, while the other half is thinking back to the sight of those poachers outside the house. I'll admit, I'm slightly concerned because good undercover field agents can role play like experts, so game poachers wouldn't have been a stretch for them. However, no one came near the house. We know this because Ross rigged up some ground movement sensors that would have triggered the outside lights.

My mind replays each point I've seen as I search for anything that may have been out of place. The three men who arrived stuck together, and I counted that all three left. Without going outside and checking, I can't know if they left behind any covert devices, or if someone jumped out of their vehicle before they stopped outside.

For all I know, there could be an operative in camouflage

lying out there in the bracken, watching the house for move-ment. Again, I wish I could do some reconnaissance, but I won't risk going out there and blowing our cover.

It's daylight outside but still early and Amelia stirs in my arms. As well as a lack of sleep I've also been fighting my feelings. My body is screaming for me to stay where I am, but it gives me enough warnings that I move and get up. I make my way out to the kitchen and find Ross is filling the kettle with water.

"I enjoyed that wee adrenaline rush during the night," he says. "Made me feel alive."

"I'm sure it was nothing, but it's easy to let my mind wander, paranoia and the wee small hours of the morning are strange bed fellows," I reply.

"Talking about bed fellows…"

"Before you let your imagination run wild, I lay on the bed beside her; she was frightened after the poacher's visit. Nothing happened."

Ross's eyes narrow and he stares for the truth in my face. He must see it when he nods, turns and puts the kettle on.

"So, what's today's agenda?" I ask, moving the conversa-tion onward.

"It's 'Fuck with Harry' day." I chuckle and Ross opens the fridge, takes out the long life milk and sniffs the carton. "This smells off," he advises me.

"All long life milk smells off. Izzy only opened it last night and it's well within date." My reassurance allows him to ignore the smell and pour some in two mugs. "Today Donaldson's reputation is going to blow up in his face, and tomorrow is voting day. I think this news about Harry all coming out this close to voters making such a vital decision will make the Scottish people see what an unsavoury char-acter the First Minister is. Would you want a guy taking you into the unknown territory of a fledgling, totally independent country with all the issues it'll bring? Especially one who can't keep his dick in his pants, and diddles in the drawers of another man's wife?"

I chuckle at how crudely Ross spells out that Donaldson's reputation will be his demise.

"I hope it's enough," I say. "What we're asking is, whether the Scottish people want independence so much that they'd be willing to ignore the two-timing behaviour of a dishonest man who will be in charge of their future, but I reckon they won't.

Ross nods in agreement. "True, it's a hearts and minds game we're playing now. There are diehards that will be driven by the cause, but the vote is close enough, and the percentages are low enough, to catch all those who make up their minds when they vote on the day. I believe they'll sway the numbers anyway."

Ross finishes making the tea and we take it into the dining room. All night long his laptops have been monitoring Amelia's place in Edinburgh, Donaldson's emails, and God alone knows what else.

"Whoop," he says sitting down, and immediately punches some keys on his laptop. There are two pictures of Donaldson kissing Miss Harper, the Scottish Education Secretary. He clicks an arrow that takes him forward and there are two more pictures: one of him sitting in what looks like an intimate restaurant holding hands with Lisa Hood, and the other which is the money shot, them both leaving a back street hotel in Bayswater, London. He clicks again and finds a credit card payment for the same hotel in the name of Mr Donaldson."

"And you thought I was the genius," Ross remarks. "My brother-in-law is my idol," he says giving credit where it's due. He then opens an email from *conscientious dot citizen*, an email account I know we've used in the past. With the IP scrambler on the phone dock, I know it would be extremely challenging trying to trace it back to us. Five minutes later he's sent all the illicit details to commence 'Fuck with Harry' day. Every national and international news desk in Ross's extensive list has been sent the images and story.

He claps his hands together. "Right, if there's nothing else I'm needed for this morning, I think I'll go back to bed."

* * *

FOR MOST OF the day Amelia and Izzy have cooked and worked on the jigsaw – which, I'd say, is now about eighty percent done – while I've watched the monitors on the laptop and stared for long minutes out of the window. I'm doing this now and everything outside looks exactly the same as it has for most of the time we've been here. The sky has changed, and in turn so has the colour of the landscape, dependent upon the sun being out or not, but the place is just the same place… apart from the weather.

As I go to stand, I freeze instead when see something move in the thick brush of bracken outside. An adrenaline rush shoots through me. I know I'm far enough from the window that I can't be seen from where I'm standing. My heart is racing as I take a deep breath and hold it. Those poachers have lowered my confidence that our position hasn't been compromised. The bracken is moving fast and there's a flattened trail from the road, coming forty feet from the house, but whatever it is has stopped moving again. I'm ready to call Ross when two rabbits pop their heads up above the brush, and an instant feeling of relief floods through me.

"Fucking rabbits," I mutter, standing and stretch my hands above my head.

Footfall in the hallway makes me turn towards the door

and Ross enters the room. "Did you say something?" he asks coming back from his rest.

"I did, two fucking rabbits out there, this wildlife here in the highlands is keeping me on my toes."

"Wish I was fucking like rabbits," Ross muses. I chuckle as a soft knock on the door makes both of us turn around.

"Dinner's ready," Amelia tells us, and her eyes meet mine. For a moment I don't move, instead I stare at her beautiful face. She looks especially appealing today.

Ross breaks the silence. "Alright, I'm starving and dying of boredom after all the inactivity today. Nothing like pigging out on good nosh to put the worlds to right." Slipping past Amelia, he exits the room and goes towards the kitchen.

"I never got to thank you for last night," she says.

I move towards her and cup her chin. "I know, I couldn't chance staying in that bed, or you'd still be thanking me yet." I wink and brush past her, our chests briefly colliding, but I keep on moving down the hallway because if I'd stayed close to her in the room, I believe I would have kissed her.

* * *

AFTER DINNER, Izzy leaves to strip the beds and change the sheets as she had done every few days since we've been here.

Ross stares pointedly at me for a few beats then shakes his head. "Oh, man," he groans, and slides his chair back. "You two have got it bad. The amount of eye fucking between you is slowly driving me mad. While you figure out how to get through the rest of the evening, I'm off to see how badly I've ruined our friend Harry Donaldson's night."

Ross exits the room and I rise to my feet. "This will soon be over," I say, not sure whether I'm reassuring Amelia or myself.

Amelia stays seated and I wander over to the doorway. I'm half in the kitchen and half in the hall when I stop and turn around. Tapping my hand on the door, I gain her attention and she looks up to meet my gaze. "I'm talking about your ordeal, Amelia. As for the rest… this," I say wagging my finger between her and me, "from my perspective this is far from over." A smile spreads on her lips and her bright hazel eyes immediately fill with desire. "All I ask is that you trust us a little bit longer." This must be hard for her, having a man she knows wants her, but he won't give in to what she wants. Resisting her is killing me. However, if we are ever going to do this properly, I don't want a relationship that's borne out of fear.

Living in microscopic conditions, like we have been, can easily fuck with our minds. And even though we've both scratched an itch, Amelia has little understanding of me as an ordinary man. She knows me as Liam, the close protection detail hired to protect her. There's a possibility she won't be interested in the real me, a man with little to offer, when her life goes back to normal.

$\mathcal{A}$melia
30th July

THE REFERENDUM IS tomorrow and I was physically sick this morning from nerves. I've kept myself strong for almost all of the way through this, but Liam and Ross have created this protective bubble. My anxiety has been quietly building during the last couple of days and nausea crept up on me as I was sorting through my laundry. I was fortunate I was in my bathroom at the time, because I couldn't keep my breakfast down.

When Izzy told Liam I had been vomiting, his face became ashen with concern, or it might have been dread and shock. I immediately knew what he was thinking; it had been a couple of weeks since we'd had sex. But I'm not pregnant; I finished my period yesterday. My sickness was due to nothing other than a straightforward case of nerves.

Who could blame me? The thought of leaving here and coming out of hiding is terrifying.

"Drink this," Izzy tells me an hour after I've been sick. She hands me a mint tea and sits opposite with a concerned look on her face.

Ross pokes his head around the door. "Are you up to me sharing something?"

"Sure," I say, standing. Nursing the tea between my hands I walk through from the sitting room to the dining room.

"Okay, hopefully this will help you feel more confident," he says. "These two areas," He points to the Welsh valleys, and the South English coast, "are where most people think you are." He chuckles. "There have been twenty-one sightings between Plymouth and Torquay and twenty-seven all over the Welsh valleys. You know the funniest part? I only used three accounts in Wales."

"What about the referendum margins?"

"Ah, I was getting to that. Donaldson's political career is in the toilet. Obviously it's too late for the First Minister to resign… although the word in Holyrood is that there will be a call for a vote of no confidence to his leadership when the referendum is over.

"The analysis from the newspapers and magazines has been more or less consistent; Harry Donaldson's name is never mentioned without reference to his relationship with the Education Secretary, *and* the Home Secretary's member of staff in London."

Liam adds, "The news articles reference both in the debates among the political parties, and interviews with the public. No one is talking about the referendum in isolation, but in relation to Donaldson's conduct and the question as to whether he's fit to lead. Every news broadcast mentions his shady affairs."

"Do we know how that's affecting the predictions about the vote?" I ask.

Liam shrugs. "The polls are saying it's too close to call

now. In another twenty four hours, this part of making you safe will be finished."

"And part two?" I ask, my anxiety creeping in.

"Well, Ross and the establishment have already sown seeds for that, Amelia. Like I said before, the public search they created means when we leave here, you'll be all over the news. No one would dare try anything after that." I must look concerned because he reaches out and tugs playfully on my shirt. "Don't worry, we have a story you can tell. You've been thinking about writing a book for a while and decided to take the plunge and do it. So you've been here in the farm-house getting a first draft down." He shrugs. "The most convincing way of dealing with this is to stick close to the truth. You've written in that diary of yours every day, right? Think about it, the house has no TV or internet, and you haven't brought any of your own devices with you, those are in your apartment, remember?"

"I can't believe it'll be that simple."

"It should be, and I'll stay close just in case. You just need to have faith this will all pan out," he says.

From the way he's already taken care of me I know I should feel as confident as he is.

I give a small smile. "I'll leave you both to talk." Turning, I walk back through the dining room, out of the sitting room door, and head into the kitchen.

"What are we going to do with the food in the freezer?" Izzy asks. "There's still a crown of lamb, pork chops, and a quarter of that side of beef left," she tells me.

I shrug. I wouldn't have known what to do with it in Edinburgh, let alone here in Glencoe.

"I'm not sure. Maybe there's a cleaning crew between lets? Perhaps they'll check the freezer." Izzy seems satisfied with my suggestion and starts emptying out the pantry. "What are you doing?" I ask.

"Taking these home with us," she replies, looking at me like I'd asked her a stupid question.

"Have you ever bought tins of soup and tuna before, Izzy?"

"Of course I have, I thought these may come in handy."

Izzy glances down towards the tins and her eyes flick back up to mine.

"How are you holding up?" she asks, packing the tins in a box.

"Holding *on* more like," I reply, "I can't lie, I'm petrified, but I trust Liam's judgement."

"You need to my dear, what else is there?"

I shrug because I have no idea.

"Cheer up, it's never going to happen," Liam says, and my body jumps at his intrusion into my thoughts.

"God, you gave me a fright there," I say with a tight smile, but I really don't feel like smiling. I'm trying to be brave today, which is a weird sensation for me, because before this I have never been afraid of much, but then again, no one has ever put me in such a position before. Being here in isolation must have made me soft.

Izzy leaves the room with a pile of sheets she folded earlier. "I'll leave a set by each bed and I'll put them on the beds in the morning."

"Put them in the linen cupboard, Izzy, the place will be put back to the way we found it by Ross's brother-in-law's crew after we've gone. Apart from them, no one will know we've been here, unless we want them to," Liam tells her.

As soon as Izzy leaves the room he reaches out and tugs my wrist. "Come here," he says, and I close the space between us. Goosebumps scatter over my skin in reaction to his touch. He opens his arms and wraps them tightly around me.

"You've been amazing, Amelia. I couldn't have asked any

more of you. You haven't complained in all the time we've been here."

"You've been mediocre at best," I respond, deadpan, and he laughs. I smile, and it's the first genuine smile I've had all day.

"This hasn't been easy, I get that. Not being able to feel the sun on your face, the wind in your hair. You've had to put up with the stale air in this house for all the time we have; it takes a tough cookie to accept restrictions on their life like that."

"Tough cookie," I reply, pointing at my face.

"Delicious cookie." Liam's blue eyes turn dark as his gaze falls to my lips and he licks his own. "You're so tempting," he mutters as he brings his lips close to my ear.

"You're only saying that because after tonight you may not see me again." The implication isn't that I don't *want* to see him after this; it's a question I leave unspoken. *But what if I don't survive?*

As if he senses my wavering confidence he leans in and brushes his lips against mine. "This is all I can give you for now, but one day I hope to be in the position to give more."

On hearing his words, my heart flutters like it used to when I had a schoolgirl crush, and they inspire confidence he feels the same as me. I shake my head, and he frowns. He stares into my eyes with concern.

"Tomorrow night we'll know where we go from here," he says and it sounds like he's backtracking because I shook my head, and he thinks he's not what I want, once this threat has passed. He's dead wrong. "We'll wait to see how the vote goes." Despite his words, I know he's confident he and Ross have done enough in respect of swaying the public to see Harry for what he is. I wish I felt the same with some degree of certainty. Footsteps near and we know it's Izzy, the tread is too light-footed and nimble to be Ross.

Liam drops his arms from me and takes two steps back but leans towards me and whispers, "I'll come and see you, later tonight."

True to his word, Liam comes to my room and our conversations about life growing up are a distraction more than romantic. We chat for hours which helps me forget why we are here for a while. It's still dark when I eventually fall asleep with Liam lying on top of the duvet beside me.

* * *

31 St July ~ Scottish Referendum Day

A headache wakes me, and I feel like throwing up again. Liam has gone and there's a dent in the duvet where he lay for most of the night. For a moment I wonder why no one thought to pack paracetamol before we came here. It's the one thing that's missing from my protectors' inventory; considering they thought of things that wouldn't have occurred to me, I'm surprised they left out those. Sure, there is a first aid box in the bathroom under the sink, but no pain medication. I'm debating wallowing in bed a while longer.

Amelia Campbell you are made of sturdier stuff than this.

I sigh heavily and throw back the duvet. When my feet hit the floor, I pad into my bathroom and drink two glasses of water in quick succession. If how I feel is down to dehydration, I'll feel better in an hour.

"Today's the day, Harry Donaldson," I say aloud with determination, but it's my reflection I see in the mirror. Turning, I lean into the shower cubicle and press the on button.

For fifteen minutes I stand under the steaming hot water, until it eventually runs cold. I turn off the shower, step out, and wrap myself in a bath sheet. Back in the bedroom I slip the towel from my body and roughly towel dry my hair. For more than two weeks I've had no hairdresser, nail technician, not even a hair dryer, not to mention my lack of a mobile phone. *Who would have thought at twenty-eight I'd spend a fort-night with a seventy-four-year-old woman, doing one ridiculous jigsaw?*

Izzy packed enough outfits to last me a week, maybe two if I swapped over the tops, slacks, sweaters and skirts, but the first thing I'll do when I get home will be to donate all of this clothing to the local charity shop. I'm sick of the sight of the same four tops, three blouses two cardigans and sweaters.

Without my phone or a wristwatch to tell me exactly, all I know is it's daytime. But when I open the bedroom door, I can hear the other three temporary members of this house-hold talking.

CHAPTER 29

$\mathcal{L}$iam
31st July -Referendum Day

"You should have stayed in bed longer," Izzy scolds. "Liam told us you were still talking at four o'clock this morning."

"It's a big day," Amelia replies but her voice sounds flat. I watch her more closely.

"I hope it's a big day for Harry Donaldson," Izzy says. "Here I am, a Scot, in Scotland and I can't even vote today."

"How would you have voted?" I ask, and it strikes me I've never asked their opinions. The referendum for us has been about keeping Amelia safe.

"If I didn't know about her position and Harry Donaldson's cunning ways, I'd have been voting yes," Izzy discloses.

"Me too," Ross says. "So that's two votes lost because we're here… well four including both of you."

"Even if I hadn't found myself in this predicament I wouldn't have voted in favour because of Harry," Amelia insists.

"You would have voted yes, Liam," Izzy states confidently to me.

"You know how I'd have voted?" I ask.

Izzy scoffs. "Yeah, a man like you would have wanted your country's independence."

"If you say so," I say, and snigger. She's right, but I don't say so.

By four in the afternoon the exit polls are still saying neck and neck.

"It's a nail biter for sure," Ross says as he pulls up the Scottish Television news online at six o'clock and we hear the turn out to vote is unprecedented. There's a clip of Donaldson, and quite a few of the Holyrood MSPs voting at their local polling stations. I can't help smiling when I see how dishevelled Donaldson looks and know with certainty, thanks to Ross, he's had a sleepless night.

"He looks exhausted," I say sounding amused.

"Serves him right. Amelia didn't sleep either, and it's all his fault," Izzy says in her employer's defence.

The newscaster is spouting the usual facts and figures, and I'm surprised to hear ninety-seven percent of the Scottish electorate registered to vote, and Ross reaches over and shuts the laptop screen.

"Dinner smells ready," Izzy says and stands.

The smell from the kitchen is orgasmic and we all follow her there. She's made macaroni cheese with bacon, using the last chunk of cheddar, bacon and long life milk, and serves it with homemade garlic bread. Amelia leans over and inhales the aroma and I have an urge to pat her arse, but I don't. Instead, I focus on the delicious dish; it's like the one I remember my granny making when I was a child. It's comfort food, and although I know Amelia is putting on a brave face, she's got to be worried. I would be in her shoes.

Izzy plays mum and we all tuck in but the mood in the

room is somewhere between waiting to go to the gallows and being set free.

"Right, we've done all we can and we're still here, so what are we going to do on our last night?" Ross asks with a glint of mischief in his eyes. As if an idea suddenly strikes, he stands from the table and leaves the room. As Izzy starts clearing the table both Amelia and I stand and help. We make light work of the dishes and stack them all away.

There are three bottles of red wine left and as it's the last night we're all aiming to drink them. We're confident we're not going to be found out now, and either way we'll be leaving in the morning. Besides the vote result probably won't be known for quite a few hours after the polls close at ten.

When we go into the sitting room, we find Ross has rearranged the furniture and he's found a game of Twister. He's got the plastic mat unfolded and he hands Izzy the spinner. I cringe when I see it, and we all scoff at his attempt to get us to play the game, but after twenty minutes of coaxing, and a glass of wine so full, it's about a third of a bottle, a mellower side to me comes out. I'm bored enough to lower myself to play the stupid game.

Amelia squeals. "It's been years since I played this at college."

The effects of the wine – after so little alcohol consumption for a couple of weeks – are stronger than they'd usually be. In normal circumstances I'd tell Ross to go fuck himself, and feel more than embarrassed at the thought of doing something so juvenile, but if Amelia is playing, I'm down for rubbing my body parts up against hers.

Amelia pours more wine, filling our glasses again. She's used one and a half bottles already. Izzy informs us she has never played Twister, and I wonder what else she's missed in her life of service the upper classes. I thought everyone had played Twister at least once in their life.

By the time we've brought Izzy up to speed, I've downed the wine and I am beginning to wonder what the fuck I've let myself in for, because I'm a serious thirty-five-year-old man.

This scene sounds like the start of a joke; there was a body-guard, his intelligence guy, a socialite and her housekeeper in a farmhouse in Glencoe...

The first spin sees Ross with his first foot two spots in. Amelia's next and she's got her hand on the first spot nearest the far edge of where she's standing, alongside Ross.

"Your turn, Liam," Amelia says, and I frown.

"It's a two-man game," I protest, picking up the box and reading the instructions.

Amelia rolls her eyes. "I'm not a man, and I believe you can have three people. Instead of starting where Ross and I are, you have to start on the red side of the mat."

"Was this part of your studies for your law degree?" I tease.

"Photographic memory," she replies, tapping her temple and I laugh.

"Alright, you've worn me down, I'll play, but if my nuts go anywhere near his it's game over, okay?"

For the next five minutes we tangle around one another, until Ross can't move anymore. As soon as he falls over, he's 'disqualified' by Izzy, a task she takes pride in doing, like she was an umpire at Wimbledon. With him out of the game it leaves me and Amelia on the mat alone; her face-up on her hands and feet.

Izzy spins the dial and instructs me, "Right foot blue."

From where I am, I need to straddle Amelia to reach it, but it'll mean I'll be hovering over her. When I steal a glance at Ross, he's already ahead of the game.

"Izzy, I just remembered I need to take down some cable.

Would you come and hold the ladder?" he asks, almost dragging her to her feet, and hurrying her out of the room. I look down at Amelia who is clearly not up to speed on my move, but when I place my leg over hers, we're positioned chest to chest, and hips to hips, with me balancing on one hand and I still have one hand free.

Grinning up at me, she has the best carefree smile I've seen since we've met.

"I've forgotten how much I enjoyed this game," she's says, chuckling.

An unexpected wave of emotion tears through me, and I push her down to the floor. Covering her body with mine, I can't help myself when I grind my cock between her legs. Rising up on my elbows, I cradle her head between my forearms, lean down and gently kiss her nose, her cheek, and all bets are off as soon as I brush her lips with mine.

For the next couple of minutes, we almost get carried away, until I hear Izzy's voice getting nearer, and I pull myself roughly out of reach. Amelia and I separate like two teenagers caught in our parents' bedroom, both breathing hard as we try to appear normal. I glance down at the destroyed twister mat on the floor, and she follows my gaze before we both burst out laughing.

CHAPTER 30

THE POLLS HAVE BEEN CLOSED for almost two hours and it's nearly midnight. Ross and Liam are talking in the dining room, and both Izzy and I are in our beds.

The moment I hear a soft knock on my door my heart skips a beat.

"Are you decent?" Liam asks before he opens it.

"Yes, come in." Shifting from lying on my side, I sit up and watch as he steps into the room and stops at the foot of the bed.

"Want some company?" he asks, nodding towards the bed. My skin flushes but I do my best to let him think I feel casual about his question.

"That would be nice, but I thought you said—"

"I did… and I meant well," he adds, in reference to keeping his professional distance. He chuckles as he toes off his shoes and climbs on the bed beside me. "It's our last night here and I thought we should just spend it in the same room."

He stretches his legs out and leans back, then obviously decides he isn't comfortable. Changing position, he shimmies himself more upright and leans his back against the headboard.

The leg he used to reposition himself stays bent at the knee and his foot is flat on the bed. "How are you holding up?"

I purse my lips. "Not sure… the wine has helped," I say turning to meet his gaze. "That and the distraction of the idiotic Twister game." We both chuckle as he cocks his head from side to side, like he's considering what I've said.

"Wine always helps, as for the game…." He shakes his head as if he still can't believe we all played it, like drunken college kids. I'm sure, had we not been so utterly bored, the game would never have happened. "I should apologise for taking advantage of you like that, but I'd be lying if I said I was sorry."

The way he's staring into my eyes makes my heart swell in my chest. For most of the time we've been here, he's fought his feelings apart from the night we arrived. But there's no mistaking the look of desire in his gaze right now.

"From the way you ravished my mouth, if you had apologised, I'd have called you a liar."

We both laugh, and he reaches out and lifts my arm nearest to him by my wrist, and laces our fingers together. Butterflies take flight in my belly with his simple gesture. "I know we've got this crazy magnetic pull towards one another, but I want you to know that I don't expect anything of you… I mean, I'll understand if you don't feel the same when you're back living your normal life."

"That's not what I want," I say. "I don't go around hooking up with hot men all the time, despite what the papers say."

"So…" he says and turns the top half of his body toward me, and then holds my chin with his finger and thumb, keeping my eyes on him. The way he wants my attention thrills me and a bolt of electricity shoots through me. "You think I'm hot?" He grins because he's caught me saying something I hadn't intended to.

"No, I said I don't hook up with *hot* men, and I *did* hook up with you so…"

His eyes widen at the inference I don't find him attractive. It's a point neither of us can deny since I've been unashamedly hitting on him from day one. Liam throws his head back and lets out a deep, hearty laugh. In an instant, he changes position and straddles me, pinning me to the mattress under the duvet, and begins to tickle my ribs. In an instant I'm screaming with laughter and it feels great. It's an age since I have.

"Say, 'Liam you're the hottest man I've ever seen,'" he says, still tickling me. I'm breathless, I can't even find the breath to tell him to stop, but I try to do what he says because he *is* hot, and something tells me he won't stop until he hears me say it.

"Liam…" I say, laughing so hard I think how unattractive I must look in this state. "You're the hottest…" He doesn't let up, and is tickling me as hard as he was when he first began. "Man I've ever seen," I squeeze out.

He immediately stops tickling me and slumps back on his side of the bed. "There, feel better?" he asks, like he's extracted something painful from me. He turns onto his stomach and stares up into my eyes. "I think this is the weirdest job I've ever had," he admits, chuckling.

"Why?"

"Because I've never played Twister, tickled, or slept with my principle during a job before."

I sense my face flush and suddenly feel shy. Liam's gaze is intense, and my chest is tight from the way he's watching me.

"Believe it or not, I've never become personally involved with anyone I guarded in the past."

I smile. "I'm glad to hear it." My eyes break his gaze, and fall to his lips and my core pulses between my legs. The thought of kissing him, like we did in the sitting room while playing Twister, sends a thrill coursing through me. In the couple of weeks since I've known this man, a deeper connection has grown with him than I've ever felt for any man in my past. Liam has seen the stripped back version of me; an insider's peep at my warts-and-all state of no make-up, mismatched clothing, and my lack of usual finesse. Yet he looks at me like I'm all consuming, and dressed in my Sunday best.

Realising I'm staring I say, "I believe you. I don't know why, but I have complete faith in you. I have from the start of all this. Most would say I have been naïve in letting you whisk me away from my home like you did. But having been here, and seeing the lengths to which you and Ross have gone to protect me, I feel lucky you came into my life when you did."

"Whatever happens after today, I just want to say it's been an absolute privilege to protect you, Amelia."

"What's next?" I ask, and I suppose my question is two-fold; for me and my fate, but with equal importance, the question I ask is about us.

"From a business perspective, we get you out in public. You need a cover story. That little journal or diary you've been keeping gave me the idea for your excuse for disappearing. As I mentioned before, you tell them you had planned to take a couple of weeks out to write a plot for a book, and you'd guessed if your friends knew of your whereabouts, they'd want to visit with you. The place you chose was secluded, and as there was no internet or phone signal you decided to leave your devices at home."

"Sounds like a reasonable excuse. Although, I can't write a book."

"That's what ghost writers are for," he replies. "Do you think all those celebrities have written their memoirs? Who says you have to publish one anyway? But forget that for a moment, if those who would harm you think you've written something no one has seen, it could also suggest that whatever you wrote would be made public if anything were to happen to you."

"You're a genius," I say, reaching up and cupping his cheek in my hand. A zap of electricity runs through me and having him here on my bed is enough to make me feel regretful that our time in this farmhouse is coming to an end.

"Do you want to get into bed?" I ask. I can hear the hope in my voice, and I feel unabashed in my attempt to spend this last night with him inside me.

"No, I'll lie on top of the covers and hold you if that's alright? I just think that you have a lot to think about, and I don't want to confuse those thoughts any further right now."

"When this is over, I'd really like to get to know you properly," I say, because telling him I want to spend time with him feels odd since we've been locked inside this house for two weeks already.

"Put the light off and try to get some sleep. Tomorrow's going to be a busy day," he says, changing the subject, and I wonder if this is him feeling his work is done.

Perhaps he thinks he's made some mistakes and now he's pulling away.

I do as he says and feel him shift on the bed until his warm breath wafts over my cheek. Lying so close in the dark like this feels even more intimate than anything sexual we've done. I wonder if it's because without light my other senses are heightened.

"Like I said, Amelia, I'm not saying no, I'm saying we'll see how you feel tomorrow when you know you've got your life back."

"You doubt how I'll feel?" I ask, my voice quieter.

"Right this minute, no I don't. But that could be because you've come to depend on me here. How we've been living during this past couple of weeks could have given you tunnel vision."

"Tunnel vision?"

"Yes, your focus has been channelled to the circumstances you've found yourself in. And as we had a connection, be that lust or something deeper, it could have made you develop more of a false infatuation you might find isn't there when we leave here."

"I don't believe that's what's happening between us. From the moment I saw you I was drawn to you. You don't get goosebumps and that electrically wired feeling because you're confined in a house with someone. Do you feel that's what's happened for you?"

Liam's fingers tighten slightly around mine and he shakes his head. "No, I don't. I know what my feelings are; it's not as if I haven't tried to keep my distance from you. There may have been times when you've thought I've behaved indifferent towards you but trying to maintain those boundaries has enabled me to do my job. It hasn't been easy. I just don't want you to wake up in the morning to find Scotland is still part of the union, and then feel obligated to me, after what you've been through. In the beginning, everything happened so fast, I'd hate for you to regret our relationship later."

"I'm not one for regrets; there's never been a single thing that I've done with you that I'd take back if I had the choice. A connection like ours has never happened to me before. And I don't just mean this insane chemistry I feel around you either. I've never had someone who knows instinctively what I'm thinking, or acts selflessly to make sure I'm taken care of. There has never been one day where you've made me feel like you see me as 'just another job.'"

"That's the last thing you are, and we're not charging for this gig. What we did here amounts to our civic duty to ensure a crime wasn't committed. It's not like you chose what you were born into. Since the moment Ross and I found out why Donaldson wanted you protected, our role changed to fit a much bigger picture. Our first duty is to you, but Ross and I both have skills gained from our time in the military to know the unrest Donaldson could bring to Scotland. I'm surprised the Crown put the focus on you. I'd have thought taking Donaldson out of the equation would have been a much better way for central government to resolve this issue.

"Agreed, that horrible man is a law unto himself. Some people are humble in power and some are reckless with that privilege. I fear Harry Donaldson wouldn't be a good prime minister for Scotland. Also, I insist on paying. Setting all of this up and being here must have cost you both a fortune … and I want to pay for the people Ross had help out too."

"Ross and I aren't poor, just common people; doing an uncommon job."

"Believe me when I say, there's nothing common about you, Liam."

CHAPTER 31

*L*iam
1st August

BEING in bed with someone I want more than anything, but I refuse to allow myself to indulge in, takes more will power than I ever knew. Nothing would give me greater pleasure than to strip bare and slide my hard cock inside Amelia. It's our last night here, and as relieved as I am her perilous situation is nearly over, I'm not sure I'm ready to not see her every day.

It's such an odd feeling to want to remain here with her, when I'm sick to my back teeth with the beautiful scenery outside. I always used to say I'd never get tired of staring at this part of Scotland in all its raw, natural beauty, but I am. If I never see another Scottish mountain again this year, it'll be too soon. Living inside four walls, with limited supplies, and not much in the way of entertainment, has felt tedious for most of the time.

"This is so hard. I want you." Amelia's whisper seems louder than usual in the dark.

"I know," I say, sliding my hand up her body and finding her cheek. "Trust me; I'm right there with you. Go to sleep," I insist, thinking it was a bad idea to come in here and lie with her like this. Then again, I've never been one for making situations easy for myself.

I stroke her hair and feel her edge closer under the covers. Lying on top of the duvet is the only sure-fire way I won't demand more from her. My hand slides down from her head to her arm that's outside the cover, and I gently stroke her soft skin. Goosebumps radiate over it, and I know I'm affecting her. We're not talking anymore, and eventually she settles, and I hear her breathing deepen, then I know she has fallen asleep.

Edging my way off the bed, I leave the room and go to see Ross. When I walk into the room, he's resting his chin on his forearms, on the table, as he watches the results of the vote.

"How is it going?" I'm eager to know our plan has worked.

Ross leans back in his chair and meets my gaze. "The *no* votes are only two percent ahead, so it's still neck and neck at the moment. Some of the larger populated area's votes are still being counted though."

"Jesus, that's tight," I reply. "I hope we've done enough."

"Oh, have faith; I'm fairly confident Donaldson's done enough damage to himself by poking his dick south of the border."

Staring at the screen is making me antsy, so I go and make us both a cup of tea. When I come back Ross tells me three more have declared and the result is now fifty three percent to forty seven percent for the *nos* of all the votes so far.

"Dare I go outside and start packing the van?"

He glances at the clock. "Crack on, we're out of here in a few hours. They should be finished in an hour or two, and either way we'll know."

For an hour I traipse back and forth, piling everything that's left in the back of the van. Thankfully it's not much, since we've eaten most of the food Ross brought. My lungs feel as if they are bursting due to all the fresh early morning air I'm breathing in for the first time in weeks. A breeze sends a chill through my body.

When the packing is done, I lock the van up, close the barn door and head back to check out what's happening with the vote.

"Yes, ya beauty!" Ross exclaims and I run into the room in time to see him punching the air. "It's a no vote! There are still three voting areas to come in, but even if anyone eligible to vote did, they don't have enough people to make a difference."

Relief flows through me, and I stare at Ross for a long moment before I speak. "Right. Next part of the plan. I'm going to speak to Amelia when I wake her up. You're heading back to Balloch where you'll put Izzy on the train to Queen Street Station, in Glasgow. Book her an onwards train to Edinburgh, and she can go home with the story we've devised for Amelia's return."

"Did I hear my name being mentioned?"

We both turn and look at Izzy standing at the door. She's in a flannel nightie down to her ankles and a night cap over her hair. I chuckle, because seeing her makes me feel like I've stepped back in time.

Izzy pouts, clasping her hands in front of her. "In a way I'm sad that the nos have won, but relieved because it helps to keep Amelia safe." It's a sentiment I'm confident all four of us feel.

* * *

Leaving the farmhouse is a mixture of relief and regret. As strange a mix as we are, we've bonded during our time in Glencoe. Ross and Izzy set off at seven this morning, with Amelia and me not far behind.

When we reached Lochearnhead Amelia knew enough of the journey to question my route. "Why are we heading east, shouldn't we be going south here?"

I glance over at her. "We would be if we were going straight back to Edinburgh, but there's one last detail I want to cover before you get there. I'm taking you to the Glen Eagles Hotel for the night. There we're going to be 'discovered' and if it goes the way I plan, then the police will check you out."

"Clever, but I don't have any suitable attire for the Glen Eagles Hotel."

I stare down at the black slacks, neatly pressed by Izzy, and the pale blue sweater she's wearing. "You look perfect to me. Besides we're not coming out of the room until tomorrow morning. By that time, Izzy will be home, and the focus will be on her. It'll look like she's been granted leave while you've been away and she's back before you."

"Am I to hide then?"

"Think of it as a night in a plush hotel with great room service, champagne instead of wine for a change, and a hot man to keep you company," I say. "Tomorrow, we'll go down to breakfast like we're oblivious the press has been reporting you missing."

"Cunning," she replies, nodding and a smile spreads on her lips. "You really have thought of everything... except paracetamol."

"Condoms... No one thought of those," I remind her. She chuckles and I know our relationship has shifted; it has from the moment we stepped out of the farmhouse and into the car.

"What do you want to happen next, Amelia?" It's a reasonable question, because once the Crown and the Palace know she's no risk to them she's free to do what she wants.

"I want to speak to James."

Her answer surprises me, but it makes perfect sense that she'd want the reassurance from the horse's mouth for herself.

"In that case I think I should be there." My response is immediate. Her eyes meet my gaze, and immediately soften when they lock with mine.

"You really are my knight in shining armour, aren't you?"

"Just doing my job," I respond.

"I call bull on that Mr McKenna." Her reply is playful, and I can hear a lighter tone in her voice.

"Let's say I'm dotting the *I*s and crossing the *T*s to ensure no harm comes to you."

We arrive at the hotel in Auchterarder and it's just after nine in the morning. I leave Amelia in the car, tucked out of sight, and sign in. In my casual clothes and with the scruff on my chin, it would take a detective to connect me to the suave looking man in the Row Nolan suit, paraded around in the better picture swapped out for my passport photo by the press.

After paying for an extra night in the hotel due to the early check-in time, I've got the key and I'm heading to the carpark again. Amelia is sitting looking down at her lap, and without talking to her I can see she's nervous. I open the door and see she's been writing in her diary again.

"Come on, beautiful, we're all checked in and our room is ready and waiting."

A nervous smile quirks her lips, and she stuffs the diary in her handbag. Exiting the car, she walks one step behind me.

She's careful to keep her head down. When the lift doors open there's no one inside. I glance towards Amelia and she looks relieved. I am too, if I'm honest.

"After you," I say gesturing her inside. Our room is on the second floor near the fire exit and overlooking the golf course. I wander over to the window and stare out for a second before drawing the curtains. "I don't know about you, but as wonderful as the wide-open space is outside, I'm tired of looking at grass."

Amelia nods before she pulls her sweater over her head. She's wearing a top that's my favourite on her. It's green in colour and that makes her eyes more vivid, and it really clings seductively to her curves. She kicks off her shoes and flops backwards onto the bed.

"Oh. My. God, this bed is orgasmic," she informs me.

She's writhing around and arching her back, her tits straining towards the ceiling. My cock stirs in my boxers, like it has hundreds of times during the past couple of weeks whenever she's made a sexy little noise or done something that flaunted a part of her gorgeous body. I must have spaced out with my thoughts when a long groan of pleasure escapes from her throat and drags my focus back to her. She's stretched out flat this time, her arms above her head. A strip of the silky skin on her flat stomach is visible where her top has ridden up.

"Damn this feels so luxurious after that lumpy four poster bed." Her action makes me stare, enthralled, and I'm frozen to the spot, enjoying her little show. As provocative as it looks, I doubt she has a clue what she's doing to me inside.

Standing off the bed again, she wanders over to me and places her hand on my chest. As delicate as it is, I feel the weight of it against my pecs, and the heat of her palm scorches an imprint over my heart. It's an innocent touch but the feelings running through me are anything but.

"I'm starving, can we order some food and drink?" she asks, looking up at me with a glint of lust in her eyes.

I clear my throat because my mouth is as dry as the desert, and I'm not sure I can speak because my tongue is stuck to the roof of my mouth.

I clear my throat and try. "It's all in hand. I ordered something to be brought up by room service within the next hour," I say in a gruff voice.

"Oh, what are we having?" she asks looking up at me through her lashes. I have the strongest urge to kiss her, so I give in, dip my head and I do. It's a gentle kiss and I pull away. I need a shower, and although I'm desperate to be inside her I want to do this right.

"I thought I'd order a fruit platter, a continental breakfast with pastries, a couple of avocado and mango smoothies, and Bucks Fizz. I don't know about you, but I've been craving fresh fruit and vegetables for over a week now."

"Can you order some champagne? We could lie back and binge on some movies today. Thank you for giving me this one last day alone with you."

"The pleasure is mine and your suggestion sounds perfect, but let's take a bath first after breakfast, and if we're going to do this properly, we should be naked in that bed."

Suddenly I'm not hungry; not for food anyway, and now that we're here and her safety is going to be assured, I'm done denying the burning desire that's almost killed me. Since that first night at Glencoe, I've been dreaming of having her again. That night we shared filled with passion has hung between us like a noose around my neck, and as each day has gone by since, it's been slowly strangling me.

My thoughts, which are normally sequential and orderly, are conflicted; on one hand my intentions are great. I want to give Amelia valuable time to think; time to reject me out of hand I suppose. But this morning when it came down to it, I couldn't let her go without this extra day to explore this undeniable, almost visceral connection we have, before the madness of whatever is coming for her begins. That's why I had Ross book this hotel for me before he left us.

Now that she's standing in front of me and there's nothing holding us back, I'm still hesitant, which is a new feeling for me. Usually, I'm dominant with my sexual partners, but this is different; *she's* different. This time, it's not about sex with another woman and simply racing towards a release. It isn't only lust that's driving me towards her, it's more than that; real feelings that make my need for this to be perfect.

melia
1st August

A CHUCKLE ESCAPES MY LIPS, despite my heart pounding as I hide behind the bathroom door; I don't know whether I find this funny or I'm feeling slightly hysterical. Perhaps it's a bit of both. Liam tips the room service staff, closes the bedroom door, and gives me a soft knock signalling for me to come out.

"Who'd have thought at twenty-eight years old this party girl would be hiding out in a hotel bathroom?" I ask with a bravado I don't quite feel. The crooked smile Liam gives me in reply relieves my tension and makes my heart flutter in my chest.

"Ah, so you normally don't hide when you're holed up in a hotel with some hot man?"

I love when he's playful like this. I've seen this side of him a few times but it's far rarer than I'd like. "I hid because you're *not* hot, remember? Can't have a woman with my reputation linked to some guy that's only mediocre," I respond.

He picks up a peach from the fruit platter and wraps his mouth around the flesh. "You know what I think?" He reaches for the TV remote but stops abruptly. A guttural groan tears from his throat at the taste of the fresh produce, and it makes my core pulse.

"No." My voice is sharper, the word is rushed in my attempt to hide what the erotic sight does to me, of him consuming the piece of fruit that looks small in his large hand. I tell myself my reaction is because I haven't been laid for over two weeks, and the last time I was, that talented mouth devoured every inch of my flesh.

When our eyes meet, Liam smiles and I'm not sure whether he's smiling because he's caught me staring, or if it's an innocent reaction because he feels happy to be here.

"I think you're totally into me," he states, and when I say nothing, I'm sure I simply confirm his words. "Come here," he says sitting down on the bed and patting the mattress beside him. I do as he says, my heart racing because when I sit and our gazes collide again, his pupils are dilated. "Taste," he says holding the peach towards me. I do as he says and he's right, the fruit bursts with flavour after we've not eaten any fresh fruit in over a week.

"Mm," I moan, and instantly his mouth is on mine and I'm being shoved back onto the bed. With no effort he climbs to hover over me. I still have my bite of peach, until Liam fishes it from my mouth into his with his tongue. Breaking the kiss, he pulls back to look at me, still chewing.

"I said taste, not bite," he chastises, grabbing my wrists and pinning them to the mattress above my head. "God, you're so beautiful," he tells me, his gaze trailing over my face. The truth in his eyes makes me fall that little bit more for him. "You have no idea how tortured I've been these past two weeks. Knowing how you feel beneath me and trying not to take you in so many ways has been the most painful experience of my life."

"Me too," I admit, my chest heaves for air under the weight of his stare, as he takes me in at his leisure.

"It's taken everything in me not to take what I want and devour you."

"Devour," I demand, hearing how brazen and determined I am. I don't care how I sound, I'm not leaving this room until he's given me what I want: all of him.

Liam chuckles. "You could at least make me work for it," he jokes and removes his hands from my wrists to skim them down the skin on my arms and then my sides. "Jesus, Amelia." His words stop when he leans down and peppers kisses all over my neck. When his lips touch my skin, my body is an instant contradictory mixture of hot and cold; my flesh burning under his skilled plump lips, in contrast to bursting shivers of delight running freely down my spine. I can't lie still and my lower body arches up towards him, seeking greater contact. It's like he understands I need more and drops his hips to mine. He's hard; so hard, and his breathing is ragged when he grinds his erect cock against my pubic bone.

"Liam?" His name sounds breathy when it falls involuntarily from my lips. The question it asks is why are you making me wait?

When he hears his name, the controlled man is back in the room. He pulls himself away from me and steps off the bed, staring down. "In my mind this happens so differently," he says running his hands through his hair, and shaking his head as he strips himself out of his jeans and pulls his T-shirt over his head. For a second, he stands in his athletic, tight boxers before he slips them down. His amazing cock bounces from the confines of his underwear and points in my direction. It's huge and his circumcised head is proud.

"It does?" I ask, as he reaches down and unfastens the button on my trousers before dragging them down my legs.

"Yeah, I wanted this to be slow and controlled, everything you deserve, but I think we're just going to fuck first, and the tenderness I want to show you will have to wait." Hearing how raspy his voice is, and how hungry he is for me matches my feelings exactly. It's the last thing he says before we're a tangle of lips and teeth, grabbing hands and tongues; exploring each other like we want but were too polite to do before.

Of all the kisses I've ever had in my life, none compares to how Liam kisses me. His mouth wipes all thoughts in my head, and his taste reaches places in my body I didn't know were alive before. Sparks course through me, flushing my skin, while I'm drenched between my legs.

"You're soaking wet," he says, confirming this after minutes of torment where his hands skated near but avoided my most intimate area. His fingers enter me, and they send a current of need running through me which is almost unbearable. But it's a relief to finally have something of him inside me. "I want to taste you and fuck you at the same time, yet I know that's impossible," he mumbles, as his fingers thrust in a rhythm that threatens to make me come.

Without warning he pulls his fingers out and sucks them into his mouth. "Oh, damn, you taste amazing," he mumbles around them. Keeping them in his mouth, he grabs his shaft with his free hand, and begins pumping his fist back and forth; it's an unhurried yet deliberate action.

"Spread your legs, you're more than ready for me," he tells me, and his voice is more masterful and demanding than I've ever heard it before.

I do what he orders me to, and he positions himself

where I want him. Sliding his forearms under my knees he pulls me towards him, and I immediately feel his wet tip glid over my entrance.

"I likely won't be gentle," he warns. "But if I hurt you, tell me." It's the only warning I get as he pushes himself steadily inside me and doesn't stop until he bottoms out. "Fuck," he says when I gasp in reaction to the raw need he displays to have me. "I'm sorry." He buries his face in my neck and my hips begin to move. "Did I hurt you?" he asks, concerned, as he lifts his head and stares down at me.

"Not at all, it feels incredible," I say, my hips gyrating gently in my effort to make him move.

When he's confident he isn't hurting me, he thrusts into me fast and slow, his technique a mixture of raw lust and reining back into gently coaxing, until my core tightens, and my orgasm explodes. White lights flash behind my eyes as my brain performs a mini meltdown I know I'll remember for days.

"Liam!" I cry out as I open my eyes, and he smiles on hearing me. I'm still coming, while he moves my shaking legs from his arms, and he rests the back of my knees over his shoulders. He leans in and kisses me; this one is slow and sensual. We haven't kissed that many times, but each time we have, it has felt different.

When I came, he slowed his pace right down, but now that my orgasm is ebbing, he's starting to quicken his movements again. In this position he feels so deep, thick and hard.

My walls pulse around him and he groans. "Damn, Amelia, you feel so tight... so good," he pulls out and moves onto his back, pulling me on top of him. Reaching up, he smooths his hands down my sides and grabs my hips. He flashes me a sexy smile and my gaze locks in with his. "Ride me," he tells me, and it's all the encouragement I need.

Gyrating and bouncing on his cock lets me take control

of the pace, while Liam pays attention to sucking both breasts, and circling my clit. "God this feels good," I confess.

This time Liam surprises me when he realises I'm about to come a second or two before I do. He quickly grabs my throat and squeezes it a little. "Do it," he orders and immediately I do. "Jesus," he blurts in reaction to how hard I squeeze his cock from inside.

Immediately his head drops back onto the bed, but without taking his eyes off me he comes. Hot jets of his seed pour from his body into mine in short, rhythmic pulses, and when he's given me all that he has I collapse in a heap over his chest.

$\mathscr{L}$iam
1st August

MY LIMP COCK slides out of Amelia and I realise I must have dozed off. She must have fallen asleep at the same time as me, and she's still asleep on my chest. It wasn't the longest sex session I've ever had, but it felt like one of the most intense. There is no denying the connection we have because it makes the sexual contact between us insane.

Usually, I'm not one who displays affection after sex, yet here I am drawing lazy circles on her back because I can't bear her lying here atop me and not using this opportunity to touch her. Her skin is so silky smooth and feminine, and she smells delicious; her citrus shampoo and the scent of her beautiful body surrounds me. I inhale deeply, savouring the moment before she wakes.

"Mm," she moans softly as she changes position from sitting astride me, and lays the length of me. She's made no move to climb off me, just make herself more comfortable. A smile curves my lips when I realise this.

"You okay?" I ask, lifting my head off the pillow to kiss the top of hers.

"I am now," she says, stretching a little lazily. She lifts her head and presses a kiss over my heart. "I've been listening to your heartbeat," she tells me.

"Yeah, did it give you any advice?"

She nods her head twice. "It did," she says, smiling up at me.

"Oh, don't tell me, it told you to run, get away from this dangerous man."

She frowns. "It did no such thing. It said, I can trust you, and I believe it."

"Ah, I see," I say nodding slowly; "it's smarter than I thought because you can."

"I'm hungry," she says in an instant change of subject, and pushes herself off me. "I need to quickly freshen up and then I'm going to scoff down most of these pastries."

"Only most of them?" I tease, shifting to sit up in the bed as I watch her gorgeous, round arse disappear into the bathroom. I hear the water running and after a few minutes she comes back out wearing a bathrobe.

"What did you say?"

"You said *most* of the pastries," I remind her.

"Oh that? I hate apricots, and that squidgy lemon stuff, so feel free to have those ones."

"You hate apricots, yet you ate my peach?" I ask, thinking they weren't that far apart in taste.

"I've never been partial to peaches either for that matter, but the way you were eating that fruit looked like you were thinking filthy things." I throw my head back and laugh because she isn't far wrong. "See," she remarks, wagging her finger. "I knew it."

We eat the pastries, drink the smoothies for our health, and drink the Bucks Fizz because it's all here. Now we're lying on the bed together, her head on my chest, and we're watching an action and adventure movie on TV.

My mind wanders to what may happen when we get back to Edinburgh, and I know that the time has come to prepare Amelia for dealing with the press, and to some extent the establishment. At least the vote for independence is no. As much as it pains me to say as a Scotsman, but from Amelia's perspective it's positive anyway.

When the movie is finished, we shower and lie in bed in our bathrobes again. She tells me about her life growing up in Edinburgh, her private school days at Gordonstoun School in Elgin until she was eighteen, followed by a three-month enrolment at a Swiss finishing school. It confirms, again, to me Amelia's world is a vastly different one to my own.

I grew up in Tomatin in the Highlands, the son of a gamekeeper and the local primary school teacher. Having your mum as your teacher is character building. Secondary school was less eventful and when I left at sixteen there were very few opportunities for careers in that part of the world, unless you were into farming, game keeping, forestry or any profession associated with it.

As I saw it back then, the army was my ticket to the outside world, and I can't deny it gave me skills I'd have never otherwise acquired, but after two tours of Iraq and Afghanistan I knew I had to get out.

Ross and I kept each other sane during the last critical assignment we were given, but it wasn't until we found ourselves in Civvy Street that our partnership in business blossomed. He had been doing some work for his brother-in-law – who is some kind of spook – at the time, although, to this day, neither of us knows who he works for. He somehow guided Ross and me as we extended our individual skillsets, until we became who we are today.

Over dinner I admit, again, to Amelia that her idea of asking James to meet her is a good one. Using James to convey her loyalty to Queen Sofia is the most direct, yet indirect way. I suggest she asks for an audience with his mother. If Amelia is as close as I think she is to the royal family, I can't see how the Queen would refuse her. However, I will insist on accompanying her to the palace if this request is granted. I'm still her protector, even if our relationship has been somewhat compromised by my inability to keep my dick in my pants around her.

Amelia discovers the hairdryer in the wardrobe, and decides to wash and blow-dry her hair because she's going to be seen in the press when she arrives back in Edinburgh tomorrow. She has no idea that the first time she's seen in public will be here at the hotel. I'm taking her to breakfast tomorrow, and I'm banking on someone recognising her and calling the police. I'm ensuring her comeback is high-profile and no one can miss her. This in itself will give her some extra security. No one would dare try anything knowing the world is watching her.

While she's applying make up in the bathroom, I put in a call to Ross on his last burner phone, from the phone in the hotel room.

"Did Izzy get home okay?"

"She did. It took Lottie all of twenty-five minutes to turn up," he informs me.

I crumple my brow. "How did she know?"

"Bribed someone at the front desk to tell her when someone showed up."

I shake my head. "Can't get good staff these days."

"Yeah, but she said he would never have told anyone

else… I think she may have given him a blow job or something." We both chuckle.

"Weren't you hot for her?" I ask.

"Uh-huh, as a one nighter, sure I was. You saw the tits on her. Not interested in anything else… unlike you. How's it going up there?" he probes, playfully.

"It's going," I reply, unwilling to be drawn into a conversation about my sex life with Amelia. I like to think I'm a gentleman most of the time.

Ross laughs. "Still keeping your lips tight, eh?"

"You know it," I reply. "All set for tomorrow. Make sure the press is outside when she gets home."

"No problem, they're being tipped off in the morning. By the time the news story is out, it'll take you a while to get back here to Edinburgh anyway."

"Yeah, true," I say, and hear the hairdryer stop. "Okay, I'll be in touch, mate, thanks for everything." I place the receiver back on the cradle as Amelia comes into view. She looks stunning, and her skin is glowing despite it not seeing sunlight for a couple of weeks.

"Well, she says?" gesturing at her hair.

"That was a waste of time," I say, nodding back at her, while looking at the perfect long curls she's sculped.

"You don't like it?" she asks, a note of disappointment in her tone.

"Love it, but you're going to have to do it all again by the time I've finished with you tonight."

"That sounds like a chore I'll look forward to," she says, smiling widely as her eyes sparkle at the unspoken suggestion of what I have in mind.

"That's as well because when I look at that delicious body of yours and this huge, ginormous bed, I know no matter how long we are here I won't have enough of you."

There isn't a hint of shyness when Amelia walks over to me. She slides her hand inside my bathrobe and cups my balls. Instantly an electric current soars through my body and my previously limp cock immediately stands to attention.

"You like that?" she whispers, her soft hand gently rolling my balls between her fingers.

"So-so," I say, playfully. "It's one thing to tickle this *hot* guy's balls, but I think if you really want to get his attention, you'd have to be blind not to notice the far more impressive appendage down there."

Amelia's head rolls back as she laughs at my corny tease, but she takes my hint in all good faith, smiles wickedly, and drops down to her knees.

CHAPTER 34

 melia
2nd August

Stepping into the lift, I catch sight of myself in the mirrored walls. Outwardly I look composed, inside I feel sick with nerves. The only reason I'm doing this is because I have complete trust in Liam's ability to keep me safe.

"Don't be nervous, darlin'. Everything's going to be okay."

I smile at his words and look up at him. His gaze is serious, and I don't see the same concern in his eyes as I've seen in mine.

"I hope you're right," I mumble, as the lift door opens and we're out in the foyer. I steal a furtive glance around, but no one is paying attention to us. Relief washes through me, but my heart is still racing. A weird feeling of impending doom settles upon me.

"Come on, darlin', this way," Liam says as he guides me to the Strathearn restaurant for breakfast. We're greeted at the door by the head waiter who looks at Liam for a long moment, then he looks at me. He studies his reservation book and checks off a name I don't recognise. I immediately know Ross had something to do with this booking.

We are led to a table that's right in the corner but facing out into the restaurant. The size of the table is far too big for the two of us, considering there are plenty of tables for two sitting empty.

Liam gestures for me to sit on the plush corner suite, and follows me on the same side. "Coffee? Tea?" the gentleman asks.

"Tea for the lady, coffee for me," Liam replies.

"Toast? White, brown, or seeded bread?"

"Seeded," we both say because we've been eating whatever Izzy has made, but now there's a real choice, we make the most of it.

The head waiter leaves the table and signals to a waitress to come to him. He speaks and she turns to look at me, but when she sees me watching her, she turns her back."

"I think they've recognised me," I whisper, while I casually pick up my napkin and throw it over my knee. My movements may look casual but inside I'm a mess.

With a pleading look, Liam says, "Relax, trust me, everything is going to be okay,"

I take a breath and try to do as he says because I do trust him. After living with him for the past couple of weeks I believe he'd lay down his life for me.

"Are you ready for me to take your order?" The girl who was watching me before is standing at the table but I didn't notice her approach.

"Yes," I blurt, touching my silverware and instantly knowing my movements are jerky.

Liam puts a hand on my knee, then finds the hand I've dropped to my lap and holds it.

"We'll both have the full Scottish please," Liam tells her calmly. "Both with fried eggs, I like mine runny, but my lady likes hers hard." He looks at me, and a smile quirks his lips. I find myself grinning even though I'm frightened half to death.

"God, I feel as if I'm going to be sick," I admit, and Liam reaches up to cup my cheek.

"You've got this, Amelia. *We've* got this. I'm just hoping I get to eat my breakfast before the police get here. It looks delicious," he says, glancing over at a table where a single guy is sitting tucking into his food. His remark makes me chuckle. "That's my girl," he says, and I stare into his gorgeous blue eyes.

"Am I?" I ask, because I don't know what we are to each other, or if I'm going to see him again when all of this is over. *Correction when all of this is over and I'm still alive.*

The breakfast arrives and Liam gives a sigh of relief without answering my question.

I gasp. "You really were worried the police would interrupt your breakfast?"

He grins. "Dead right I was. Do you know how much bed and breakfast costs here? If the police had turned up, I'd be asking for mine to go."

I laugh and it's loud; louder than I expected it to be. *It must be due to my nerves,* I think. Liam leans in and kisses me. It's unexpected but it feels perfect for the moment.

"Eat, it may be a long morning," he warns, leaning back and pointing at my plate with his fork. "We're a couple remember?" he says, reminding me of the story I'm going to tell. Part of it is a story, but the part about us is still blurry.

I manage to eat two pieces of bacon and half a slice of toast that Liam buttered for me.

"You don't want that sausage?" he asks before stabbing it with his fork. He polishes it off, and another piece of toast, before he places his hand over mine to stop me fiddling with the butter knife I haven't used. "Do you want anything else?"

I shake my head. "No, I'm too nervous."

"All right, let's get this over with," he says, standing. He moves away from the table so that I can get out on the same side as him.

"I thought we were waiting for the police?"

"They've been here for a good ten minutes," he informs me.

"They have?"

He chuckles. "Yeah, this isn't a Wetherspoon's pub, Amelia. The relationship between a hotel like this and the local police is much more discreet.

"Wetherspoon's?" I ask.

Liam laughs and shakes his head. "I'll take you there sometime, and let you compare the difference."

"Are you asking me on a date?" I ask, wondering what the hell I'm focusing on this for, when the police are waiting to grill me.

"If you're lucky," he replies. "Let's see how lucky you are after today is over."

$\mathcal{L}$iam
2nd August

THE LOOK of surprise on Amelia's face is entirely convincing when the police interrupt us as we're leaving the restaurant. They do their job well in separating us; the female police officer going off with Amelia and the sergeant, while the third officer, an overweight man in his mid-fifties who looks nearing retirement, is left to detain me.

I pretend to protest at our separation when he ushers me into the cocktail lounge without my girl, while Amelia is taken behind the reception desk and into an office. Normally, I'd have put up a fight and not let them separate me from my principle, but this is Auchterarder and Amelia and I are sticking to our script.

When I see the officer tasked to guard me asking for a cup of coffee, I wonder if the two police patrol cars that have turned up represent the whole local force on duty this morning. I know the number of law officers in the Highlands of Scotland, on any one shift, can tend to be light in numbers.

PC Munro collects his coffee from the waiter and walks towards me, balancing the coffee on his saucer. His tongue is out in concentration as he tries not to spill it. He places it on the table beside me, pulls out a seat and squeezes himself into it. He's got beads of sweat on his brow and he's done very little since he's been here as far as I know.

"Now then," he says taking out his old school black notebook. He fishes a pen out of his pocket and clicks it several times. "What is your relationship to Miss Campbell?" he asks, pen poised to write.

"Why?" I ask sounding indignant as I stare him down. When he says nothing, I eventually sigh. "She's my girlfriend," I reply, still staring him straight in the eye as I will him to contradict me. My statement isn't technically true, but we do have some kind of relationship, although I can't define it right now because it's too soon to know what we are. We've been forced into this fucked up situation which has prevented us from exploring *us*... If there is an 'us' at all.

"Girlfriend? Does she know this?" he scoffs, and I can see how he thinks we'd make an odd couple. It isn't that I'm not a good-looking man, I know this without being vain, but with her breeding I can see how he would wonder if I'm with her because she likes her men rough. I consider my current unshaven face, faded jeans and blue T-shirt. I do fit that mould, I decide.

"Do you know the whole country has been looking for Miss Campbell?" he asks, coming closer. I sit back in my seat, assaulted by a whiff of halitosis, mingling with the coffee, on his breath.

I scrunch my brow. "Really? What for?" I ask, sounding amazed as I give the performance of my life.

He doesn't answer my question but poses one of his own. "Where have you been?"

"In a house in Glencoe. We went there for solitude so that Amelia could write."

He smirks knowingly. "Without her phone and laptop?" He thinks he's caught me out in a lie.

"Yes, she's handwritten a journal. Surely you know there's no point in taking devices to the glens. When was the last time you had a signal up there?"

He considers my answer and nods. "Well, we'll know soon enough if your story fits when my colleagues come back. Miss Campbell will tell us the truth of the matter."

"Indeed," I say stretching my arm along the velvet seating and stare towards him innocently.

When he realises I'm not going to talk of my own volition, he stands and moves to the door.

"Don't go anywhere," he warns, but as he's blocking the only door, I think he'd know if I tried.

Fifteen minutes later, Amelia comes rushing in; the police are standing behind her. She's holding her cheeks like she's embarrassed and she's laughing. "Isn't this ludicrous? Did they tell you what's been going on while we've been away?"

"Not much, except people have been looking for you. Didn't you tell everyone we were going away?"

She shrugged. "I know I should have," she says in a pleading tone, "but you know how everyone is, there would have been demands to know where I was going, and we wanted this time alone."

"I get that," I say, my eyes softening towards her, and I cup her cheek. We portray the perfect couple and I bend, pressing my lips to hers.

"Who has been looking for her?" I ask, ignoring that the policeman had said the whole country is looking for her, like I've accepted it's an exaggeration.

KAREN FRANCES

"Everyone. They think you abducted me," she informs me, covering her mouth with her hand, and she giggles.

"I did, darlin'. Two weeks in the wilderness alone with you has been fun."

"No, they really do think you've abducted me," she insists, and I stare at her like the penny is only just dropping.

Eventually, the police accept that Amelia's in no danger. They leave with their apologies, satisfied we are a couple. Afterwards we pack up our belongings, get in the car and we head back towards Edinburgh.

Less than twenty minutes into our journey there's a news bulletin declaring Amelia's been found, that she's safe and the search for her has all been a misunderstanding. We chuckle as the story is relayed and there's even a short segment of the police sergeant on the phone telling the radio station that it's all been a misinterpretation of the truth.

* * *

AMELIA SPOTS the reporters from halfway down the street as we drive up towards her building. "I'll park out front and you can give a statement." I clasp her fingers in mine and kiss her knuckles. "It's nearly over, Amelia, you've been incredibly brave. I know how anxious you must be feeling, but everything's going to be fine."

As we draw up to the building camera bulbs flash even though it's daytime. It's a grey day in Edinburgh and there's not much natural light.

"Miss Campbell, can you tell us where you've been?" someone shouts before she's fully out of the car. She steps out on the pavement and I close the door quietly. She reaches for my hand and I take it. I give it a squeeze of reassurance.

Looking directly towards the press, Amelia smiles sweetly and waves her free hand. "Wow, what a welcome home. I'm

264

so sorry you have all been on what seems like an amazing wild goose chase. I had no idea I was... missing." She shrugs, holding her hand out. "I happened to mention to Liam I was thinking of writing a book, and he suggested a writing retreat. I thought it was a great idea. As I have all summer free, I thought it would give me some time to collect my thoughts. So... we went off the beaten track for a while that's all."

"Without your mobile phone?"

"You know I didn't take that with me?" she asks, her mood shifting in a heartbeat as she turns on the reporter that's asked the question, a scowl on her face.

"Left all your devices the report says," he probes.

Her nostrils flare. "What report? And someone would know this *how*? Has someone been inside my apartment? What business is it of anyone's what I take or don't take from my home?" The change in her tone is abrupt and in keeping with someone who has had their privacy violated. She looks and sounds pissed off.

I glance towards her and she turns her head to look me in the eye. Pissed off is a great look on her, even when she's pretending.

Addressing the reporter again she says, "I'll have to look into this. If you must know, I left all my electronics behind because I knew there was no signal where we were going and I wanted to write the old fashioned way. Plus..." She sounds hesitant. "Some of my friends are so persuasive and insistent, I knew they'd wear me down and want to join us. My partner, Liam, and I wanted time to ourselves with no interruptions." She looks for me and I step forward, wrapping my arm around her waist.

"Where did you go?" asks another reporter.

"Where else would I, a Campbell, choose to take soul searching reflection, other than near the battlefield where my ancestors fought?" There's a glare in her eye now, and it's the right reaction to have if she had simply been on holiday and arrived back to the third degree from the press. "If you'll excuse me, everyone. I want to thank all those who've been concerned, but I think when you look at this gorgeous man beside me most would understand my need for alone time, and the lack of my mobile phone."

Without waiting for anyone to come back at her statement, she turns with me and we walk inside the building. "Can you park the car outside in the garage, Edward?" she asks one of the two security guards on reception.

"My pleasure, Miss Campbell, it's great to have you back."

I toss him the car key, and Amelia pulls her key card out of her purse. The lift door opens and we both step inside. As soon as the door swishes closed, Amelia turns to me, buries her face in my chest and begins to cry.

CHAPTER 36

$\mathcal{L}$iam
2nd August

AMELIA KNOWS the easy part of showing herself is over, and the most worrying meeting with Prince James, and possibly Queen Sofia, is yet to come. One thing I've discovered is the prince's engagement hasn't yet been announced. Are they still hoping Amelia will change her mind and marry Prince James? I smile at the thought because if this is the case, then they're dead in the water. Following the earlier news reports of our relationship, Amelia herself shared with the world, she made it clear I'm the man she wants.

The lift barely opens before Lottie comes rushing down the stairs, pulls Amelia out of my arms and wraps her whole self around her. Watching them rock from side to side, while they both laugh and cry, tells me their relationship means a lot to one another.

"Oh, God, I missed you," Lottie gushes, pushing her friend back to arm's length and checking her out from head to toe.

"Apart from your hair and nails you look as good as ever." Lottie turns to me and scowls, tears running down her face. "I hate you for taking her away like you did, but I love you for keeping her safe."

"Lottie," Amelia warns.

"Don't '*Lottie*' me," she tells her and turns to look at me, then addresses Amelia again, saying, "And I hate you too right now." Her eyes blaze with fury. "Don't you *ever* run off without me again, you hear?" she shouts angrily, before she pulls Amelia to her chest and starts crying again.

They hug again tightly, and a sweet chuckle leaves Amelia's mouth. "You know what? I still say that honesty of yours is going to get you into trouble."

"Oh, tell me something I don't know," Lottie replies with a wicked grin like 'Trouble' is her middle name.

When the two women part I place my hand on Amelia's back and say, "Shall we get out of this hallway and up to the living room?" My move isn't missed by her friend and her eyes flit to mine. She smiles knowingly like she's aware there is more to us than me merely protecting her, but, thankfully, she says nothing.

Lottie drops back behind us as we climb the stairs and I hear her sniff as she dries her tears. When we reach the kitchen, Izzy runs forward pulls Amelia out of my arms and she too hugs her tight.

"Oh, come here, child," she says, pulling her head down to her shoulder. Amelia bursts into tears again, and I figure it's a mixture of relief at being back here, and fear of facing what comes next. I'm glad she has Lottie and Izzy to support her, and I know she'll need them in the coming days.

Izzy sighs. "Thank goodness, you're okay. I mean, I knew you would be fine with Liam taking care of you, but..." She shrugs meeting my gaze and I chuckle. "I feel better seeing you here for myself."

"No offence taken," I say, giving her a good-natured smile. I've grown to like Izzy, she's an uncomplicated woman with a big heart, and the fact she's so adaptable has helped keep Amelia on a, mostly, even keel during these past weeks.

Lottie is quizzing Amelia about the previous two weeks, but I can see Amelia doesn't really want to relive it just yet. However, something tells me when the time is right, Lottie will know every last memory her friend has of it.

Fortunately, Izzy has set the table for afternoon tea, which I realise is the most appropriate food for the time of day, and this is enough of a distraction for Lottie to focus her attention away from Amelia. While we sit at the table, I notice Amelia looks preoccupied and is fingering the same small triangle of sandwich, while everyone else at the table talks and tucks in.

"Shall we go to your office?" I ask, sensing she needs to speak her mind, and perhaps feels she can't say certain things in front of the other two women.

"Sure," she says, giving me a grateful glance and stands. We leave the table and head upstairs to her office, and once there she slumps into her seat, places her forearms on her desk, and drops her head onto them.

"This is about making the call, right?"

Instantly her head whips up and she stares straight through me. "Are you inside my head?"

"No, but I know what would be running through my mind right now, if I were you, so I understand."

She clenches her jaw. "I'm better than this. We've come this far, and you're right, this will only be over if I take control of this situation. The vote was no and that should be all I need to finish this, right?"

"Right," I say, careful to smile in the hope it inspires confidence.

I turn to leave. "No stay," she says quickly, her arm

outstretched, and her hand grabs for mine. I move closer and she nods at the seat facing the side of her desk. I sit, and once I do, she takes a deep breath to compose herself and swallows roughly. "Okay, here goes nothing."

With another deep inhale she lets go of my hand, toys with the phone, exhales slowly and shakes her head. Lifting the landline handset from the cradle, she dials Prince James' number by heart, which surprises me. I don't even know my mother's phone number in my head. The moment he answers her body steels with tension, her eyes widen and flick to mine as if she's drawing strength from looking at me. Quietly, she slowly blows out a breath and clutches my outstretched hand again.

"James?" His name is a question, and her face immediately flushes from nerves. My heart clenches at how brave she's being. She squeezes my hand the moment he speaks, and I can feel the tension in her body just from hearing his voice. I run my fingers gently over her knuckles and she nods, draws another breath, and this time when she releases, I see her shoulders sag a little more. It's then I know she's temporarily got her anxiety under control. I lean in and listen.

$\mathcal{A}$melia
2nd August

"AMELIA, WHERE HAVE YOU BEEN?" Prince James sounds like a father scolding his wayward child.

"No, *hello, Amelia?*" I counter, and my sassy question makes Liam smile.

"I can't believe you dropped out of sight like that."

"No, *I've been concerned, Amelia?* Or *did you miss me?*" I ask, knowing I sound indignant. "I mean it's only been just over two weeks since you asked me to be your wife… or have you conveniently forgotten about that?"

"Amelia," the sharpness in his tone indicates he thinks he's the one who matters.

"I think you already know the answer to your question, James. I mean, you'll have watched the news, or someone will have informed where I was by now."

"Disappearing was a foolish move." His tone is flat, but I sense he's trying to stay calm.

She scoffs. "Foolish? No, you have me confused with

whomever has been looking for me. I'm not as naïve as you all thought. And I regard what I did as the only option open to me at the time. How dare those people invade my privacy and target me because of my birthright? I already gave you my word I had no intention of threatening the Crown. Shouldn't Harry Donaldson have been the focus for the monarchy's attention?"

James falls quiet for a moment, and the paranoid part of my mind wonders if someone is listening, and if there's already a team of operatives winging their way to my home. I look towards Liam and he squeezes my hand again. His gaze immediately calms me, and I feel some of the strain melt, taking my anxiety down a notch or two. But it's not enough to diminish the conflict within me in the same way it has on several occasions before. It dawns on me that this part of my problem is out of his control. He's not the one that can stop any order that's out there about me, if one actually exists.

"The referendum result was no, and the First Minister's intentions will have changed. It sounds as if he'll be out of a job in the next few weeks. Therefore, I need to know what happens now?"

James pauses before speaking. "I agree, your connection to James Edward isn't of interest to anyone, for now."

"*For now?*" His last two words shock me. They don't inspire confidence that my safety is secured, and I immediately go on the attack. "I'm deeply offended by all of this, James. Did I run to the press about the visit you made to me? No, I didn't. What's to stop me going public with all that I know? Even with the no vote in Scotland's referendum, I could cause quite a stir within political circles if I were to do this. How do you think the people of Scotland would regard you if they knew you came into my home with an outlandish proposal? More to the point how would Effie react to that?"

He quietly considers what I say and sighs. "Like you said, the vote was no…"

"James, I know I'm breaking the rules to make demands of the Crown, but I need a guarantee my life isn't going to be disrupted by someone. You appear to forget, having studied law, I have more awareness than most of the political corruption within our institutions. I've heard how decisions are made which discard people at will." The authority in my tone ensures that he knows I mean every word that I say.

"What were you writing?" he asks, and I immediately understand he's picked up on the point that's been made about this in the press." *Good. Does he think I'm going to give him anything that they could give a counter response to? Besides I have nothing. Perhaps writing something that I can have stored for safekeeping may be necessary after all. The few odd things I have written in my diary bear no relation to my current situation and are more about my feelings towards Liam.*

"Nothing that will be published, unless something happens to me before I'm old and grey," I say, leaving a veiled threat of my own hanging between us.

"What is it you want, Amelia?" The tone he uses is sharper than I've ever heard him use before. But his language has changed. He's agitated but wary now, and I remind myself, he, more than anyone, has more to lose if I've written something damaging to his reputation.

"An audience with Queen Sofia," I state, brazenly, knowing I'm asking for the world, but after the last couple of weeks in isolation, I feel a sense of entitlement. Liam grins and brings my hand up to his lips. He presses a kiss to my knuckles and winks at me. This small move fills my chest with a feeling of power which has previously been missing in all of this. I realise now my true personality is shining through for the first time since this started. I sound and feel like the same person I was before this stupid situation took over, when Harry selfishly wanted to use my connection to the Crown for his own gain.

"You want to meet with my mother?" His tone is mocking, like I'm asking him for the moon, but she's my queen, I am one of her subjects and she was complicit in her son's proposal of marriage.

"Talk to her, James. You have twenty-four hours to get her to agree, and remember what I've told you; anything happens to me, no one who has been involved in all of this will emerge unscathed."

I don't conclude the call with words, but simply replace the receiver. Every nerve in my body is vibrating and my cheeks are burning. My heartbeat is running at a mile a minute, and nausea rises up from my chest. Glancing anxiously at Liam, I know the look in my eyes seeks his approval for how I handled the call. It's a once-in-a-lifetime request, I've made, and I know my demand will be viewed as insolent at best. Fear streaks through me and my confidence is fragile again.

"Amazing." Liam praises me as he rises from his seat, leans forward, cups the back of my head and presses a kiss to my forehead. "Nearly there, Amelia. Stay strong, darlin'. It's just a little while longer now. Scotland may not have its independence but we're going to ensure yours."

CHAPTER 38

*L*iam
    3rd August

SINCE AMELIA ARRIVED HOME YESTERDAY, she hasn't hidden her feelings for me in front of Charlotte or Izzy. Once again, I'm in her bed, lying beside her, and I've been staring at her beautiful sleeping face for almost an hour. It's early morning, but the hum of traffic has slowly been growing as Edinburgh wakes up.

The intercom buzzes and there's a soft knock on the bedroom door. I slide out of bed as Amelia stirs, and I crack the door open.

"There's someone downstairs for Amelia," Izzy informs me.

Grabbing my jeans, I pull them on, slip out of the bedroom, and go to the intercom on the wall near the lift. When I look at the screen, I don't recognise the man, who, at a guess, I would say is in his early sixties – he may be older but looks as if he's lived well. He's dressed in an expensive suit, and is very well groomed.

"Please let me speak to him," I tell the security man on the desk. I watch him pass the handset over and the man puts it to his ear.

"Please state your business with Miss Campbell," I say in an authoritative tone.

"My name is William Alexander, one of Her Majesty the Queen's representatives at Balmoral. I have personal business, on behalf of Her Majesty, with Miss Amelia Campbell."

"Please wait, I'm coming down," I tell him before replacing the handset. I ask Izzy to stay waiting in the hallway and go back into Amelia's bedroom. Grabbing my T-shirt, I slip it over my head and run my hands through my hair before going over to the bed and kissing Amelia's head.

She stirs and wakes, but her eyes widen when she sees I'm already dressed.

"What time is it?" she asks, looking startled.

"Everything's okay," I reassure her even though she hasn't asked if anything's wrong. "I think you're going to need to get up and get dressed. There's a representative of the Queen downstairs, and if my guess is correct, he's likely got a handwritten note. I'm going down to meet him, but the chances are he'll have to come up here and give it to you himself."

She hurries out of bed and riffles through a set of drawers for clothes. "God, do you think she's really going to grant me an audience?" she asks.

"It's looking hopeful, I mean, it's still early, and he's here… and it's within the twenty-four-hour deadline you gave James. Izzy's outside the door, I'll send her in to help you. I'll give you five minutes before I bring him up." Pulling her to my chest I kiss her forehead again, push her back a little and cup her cheeks. "You've got this, Amelia. Don't doubt yourself now," I say, before I turn and head out the bedroom door.

Slipping on my shoes I grab the key card and make my way down to the foyer. The gentleman is sitting on one of the reception chairs reserved for the building's guests.

"Mr Alexander?" I ask, even though I already know it's him.

"Yes?" he asks, taking in my attire and I can see he isn't impressed.

"My name is Liam McKenna, Miss Campbell's partner. "How was your journey down from Balmoral today?"

"Uneventful, and thankfully it didn't rain. I hate helicopters at the best of times, but it's much worse in poor weather."

"I agree, it can feel a precarious trip over the hills if there's driving rain."

We continue to exchange small talk regarding the weather, Edinburgh, and he knows we've been in Glencoe, so there's a small conversation about this, and after I check his identity, I lead him to the lift.

The short journey up to the penthouse is quiet and strained as we both stand facing forwards. I have little in common with a man whose only purpose is to act as go between for the Queen.

After entering the apartment. I lead him upstairs, but when he asks to speak to Amelia alone, she denies him and asks me to stay with her.

"Liam and I have no secrets from one another. He probably knows more about what's in that envelope you are carrying than you do," she states, not so much as to put the man down, but to let him know what Queen Sofia is dealing with. No doubt he'll be questioned on his return about how the invitation was received.

Mr Alexander passes the envelope to Amelia and gives

her a small bow before he steps back. I'm not sure why he does this, other than he's obviously very adept at bowing a lot for a man in his position.

Amelia breaks the seal and opens the expensive looking paper that's been folded horizontally into three. She reads for a moment and glances up at me before she folds it again and places it on her coffee table.

"I need this invitation to extend to Liam, I'm not going up there without him," she states, flatly.

Mr Alexander looks flabbergasted at Amelia's response, and I suspect it's because no one usually states their demands when the Queen requests their presence. Following this, he decides to leave the apartment, saying he will call back when he receives his instructions from the royal household and that he'll contact us in due course.

We watch him leave and I immediately call Ross to bring me a fresh suit and shaving gear. "She's gone this far, she's not going to say no now," I state with confidence. "Can I suggest you don't go overboard on your attire?"

"Trousers, a sweater, dress jacket and flats?"

"Sounds about right," I agree. "Come on, we need to get on it. Unless I don't know what I'm talking about, my money's on him being back in a couple of hours."

* * *

4TH AUGUST

Yesterday, my prediction about Mr Alexander's return proved correct and subsequent arrangements were made for Amelia to be taken to meet with the Queen. Today, Mr Alexander picked us up in a town car, and we were driven to a waiting helicopter on the outskirts of Edinburgh.

Amelia has been talking about anything and everything other than where we are going, during the journey and I smile at her when her eyes meet mine and her cheeks flush. I know she's nervous and she's babbling, but to those that don't know her well, she looks the ultimate in calm and collected.

After a pleasant flight in good weather, we circle the Balmoral estate and the helicopter lands. Mr Alexander looks relieved when he clambers out of the door and stamps his feet on the helicopter pad to shake his trousers back in place. I turn and look at Amelia and she inhales a deep breath.

"We'll go out and celebrate tonight," I tell her. "Hell, when this is over, I might take you to Wetherspoon's for a meal," I joke, before the pilot opens my door and I step out. Taking Amelia's hand, I help her down from the chopper and I know my joke has gone over her head because I still haven't explained what Wetherspoon's pubs are like inside.

The castle itself is grand, perfectly positioned in a prime location in Royal Deeside, dwarfed by the land around it. We don't get to see much of the exterior as we're quickly ushered through the entrance.

Once inside we are met by a footman who leads us into a drawing room not far from the doors we've just entered by. He sits us down and tells us someone will be along momentarily to brief us on etiquette before we see the Queen.

"Relax," I say, feeling slightly nervous myself, since I'm in the position whereby I've practically gate-crashed the meeting from the Queen's perspective. "It's not like this is the first time you've met her, right?"

She nods. "I've met her many times before, but it's been in much less formal circumstances. It's usually been an introduction by one of her children, or another relative, whenever she's made an impromptu visit to them, or a garden party. This feels… different, like detention, except with the possibility of facing a guillotine."

Voicing her assessment of her situation makes her even more nervous and she chews the inside of her cheek. "Tell me something good," she blurts, needing a distraction. Her knees are crossed, her leg bouncing up and down. She's hunched over as if subconsciously aiming to protect herself. Seeing her like this makes me want to kill the Queen with my own bare hands for stressing her out this way.

I clap my hand on her ankle, stilling her foot immediately. I squeeze it gently but it's enough to gain her full attention from her thoughts.

"Put your foot on the floor and sit up. Remember you're not the one that's done anything wrong," I say sternly. When her eyes meet with mine, I can see my tone has shocked her, but she does as I say, and I feel my eyes soften at her vulnerability. "Look, I won't have you wrecked like this. It's the Queen who should be shitting her pants, not you." She giggles nervously when I say this, and I smile. "It's true. If things had panned out differently in the past you could well have been where she is now. If that was the case this would have been your house, not hers. When the time comes, you're going to walk in there like you have a huge set of balls swinging between those gorgeous shapely legs. "You. Are. In. Control."

"Interesting mental image right there," she says, and we both laugh. As we do another door opens on the far side of the drawing room and a different man in a smart, black suit enters with purpose. This one's mannerisms aren't so different from the stiff brigadier general Ross's uncle knows. All that's missing is a formal army uniform, a whipping stick under his arm, and a monocle.

He begins talking to us like an army instructor and we're the rookie squaddies: how we're to stand, likely actions the Queen may take and how to respond, when and how to address her, as well as when to move and how to communicate. Amelia looks bored and I can tell she's been in this position many times before. For me it's a first. I smirk when I think I'm sharing my first, *'first'* with her. My mind corrects me because there have been many firsts with her during our brief time together. Her first can of soup that she knows of and her first time being smuggled out of Edinburgh, to name but two.

"Her majesty will see you shortly," the man says and retreats from the room, one arm swinging by his side. You can take a man out of the army, but you can't take the army out of the man.

"Your Majesty, then ma'am," she reminds me, but I have no clue why she's telling me. My role is that of a fly on the wall, I won't be there as far as the Queen is concerned.

The original door we came through opens and the original footman who led us in here is standing in the doorway.

"Her Majesty the Queen will see you now. If you'd like to follow me."

Amelia jumps to her feet, and as the footman has gone out of sight, I grab her, pull her back and kiss her roughly. It's not a long kiss but when I draw back her eyes are wide, and I can see what I've done has had an effect. "Remember huge balls," I say and wink.

* * *

THE DISTANCE between where we were waiting, and where the Queen is situated for our audience, is not far at away at all. The footman opens the door and ushers us in, halts us and steps aside.

"Miss Amelia Campbell and Mr Liam McKenna, Your Majesty," he says, bows and steps back. The Queen is sitting on an armchair and she's dressed in a pair of flat brown brogues, brown tweed trousers and a mustard woollen sweater. A degree of disappointment strikes me at how she's dressed like an ordinary granny.

"Come forward, Amelia," she says beckoning her to the edge of the carpet. The drawing room we are in looks drab with the thick, dark oak furniture and the gilt framed ancestor's portraits hanging on the wall. The conversation sounds quiet in the high-ceilinged space of the room.

Amelia does as instructed. "Your Majesty," Amelia says, drops a perfect curtsy, and the Queen gives a smile. Amelia does have great deportment and looks very elegant in her greeting.

"Please sit," the Queen says, signalling for Amelia to take the armchair across from her. "I believe you wanted to see me." The Queen's tone is clipped.

"Thank you for agreeing to my request," Amelia says quickly.

"Well, you're here, so should we not get on with it?" the Queen asks, sounding arrogant and rude. Considering what Amelia has been through, it would appear the royal position is to feign their ignorance on the matter.

"May I speak, frankly?" she asks. The Queen looks bored and nods. "I won't be insulted by anyone, royalty or otherwise, when it comes to my life. You and the Crown may not see my life as important as those in the royal household, but I want to remind you of the discretion my ancestors have given the monarchy for centuries now. It has never been my intention to bring your position into question; yet you or those acting on your behalf felt the need to send your son to ask for my hand in marriage to protect your position."

The Queen raises her eyebrows. "An honour you threw back in his face," she interjects.

"You call it an honour, when, in fact, your son's intrusion drew more attention to me than at any other time in my life? At my home no less? Your son's purpose was to use me as a pawn not to take me as someone he'd cherish. Do you know what it means to live a good life with no intention of anyone knowing how connected I am to the throne of my country or to yours for that matter? Forgive me, ma'am, but I've been in hiding and if it wasn't for this man here, goodness knows where I would be." Amelia points to me, but the Queen's gaze doesn't follow. Her focus is squarely on Amelia and the way she shifts in her seat tells me she isn't comfortable with the confrontation.

"It saddens me that I should have been placed in this position. No one has asked how I felt knowing that someone was plotting to use me in the name of Scotland to question the monarchy and the potential harm it could do to all of the nations of the UK." Amelia's chest is heaving from her outburst and I see her take a deep breath to calm herself down.

"As James told you, the problem has now passed, so you're safe. No one is interested now that Scotland's people wisely voted no."

"I would disagree with how wise the result is. It is what it is because of Donaldson's foolish actions. And the vote is no for my generation, but what if another vote happens during my children's lifetime? Are they going to face the same fate as me?"

"The vote was no by almost ten percent," the Queen retorts.

"This time," Amelia interjects. The insistence in her tone makes me proud. "I know I'm speaking out of turn... and you're likely not used to this, but you have to hear what I'm saying. I'm past caring what happens to me afterwards." She turns and points to me. "I would go as far as to say this man and his partner saved my life. Their work also saved your United Kingdom from potential infighting. It's due to their intelligence and protection that I'm here speaking to you and that Harry Donaldson's reputation brought the vote into doubt. They guaranteed the question of your reign over all four nations of the UK remains unchallenged."

Amelia went on to explain in detail some of the lengths that we'd gone to in order to keep her safe, and to expose Harry. She also disclosed the name of the secretary within the Home Office that shared the information about her lineage in the first place. When she was finished, she took a deep breath and wrung her hands.

I can see that Amelia's fierce dressing down has gained the Queen's undivided attention now.

"Your Majesty, you are my Queen, you're his Queen." she said pointing towards me. "Now and until the day you die. I'm a Campbell, and I don't need to tell you what that means to the previous Kings and Queens of our kingdom."

"You have to understand the damage Mr Donaldson could have caused, the harmony of our nations was at stake," the Queen insists.

"My life could have been at stake," Amelia implored. "It still might be until you tell whoever is out there to back off. I trust you, my Queen, to defend your subject, to act with fairness and be above reproach, as much as I have been in my loyalty to you. Indeed, the Clan Campbell pledged their allegiance to the Crown yearly for centuries and fought in King's and Queen's names. How would they feel if they knew of this turn of events?

The Queen sits motionless for a few moments collecting her thoughts before she rises, and Amelia immediately does the same.

"By insisting to have an audience with me, I can see for myself how much you and your people have done to ensure the unity of our four nations. In doing this, you have also shown your loyalty to me and the throne. It will be sanctioned that your life has to be protected at all costs, and that you and those loyal to you, are able to live your lives free from all threat of the Crown."

"I trust that my Queen's word is her sacred bond and will ensure that my written account of this past few weeks will remain in very discreet storage unless myself or the generations after me should find themselves in a similar situation in the future."

The Queen's hands squeeze together gently in reaction. To Amelia it may look as if there has been no response, but to the trained eye, I can see her pointed comment has hit home.

Amelia curtseys and thanks the Queen for her generosity, which pisses me off because nothing that's happened to her, by her statement, has been a gift.

"Come," the Queen states waving me over and pointing to the spot just off the carpet. I step forward.

"Your Majesty," I say and bow.

"Remind me of your name?" she asks her gaze meeting mine.

"Liam McKenna," I reply.

"Well, Mr McKenna, I hear you gave quite a lot of people the run around wouldn't you say?"

"Indeed, ma'am," I say, because it's a fair assessment, and I imagine she's a woman that can smell bullshit at a hundred paces.

"Thank you for keeping Amelia safe, I've always had a soft spot for the girl."

"You and me both, ma'am," I joke, and she steps away. Turning her back she wanders over to her sofa table and rings a small bell.

The footman opens the door. We're being dismissed, and as we both turn to go the Queen calls out to Amelia. "There's a new date for James' engagement party, the invitations will be going out in the mail."

CHAPTER 39

*A*melia
4th August

MY LEGS FEEL like jelly and my heart pounds in my chest as
we walk back toward the helipad for our flight home. As we
take to our seats on the helicopter again, Liam pulls out his
phone and fires off a text. I guess it's to Ross to tell him we've
had our meeting, and it was successful. Apart from
constantly holding my hand in public since we left the farmhouse, he's behaving exactly like the same quietly protective
man I've grown to depend on.

I think about what it's meant to me, what it still means to
me to have him by my side. I didn't fall for him in the short
time I've known him, I crashed. In the past when I heard
friends say they were head over heels in love, I used to think
them pathetic; that their comments were benign, and a gross
exaggeration of the truth. However, now I've met the right
man for me, I know their words are true, or that I'm just as
pathetic as I judged them to be.

On the journey back to Edinburgh there's no opportunity

to talk because we have headphones on, and our communication can be heard by the pilot. So, we sit and spectate all the way and in silence.

During the flight, Liam doesn't distract me at all. It's as if he senses I need time to process what I've just done. He gives me strength as he sits beside me, his shoulder touching mine like an anchor keeping me grounded.

Since my audience with the Queen, the quiet has given me some time for reflection. Time where all I can do is recount what I said and how she responded. Queen Sofia doesn't say anything she doesn't mean. Her reputation for being rigid and stubborn is world renowned. And for years I've heard her children whine continually to this effect.

There was truth in her eyes when she told me she'd guarantee my safety and I have to believe my Queen will keep her word. My insurance policy doesn't exist, and I make a mental note to document what has happened… just in case.

From my own perspective, it gave me no joy to speak out the way I just did. But I've reconciled this by my need to advocate for freedom to live my life without fear of retribution from those who feel threatened by my mere existence.

The helicopter descends quickly, and lands on the same helipad on the outskirts of Edinburgh we'd taken off from five hours before. I see a town car waiting and instinctively know it's here to escort us back to my building.

"Hungry?" Liam asks leaning his face close to my ear. His breath is warm, and I immediately turn to look at him. When our eyes meet, he smiles and cups my cheek but says nothing. His question reminds my stomach I haven't eaten, and it grumbles for food.

"Yes, I haven't eaten today," I tell myself as much as him, and turn as the pilot opens the door. Liam jumps down and with strong hands either side of my waist he lifts me onto the ground. His hands linger and he leans in and brushes my lips with his. Turning, Liam thanks the pilot and we begin to walk the short distance to the car.

"Me neither, you'd think the Queen would have offered us a biscuit at the very least," he says, in a tone that sounds annoyed, but I know he's being sarcastic. I love his dry humour.

"She's English. There's nothing like our Scottish hospitality," I say playfully, and we chuckle.

We settle into the car and Liam gives the chauffeur an address, and I hear the name Wetherspoon's before I happen to catch a horrified look in the driver's eyes. I think he realises who I am, and all the uproar about me being missing is what's on his mind.

We chat in general terms about up-and-coming dates in my calendar for when I resume my charity work at the end of August, until the car stops in Leith Street, just off the Royal Mile and we get out. I glance up and see *The Playfair* pub and shrug.

"This is a Wetherspoon's pub." Liam tugs me close to the door and opens it. Immediately a strong smell of beer assaults my nostrils, and there are workmen in high visibility jackets, each of them sitting eating something and chips, with a pint of beer or lager. Liam closes the door and pulls me back out to the pavement and away from the door. "I promised I'd take you and I have. Liam McKenna never breaks his promises."

I grin. "Do you think I'm too posh to eat there?"

"I'm too posh to eat there," he tells me with a serious look on his face. "This suit cost me over three grand." He holds one side of his suit jacket out for me to inspect the label on lining.

I laugh and he puts his arm around me, pulling me into his side. Our eyes meet and he presses a kiss to my cheek.

"So, where are we going?"

"I thought, since one Balmoral didn't feed you, that I'd strike a balance and make sure the other one does. We stroll along Leith Street to where it merges into Princes Street, and we see the Balmoral Spa Hotel.

"Don't we need a reservation?" I ask.

"We have one… Ross," he replies and winks.

"When did you think of this?" My heart is racing because he's planned this, but when and how?

"I texted Ross on the way back and asked him to book us a table. You can thank the Queen for being so miserly, as that gave me the idea. How much would it have cost to give us a cup of tea and break open a packet of Abernethy biscuits?"

I laugh and he looks down at me, smiling. "You really are my hero, aren't you?"

"I could be… if you play your cards right," he jokes before he shudders. "God, if I never see another packet of playing cards again, it'll be too soon."

"Or a jigsaw," I agree, and we laugh. "I hate jigsaws."

"Twister, on the other hand, lame game, but could be a lot more entertaining if it was played naked," he tells me, waggling his eyebrows.

The thought of naked Twister and Liam sounds a little more than intriguing. "The look on your face says you've imagined this," I say through a chuckle as we reach the desk at the entrance to the restaurant.

He shrugs. "Obviously." He talks to the maître d' who checks off our reservations before he guides us to a quiet table in a corner. It's the time of day between afternoon tea and dinner, but he hands us the à la carte menus and steps away. Immediately there's a waiter offering us a wine menu.

"We'll have a bottle of vintage Dom Perignon," Liam says, and it instantly takes me back to the night I first saw him when Lottie and I were kind of sloshed.

"That's expensive," I mumble, and he shrugs.

I stare at this gorgeous, considerate man who is with me, not through choice, but more by design, yet he's perfect for me in every way. Tears well in my eyes when I suddenly realise that after today there's no obligation for him to stay with me. The thought of letting him go instils a sense of panic. From what he's said before I know he feels our connection, but what does this mean now his work with me is done?

"We spoke about my plans in the months ahead. What about yours?" I ask because I need to know where I fit in, *if* I fit in.

He shrugs as the waiter brings an already chilled bottle of champagne over and pours us each a glass. After glancing up at the waiter he waits for him to leave before his blue eyes reconnect with mine.

"On to the next job I suppose."

My heart sinks in my chest, and the feeling I'm losing someone dear to me makes it squeeze tight. Immediately I look to my drink and I toy with the stem of my champagne flute. A lump has grown in my throat and if I try to say anything, I think a sob may escape. Intuitively, he appears to sense my distress, lifts my hand from my glass and places it in his.

His strong fingers wrap around mine and he gives them a squeeze. "If I can take a moment, there's something I'd like to say. In case you haven't noticed, I could easily be all in with you. That said, I understand that you may need a little time to think about what you want, since you've had to rely heavily on me when your decisions in life weren't your own."

"Stop. I want you. How I feel about you is the one thing I don't have to process in all of this. Let me tell you something, I've never known a man who gives me goosebumps with a simple touch, like you do. I've never felt my heart flutter in the way it does from how you look at me. Giving me time won't change these feelings. I don't fall easily, Liam. Despite how I look on the outside, I'm usually a hard nut to crack."

"Damn, all that and I'm mediocre. Thank God, you don't think I'm hot or your pants may have combusted by now. I mean, Izzy's great at what she does, but I'd have hated to see her trying to deal with that." He's grinning as he shifts our hands until our fingers are clasped together. The waiter approaches our table. "We need a minute," Liam says to the server without taking his eyes off me. The waiter quickly turns and retreats.

A smile curves my lips as Liam lifts our hands and runs the back of my mine over his lips.

He drops them back to the table and tilts his head to one side. "Amelia." My name is laced with affection. "I've never met anyone like you." His gaze grows intense as he pauses to let what he says sink in. "What I feel is more than attraction. This is a seriously wired connection we have," he clarifies, and my smile widens. "I've had time to think, God, have I had time," he says with passion in his tone. "You've been my first and last thoughts since I met you, and not only because of work." He chuckles. "The time we were at the farmhouse could have been better spent, had there not been the matter of your safety. My attraction to you has never been in question."

"Is it weird I felt sad to leave?" I ask, not because of the uncertainty of my situation at that time, but because it brought the possibility that we may lose the closeness that had grown in the time we'd been living together.

"We're very different people, Amelia," he says. I open my mouth to protest but he squeezes my hand, and it tells me he has more to say. "I feel I'm somewhere between just enough and not enough to make you happy. It isn't that I feel intimidated by who you are, or the circles you move in. I don't. My concern lies in what I do for a living and how compatible it is with the lifestyle you lead."

"Funny, I had a similar thought myself. You're amazing at what you do. I wouldn't dream of coming between you and your career, but if I'm honest it makes me nervous. It doesn't come without risk. If all the jobs you do are like mine, and you were sitting in some farmhouse in the hills, I think I'd have nothing to worry about, having gone through this myself. But I'm not naïve, and I know not all the commissions you receive will be smooth sailing like mine," I admit.

"You live so differently with your penthouse apartment, your charity luncheons and dinners. My life has been travelling and living out of backpacks. Hell, I don't even have a proper place to live I'd dare take you to. Although after seeing your place, it has given me the push I need to finally find a real home of my own."

"What I'm hearing are obstacles, when we're just starting out…" I protest.

"I'm just being straight with you. There's a lot for you to think about. How would you feel if you had some event planned and I wasn't there to escort you to it?"

"I'd be hoping you were safe and knowing you were somewhere more important than attending a dinner with me. It isn't as if I haven't been to hundreds of galas, balls and dinner engagements without a man on my arm before. Besides, most of those evenings would bore you to death, and Lottie would miss out if you were always with me."

"My job will get in the way and I'll hurt you."

"You'll hurt me more if you can walk away from this without giving us a real shot to be happy."

Liam closes his eyes briefly. "That's not what I'm doing. Crazy as it sounds, my heart is already yours. How to be with you, and make what we have work, is all I can think about. But we can't live in a bubble, Amelia." His penetrating stare confirms the depth of his words, and the fact he's flagging the negative aspects about himself, tells me he wants my happiness more than his own. It's typical of how he's always put me first since we met.

"Then be with me, Liam. Take the risk and I'll make it worth your while." I smile.

He chuckles. "Thank you, God," he says, rising his eyes towards the ceiling. "Risk is my middle name; in case you haven't worked that out for yourself. I'm already with you, darlin' it would kill me to walk away. So, if you're sure this is what you want, and you think you can deal with a disjointed lifestyle, I'm definitely all in."

Unclasping our fingers, he sits back in his chair. He gives me a long look like he's digesting the conversation we've just had. I lift my drink and hold it out for him to toast with me and he holds his glass close to mine.

We clink glasses as I speak. "Thanks to you and Ross, I may not be Queen of Scotland, but I'm the Queen of my own independence."

EPILOGUE

*L*iam

One Year Later

Within weeks of Amelia's return to society, it became glaringly clear covert operations were beyond a man in my position. Being associated as the partner of a high-profile public figure did nothing to help me blend, an essential skill in my line of work. What use was I to anyone if, as the security guy, I drew more attention to the principle?

Fortunately, the thought of leaving my girl for months at a time also left a hole in my chest, which was enough for me to re-evaluate how I moved forward in my career. After several long discussions with Ross and his brother-in-law, I drew up an alternative business plan. Almost six months to the day from the first time I was hired to shadow Amelia, my new close protection security business took off.

My role these days is as trainer and recruiter, and with Ross as my partner in crime, so to speak, we've got six pairs of great operatives working in teams. Our men and women come from highly skilled backgrounds related to the fields of security, intelligence and surveillance. Playing my new role brings me the best of both worlds. I get to experience some of those adrenaline rushes, but through exercises in training, rather than putting my life at risk on a daily basis.

Occasionally Ross and I will jump in on a job when extra hands are required, but it's things we can do at a distance without comprising our assets.

As for life with Amelia? I know I couldn't be happier, and I hope she would say the same. She

lights up my world with her beauty, straight-talking, and confident ways. Love isn't the word I would use to describe what we have; it feels like a spiritual connection between old souls. A year

ago, I didn't know she existed and a year later, I know I can't live without her. The air I breathe is cleaner when she is near me.

When I met Mr Donaldson, I disliked the man on sight. Now, I owe him more than he will ever know, for placing me at Amelia's side. Strange how the actions of a few power-hungry people can change the course of history. It's a pity these lessons only come to light long after they cease to exist, with the benefit of hindsight.

Amelia

Despite Lottie's disparaging remarks about Lady Effie Bower, she looks elegantly stunning in the white lace and satin A-line wedding dress. As she enters Westminster Abbey, she looks like a frightened rabbit, but her smile is radiantly bright. Prince James looks transfixed, the smile on his face as genuine as the one worn by his bride-to-be, and I'm delighted for him. Effie is a great match for James, and she will make a fabulous royal wife. I never did get to that engagement party.

Liam's hand connects with mine as she passes, almost as if he's aware that, had I bowed to James' demand a year before, the bride currently walking past, could easily have been me. My mind fleetingly wanders, and I remember how far I've come since then, *we've* come since then. I

turn to look into my husband's eyes and we both smile at one another as the organist softly plays Pachelbel's Canon in D Major. The mellow music is a far cry from the bagpipe music we had when we married at Gretna Green on a whim almost nine months ago.

My nerves were on edge for thirty days after we submitted our paperwork at the registrars in Dumfries, in the hopes the press wouldn't discover our plan before our big day. Thankfully, we escaped their attention and we finally stood, hand in hand, in the Original Marriage Room in Gretna. Our audience was as small as it gets, with Lottie, Ross, Izzy and Liam's parents as our only witnesses and guests. The Original Marriage room dates back to the 1800s, and it felt fitting to be married in a place of significant Scottish history, since it was history that brought Liam and I together in the first place.

The music stops, drawing me out of my reverie, and the Archbishop of Canterbury, the head of the Church of England, officiates the marriage ceremony between the couple. His voice echoes loudly around the ancient Abbey by the power of modern-day technology. It strikes me as impersonal, and detached from the perfectly intimate anvil ceremony Liam and I had.

I allow my eyes to wander and realise my thoughts couldn't be more truthful, as Heads of State, politicians and dignitaries from other countries, as well as celebrities, make up the congregation here to witness the joining of the royal couple in matrimony. I immediately throw up a silent prayer of thanks in God's house for not choosing this path for me.

When the service is over and the couple are ready to leave the Abbey, the Wedding March begins to play. We stand and wait as the wedding party take the long walk back up the aisle and out to towards the warmth of the sunshine. I know the moment they get there from the roar of the crowds outside and immediately after this the rest of the royal party begin to file up the aisle towards us. The Queen is at the front on my side with Effie's father, Lord Bower, by her side.

As she approaches, my heart begins to pound because it's the first time I've seen her face to face since our encounter at Balmoral. Liam squeezes my hand, but my eyes are stuck firmly on hers as she comes alongside me.

"Your Majesty," I say, and nod because our eyes meet. She smiles and nods but says nothing more as she walks past us. I don't know what it means, but I choose to take her acknowledgement of me as a mark of respect for the part I've played in us all being here today.

Heads turn to look at me, and I ignore them, turn, and look up at my husband. "You're right, you'd have hated a life like this, besides," he says, "she may have her throne to sit on, but you'll always be my Queen."

The End

ABOUT THE AUTHOR

Karen Frances author is a wife, mum of five-not-so-wee kids anymore. Who are all wonderful when they are sleeping. She is a lover of words and happy-ever-afters.

Karen lives in Glasgow, Scotland with her husband of twenty-two years and four of their five children.

Her busy days include helping her husband manage their family business.

She finds escape from the chaos of everyday life in good books, particularly stories of passionate romantic relationships. She enjoys taking her readers on an emotional ride within her stories.